LONGTUSK

Also by Stephen Baxter

SILVERHAIR
RAFT
TIMELIKE INFINITY
ANTI-ICE
FLUX
RING
THE TIME SHIPS
VOYAGE
TITAN
MOONSEED
VACUUM DIAGRAMS
MANIFOLD: TIME
MANIFOLD: SPACE
THE LIGHT OF OTHER DAYS
(with Arthur C. Clarke)

STEPHEN BAXTER

LONGTUSK

An Imprint of HarperCollins*Publishers*

EOS
An Imprint of HarperCollins *Publishers*
10 East 53rd Street
New York, New York 10022-5299

Copyright © 1999 by Stephen Baxter
ISBN: 0-380-81898-1
www.eosbooks.com

Library of Congress Cataloging-in-Publication Data

Baxter, Stephen.
  Longtusk / Stephen Baxter.
    p. cm.
  ISBN 0-380-81898-1 (pbk.)
    1. Mammoths—Fiction. 2. Neanderthals—Fiction. 3. Prehistoric peoples—Fiction. 4. Bering Sea Region—Fiction. I. Title.

PR6052.A849 L6 2001
823'.914—dc21   00-046627

A previous edition of this book was published in Great Britain in 1999 by the Orion Publishing Group Ltd.

First Eos trade paperback printing: June 2001

Eos Trademark Reg. U.S. Pat. Off. and in Other Countries,
Marca Registrada, Hecho en U.S.A.
HarperCollins® is a trademark of HarperCollins Publishers Inc.

Printed in the U.S.A.

10 9 8 7 6 5 4 3 2 1

To my niece, Jessica Bourg

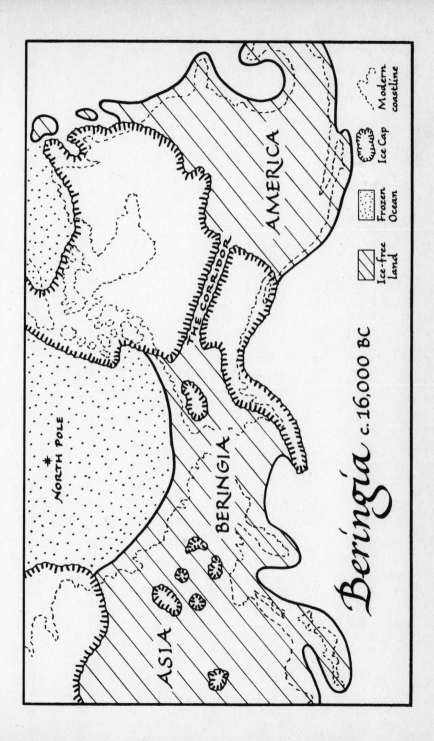

ASIA

NORTH POLE

BERINGIA

THE CORRIDOR

AMERICA

Beringia c. 16,000 BC

Ice-free land

Frozen Ocean

Ice Cap

Modern coastline

Prologue

A vast sheet of ice sits on the North Pole: immense, brooding, jealously drawing the moisture from the air. Glaciers, jutting from the icecap like claws, pulverize rock layers and carve out fjords and lakes. South of the ice, immense plains sweep around the planet, darkened by herds of mighty herbivores.

The ice has drawn so much water from the oceans that the very shapes of the continents are changed. Australia is no island, but is joined to southeast Asia. And in the north, America is linked to Asia by a neck of land called Beringia, so that a single mighty continent all but circles the North Pole.

The ice is in retreat, driven back by Earth's slow thaw to its millennial fastness at the poles. But it retreats with ill grace, gouging at the land, and all around the planet there are catastrophic climatic events of a power and fury unknown to later ages. And, retreat or not, the sites of the cities of the future—Chicago, Boston, Edinburgh, Stockholm, Moscow—still lie dreaming under kilometers of ice.

The time is sixteen thousand years before the birth of Christ. And every human alive wakes to the calls of mammoths.

PART 1
NOMAD

The Story of Longtusk and the She-Cat

Who was Longtusk?

I'll tell you who Longtusk was (Silverhair said to her daughter, Icebones). He was the greatest hero of the Cycle—and the only Bull hero in all the Cycle's long history.

My Matriarch used to say I had a little of Longtusk's spirit in me too. And I don't know why you think that's so funny, Icebones. I wasn't *always* so old and frail as this . . .

Tell you a story? Another?

Very well. I'll tell you how Longtusk defeated Teeth-of-Death, the she-cat.

This is a story of long ago, when the world was new and rich and cold, and there were no Lost, anywhere. The mammoths were the strongest and wisest of all the animals, so much so that the others grew to rely on their strength, and the way they re-made the landscape, everywhere they went.

The mammoths were the Matriarchs of the world. Everybody agreed.

Well, almost everybody.

Teeth-of-Death was a she-cat. In fact she was the ruler of the saber-tooth cats, for she was the strongest and most agile, her teeth and claws the longest and sharpest, her mind the most inventive, her cruelty the most relentless.

Every animal feared the saber-tooth cats. Every animal feared Teeth-of-Death. Every animal save the mammoths.

The mammoths were too big, too powerful. Oh, the cats could bring down a mammoth from time to time, but only the very young or the very old or the very sick. It was not an honorable business. In fact, as they glided back and forth on their great migrations, the mammoths barely noticed the cats even existed.

This, of course, drove Teeth-of-Death insane with jealousy and hurt pride.

Now, as you know, when he was a young Bull Longtusk left his Clan and traveled far and wide: from north to south, even across the seas and the lakes and the ice. Everywhere he went he gained in wisdom and stature; everybody he met was impressed by his bearing and grace; and he had adventures which have never been forgotten.

And it was this Longtusk, Longtusk the nomad, who happened upon Teeth-of-Death.

The great cat confronted Longtusk. She said, "This cannot go on."

Longtusk had been feeding on a rich stand of willow. He looked down his trunk to see what was making so much noise, and there was the spitting, agitated cat. He asked reasonably, "*What* can't go on?"

"Either you rule the Earth, or I do. Not both."

"Don't you think there are more important things to worry about than that?"

"No," Teeth-of-Death snapped. "Ruling is the most important thing. More important than life."

"Nonsense," said Longtusk. "If it makes you happy, I hereby pronounce you the world's most fearsome animal. There. Now we don't have to argue, do we?" And he turned to walk away.

For, you see, he was wise as well as brave, and he knew that an unnecessary fight should not be fought.

But that would not do for the she-cat.

With an agile bound she ran before Longtusk and confronted him. "No," she said. "I cannot live while I know in my heart that you do not respect me."

She was surely an intimidating sight: an immense cat with jaws spread wide, sharp teeth gaping, claws that with a single swipe could disembowel even an adult Bull mammoth—if she ever got the chance.

"You are very foolish," said Longtusk. But he faced her warily, for he knew he must meet her challenge.

And so it began. When news of the contest spread, all the animals of the world gathered around, pushing and staring.

Teeth-of-Death attacked Longtusk three times.

The first time she leaped at his face, reaching for his eyes and trunk. But Longtusk simply raised his tusks and pushed her away.

For her second attack Teeth-of-Death clambered up a spruce tree. She leaped down onto Longtusk's back and tried to use her great saber teeth to gouge into his flesh. He could not reach her with his trunk to dislodge her. But she could not bite through his fur and skin. After a time he simply walked beneath a low tree and let its branches scrape the cat from his back, and that was that.

For her third attack Teeth-of-Death hid in a bank of snow. She had decided that when Longtusk came close enough she would leap at him again, trying to reach the soft flesh of his belly or trunk. It was a clever strategy and might have succeeded, even against a hero so strong as Longtusk, for cats are adept at such deception. But, obsessed with her ambition, Teeth-of-Death forced herself to lie still in her snowdrift for several days, waiting for her opportunity.

And when Longtusk at last came by Teeth-of-Death was cold, half-starved, exhausted.

She sprang too early, made too much noise. To fend her off, Longtusk simply swept his great tusks and let their tips gouge furrows in Teeth-of-Death's beautiful golden coat.

They faced each other, Longtusk barely scratched, Teeth-of-Death bleeding and exhausted.

Longtusk said, "Let us reach an agreement."

Teeth-of-Death said warily, licking her wounds, "No agreement is possible."

For answer, he went to the snowdrift where she had been hiding. He scraped away the snow and the hard ice that lay beneath, revealing bare earth. Then he dug deeper, and he exposed another layer of ice, hidden beneath the dirt.

"The ice comes and goes in great waves," he said. "This old ice was covered with dirt before it had time to melt. Now the ice has come again and covered over the land. So here we have two layers of ice in the same place, one on top of each other."

The cat hissed, "What relevance has this?"

"Here is my suggestion," he said. "We will share the world, just as these ice layers share the same patch of ground. But, just like these ice layers, we will not touch each other.

"You cats eat the meat of animals. We mammoths do not hunt; we do not covet your prey—"

"Ah," said the cat. "And you eat the plants and grass and trees, which we do not desire. Very well. We will share the world, as you suggest." But her eyes narrowed.

And so it was concluded.

But when Longtusk was turning to go, the cat mocked him. "I have tricked you," she said. "*I* will eat the finest meat. *You,* however, must eat dirt and scrub. What kind of bargain is that? You are a fool, Longtusk."

And Longtusk reflected.

The she-cat thought she had won: and in a way she had. She would become the steppe's ruling animal, its top predator. But Longtusk knew that though its food may be richer, a predator

6

needs many prey to survive. Even a mighty herd of deer could support only a few cats, and the numbers of the she-cat's cubs would always be limited.

But the steppe was full of dirt and scrub, as she had called it. And Longtusk knew that thanks to his bargain it was his calves, the mammoths, who would grow in number until they filled the steppe, even to the point where they shaped it for their needs.

"Yes," he said gently. "I am a fool." And he turned and walked away.

. . . I know what you are thinking, Icebones. Is the story true? Are *any* of the stories of Longtusk true? It seems impossible that one mammoth could cram so many acts of impossible heroism and matchless wisdom into one brief lifetime.

Well, perhaps some of the stories have become a little embellished with time. They are after all stories.

But I know this. Longtusk was real. Longtusk encountered great danger—and in the end, Longtusk sacrificed his life to save his Clan.

He was the greatest hero of them all.

1

The Gathering

The greatest hero of them all was twelve years old, and he was in trouble with his mother. Again.

Yellow plain, blue sky; it was a fine autumn afternoon, here on the great steppe of Beringia. The landscape was huge, flat, elemental, an ocean of pale grass mirrored by an empty sky, crossed by immense herds of herbivores and the carnivores that preyed on them. Longtusk heard the hiss of the endless winds through the grass and sedge, the murmur of a river some way to the west—and, under it all, the unending grind and crack of the great ice sheets that spanned the continent to the north.

And mammoths swept over the land like clouds.

Loose wool hung around them, catching the low sunlight. He heard the trumpeting and clash of tusks of bristling, arguing bachelors, and the rumbles of the great Matriarchs—complex songs with deep harmonic structure, much of it inaudible to human ears—as they solemnly debated the state of the world.

This was the season's last gathering of the Clan, this great assemblage of Families, before the mammoths dispersed to the winter pastures of the north.

And Longtusk was angry, aggrieved, ignored. He

worked the ground as he walked, tearing up grass, herbs and sedge with his trunk and pushing them into his mouth between the flat grinding surfaces of his teeth.

He'd gotten into a fight with his sister, Splayfoot, over a particularly juicy dwarf willow he'd found. Just as he had prized the branches from the ground and had begun to strip them of their succulent leaves, the calf had come bustling over to him and had tried to push him away so she could get at the willow herself. *His* willow.

In response to Splayfoot's pitiful trumpeting, his mother had come across: Milkbreath, her belly already swollen with next year's calf. And of course she'd taken Splayfoot's side.

"Don't be so greedy, Longtusk! She's a growing calf. Go find your own willow. You ought to help her, not bully her . . ."

And so on. It had done Longtusk no good at all to point out, perfectly reasonably, that as *he* had found the little tree it was in fact *his* willow and the one in the wrong here was *Splayfoot*, not him. His mother had just pushed him away with a brush of her mighty flank.

The rest of the Family had been there, watching: even Skyhump the Matriarch, his own great-grandmother, head of the Family, surrounded by her daughters and granddaughters with their calves squirming for milk and warmth and comfort. Skyhump had looked stately and magnificent, great curtains of black-brown hair sweeping down from the pronounced hump on her back that had given the Matriarch her name. She had rumbled something to the Cows around her, and they had raised their trunks in amusement.

They had been mocking him. *Him*, Longtusk!

At twelve years old, though he still had much growing to do, Longtusk was already as tall as all but the oldest of the Cows in his Family. And his tusks were the envy of many an adult Bull—well, they would be if he ever got to meet any—great sweeping spirals of ivory that curved around before him until they almost met, a massive, tangible weight that pulled at his head.

He was Longtusk. He would live forever, and he was destined to become a hero as great as any in the Cycle, the greatest hero of them all. He was sure of it. Look at his mighty tusks, the tusks of a warrior! And he raised them now in mock challenge, even though there was no one here to see.

Couldn't those foolish Cows understand? It was just unendurable.

But now he heard his mother calling for him. Grumbling, growling, he made his way back to her.

The Cows had clustered around Skyhump, their Matriarch, and were walking northward in a loose, slow cluster. They grazed steppe grass as they walked, for mammoths must feed for most of the day, and they left behind compact trails of dung.

The Clan stretched around him as far as the eye could see, right across the landscape to east and west, a wave of muscle and fat and deep brown hair patiently washing northward. Skyhump's small Family of little more than twenty individuals—Cows with their calves and a few young males—was linked to the greater Clan by the kinship of sisters and daughters and female cousins. Where they passed, the mammoths cut swathes through the tall green-gold grass, and the ground shuddered with their footsteps.

Longtusk felt a brief surge of pride and affection. This was his Clan, and it was, after all, a magnificent thing to be part of it—to be a mammoth.

11

But now here was his mother, shadowed by that pest Splayfoot, and his sense of belonging dissipated.

Milkbreath slapped his rump with her trunk, as if he were still a calf himself. "Where have you been? . . . Never mind. Can't you see we're getting separated from the Family? We have to hear what she has to say."

"Who? Skyhump?"

Milkbreath snorted. "No. Pinkface. The Matriarch of Matriarchs. Don't you know anything? . . . Never mind. Come *on!*"

So Longtusk hurried after his mother.

They joined a cluster of Cows, tall and old: Matriarchs all, slow and stately in their years and wisdom. He was much too short to see past them.

But his mother was entranced. "Look," she said softly. *"There she is.* They say she is a direct descendant of the great Kilukpuk. They say she was burned in a great blaze made by the Fireheads, and she was the only one of her Family to survive . . ."

He could still see nothing. But when he shut out the noise—the squeal of calves, the constant background thunder of mammoths walking, eating, defecating—he could hear the Matriarchs rumbling and stamping at the ground, debating, sharing information that might sustain a few more lives through the coming winter.

Longtusk spoke quietly, with soft pipings of his trunk. "What are they saying?"

"They're talking about the changes." His mother's small ears stuck out of her hair as she strained to listen.

"What changes?"

"You're too young to understand," she snapped irritably.

"Tell me."

She growled, "To the north the ice is shrinking back.

And to the south the forests are spreading, more trees every year."

He had heard this before. "We can't live in the forests—"

"Not only that, there's talk that the Fireheads aren't too far to the south. And where the Fireheads go the Lost can't be far behind . . ."

Fireheads and Lost. Monsters of legend. Longtusk felt cold, as if he had drunk too much ice water.

. . . But now, without warning, the Matriarchs shifted their positions, like clouds exposing the sun. And he saw the Matriarch of Matriarchs.

She was short, her tusks long and smooth. And her face was a grotesque mask: pink and naked like a baby bird's wing, free of all but a few wisps of hair.

Longtusk burst out, "She's too young!"

The Matriarchs stirred, like icebergs touched by wind.

Milkbreath grabbed his trunk, angry and embarrassed. "Wisdom comes to all of us with age. But some are born wise. Wouldn't you expect that the Matriarch of Matriarchs, the wisest of all, would be special? *Wouldn't* you?"

"I don't know . . ."

"You're so much trouble to me, Longtusk! Always wandering off or getting under my feet or fighting with your sister or embarrassing me—sometimes I wish you were still in my belly, like this little one." She stroked the heavy bulge under her belly fur.

Longtusk fumed silently.

Splayfoot came galloping up to him. His sister was a knot of fat and orange fur, with a trunk like a worm and tusks like lemming bones, and her face was rounded and smoothed-out, as if unfinished. This was her first summer, and her new-born coat of coarse underfur and light brown overfur was being replaced by thicker and longer fur—though it would be her second year before her coarse guard hairs began to appear. "You're so much trouble, Longtusk," she squeaked up at him gleefully. She started butting his legs with her little domed forehead. "I'll be Matriarch and you won't. Then I'll tell *you* what to do!"

He rumbled and raised his huge tusks over her head, meaning to frighten her.

The calf squealed and ran to her mother, who tucked Splayfoot under her belly. "*Will* you leave this little one alone?"

"It wasn't my fault!" Longtusk protested. "She started it . . ."

But Milkbreath had turned away. Splayfoot burrowed at her mother's chest, seeking her dugs. But Milkbreath had little milk. So, with a deep belch, she regurgitated grass and with gentle kisses fed the warm, pulped stuff to her daughter.

As she fed, Splayfoot peered out from under a fringe of fur, mocking him silently.

It wasn't so long since Milkbreath had fed *him* that way, murmuring about how important it was for him to eat the food that had been inside his mother's belly, for it contained marvelous substances that would help him digest. It hardly seemed any time at all.

And now look at him: pushed away, snapped at, ignored.

He stomped away, not looking back, not caring which way he went.

2

The Bachelor Herd

He came to a track.

It was a strip of bare brown ground a little wider than his own body. Where the muddy ground was firm he could see the round print left by the tough, cracked skin of a mammoth's sole, a spidery, distinctive map.

He turned and followed the trail, curious to find where it might lead.

To human eyes the mammoth steppe would have looked featureless. It was an immense plain that swept over the north of Eurasia, across the land bridge of Beringia and into North America. But to a mammoth it was as crowded with landmarks as any human city: rubbing trees, wallows, rich feeding areas, salt licks, water holes. And these key sites were linked by trails worn by centuries of mammoth footsteps, trails embedded deep in the mind of every adult Bull and Cow, patiently taught to the calves of each new generation.

Indeed, the land itself was shaped by the mammoths, who tore out trees and trampled the ground where they passed. Other creatures lived in the shadow of the mammoths: depending on the trails they made, using the water sources they opened up with their intelligence and strength. Even the plants, in their mindless way, relied on the scattering of their seeds over great ranges in mammoth dung. Without mammoths, the steppe would not have persisted.

Longtusk stomped through his world, still angry, obsessed. But he thought over the Matriarchs' conversation: Fireheads and Lost and huge global changes . . .

He had never seen the Fireheads himself, but he'd met adults who claimed they had. The Fireheads—said to be ferocious predators, creatures of sweeping, incomprehensible danger—seemed real enough, and every young mammoth was taught at a very early age that the only response to a Firehead was to flee.

But the Lost were something else: figures of legend, a deep terror embedded at the heart of the Cycle—the nemesis of the mammoths.

It all seemed unlikely to Longtusk. The mammoths were spread in enormous herds right around the world, and even the great cats feared them. What could possibly destroy them?

And besides, his curiosity was pricked.

Why were all these changes happening *now*? How quickly would they happen? And why did the world have to become a harder place when *he* was alive? Why couldn't he have lived long ago, in a time of calm and plenty?

And, most important of all, why didn't anybody take him seriously?

Oh, he knew that there came a time when every Bull became restless with his Family; sooner or later all Bulls leave to seek out the company of other males in the bachelor herds, to learn to fight and strut and compete. But it didn't do him any good, here and now, to know that; and it drove him crazy when all this was patiently *explained* to him by some smug, pitying aunt or cousin.

After an unmeasured time he paused and looked back. Preoccupied, he hadn't been paying much attention where he walked; now he found he'd come so far he couldn't see the mammoths any more.

He heard a thin howl, perhaps of a wolf. He suffered a heartbeat of panic, which he sternly suppressed.

So he had left them behind. What of it? He was a full-grown Bull—nearly—and he could look out for himself. Perhaps this was *his* time to leave his Family—to begin the serious business of life.

Anyhow—he told himself—he was pretty sure he could find his way back if he needed to.

With a renewed sense of purpose—and with those twinges of fear firmly pushed to the back of his mind—he set off once more.

He came to a river bank.

Mammoths had been here recently. The muddy ground close to the river's edge was bare of life, pitted by footprint craters, and the trees were sparse and uniformly damaged, branches smashed, trunks splintered and pushed over.

The water was cold. This was probably a run-off stream, coming from a melting glacier to the north. He sucked up a trunkful of water and held it long enough to take off its first chill. Then he raised his trunk and let the water trickle into his mouth.

He pushed farther along the cold mud of the bank. It wasn't easy going. The river had cut itself a shallow valley which offered some protection from the incessant steppe winds. As a result spruce trees grew unusually dense and tall here, and their branches clutched at him as he passed, so that he left behind clumps of ginger hair.

Then, through the trees, he glimpsed a gleam of tusks, a curling trunk, an unmistakable profile.

It was another mammoth: a massive Bull, come here to drink as he had.

Longtusk worked his way farther along the bank.

The Bull, unfamiliar to Longtusk, eyed him with a vague, languid curiosity. He would have towered over any human observer, as much as three meters tall at his shoulder.

And he towered over Longtusk.

"My name," the Bull rumbled, "is Rockheart."

"I'm Longtusk," he replied nervously. "And I—"

But the Bull had already turned away, his trunk hosing up prodigious volumes of water.

The Bull's high, domed head was large, a lever for his powerful jaw and a support for the great trunk that snaked down before him. He had a short but distinct neck, a cylinder of muscle supporting that massive head. His shoulders were humped by a mound of fat, and his back sloped sharply down toward the pelvis at the base of his spine. His tusks curled before him, great spirals of ivory chipped and scuffed from a lifetime of digging and fighting.

And his body, muscular, stocky, round, was coated by hair: great lengths of it, dark orange and brown, that hung like a skirt from his belly, down over his legs to the horny nails on his swollen pads of feet, and even in long beard-like fringes from his chin and trunk. His tail, raised slightly, was short, but more hair made it a long, supple insect whisk. His ears were small, tucked back close to his head, all but lost in the great mass of hair there.

Suddenly the ground shuddered under Longtusk's feet, and the river water trembled.

More mammoths, a crowd of them, came spilling down the bank, pushing and jostling, clumsy giants. They were all about the same size, Longtusk saw: no Cows, no infants here.

It was a bachelor herd.

Longtusk was thrilled. He had rarely been this close to full-grown Bulls. The Bulls kept to their own herds, away from the Cow-dominated Families of mothers and sisters and calves; Longtusk had seen them only in the distance, sweeping by, powerful, independent, and he had longed to run with them.

And now, perhaps, he would.

The Bulls spread out along the river bank. Before passing on toward the water, one or two regarded Longtusk: with mild curiosity over his outside tusks, or blank indifference, or amused contempt.

Longtusk followed, avid.

For half a day, as the sun climbed into the sky, the Bulls moved on along the river bank, jostling, jousting, drinking and eating.

Their walk, heavy and liquid, was oddly graceful. Their feet were pads that rested easily on the ground, swelling visibly with each step. Their trunks, heavy ropes dangling from the front of their faces, pulled the mammoths' heads from side to side as they swayed. Even as they drank they fed, almost continuously. They pulled at branches of the surrounding trees with their trunks, hauling off great leaf-coated stems with hissing rustles, and crammed the foliage into their small mouths.

The soughing of their footsteps was punctuated by deep breaths, the gurgle of immense stomachs, and subterranean rumbles from the sound organs of their heads. A human observer would have made little of these deep, angry noises. But Longtusk found it very easy to make out what these Bulls were saying to each other.

". . .You are in my way. Move aside."

"I was here in this place first. *You* move aside."

". . . This water is too cold. It lies heavy in my belly."

"That is because you are old and weak. I, however, am young and strong, and I find the water pleasantly cool."

"My tusks are not yet so old and feeble they could not crack your skull like a skua egg, calf."

"Perhaps you should demonstrate how that could be done, old one . . ."

Longtusk, following the great Bull Rockheart, was tolerated—as long as he didn't get in anybody's way—for he was, for now, too small to be a serious competitor. His tusks were, despite his youth, larger than many of the adults—but they only made him feel self-conscious, as if somehow he wasn't entitled to such magnificent weapons. He walked along with his head dipped, his tusks close to the ground.

Being with the Bulls was *not* like being with his Family.

Even the language was different. The Cows in the Families used more than twenty different kinds of rumble, a basic vocabulary from which they constructed their extremely complex communications. The Bulls only had four rumbles!—and those were to do with mockery, challenge and boasting.

His Family had been protective, nurturing—a safe place to be. But the bachelor herds were looser coalitions of Bulls, more interested in contest: verbal challenges, head butts, tusk clashes. The Bulls were constantly testing each other, exploring each other's strength and weight and determination, establishing a hierarchy of dominance.

This mattered, for it was the dominant Bulls who mated the Cows in oestrus.

Right now, Longtusk was at the very bottom of this hierarchy. But one day he would, of course, climb higher— why, to the very top . . .

"You have stepped on the hair of my feet."

Longtusk looked up at a wall of flesh, eyes like tar pits, tusks that swept over his head.

He had offended Rockheart.

The great Bull's guard hairs—dangling from his belly and trunk, long and lustrous—rippled like water, trapping the light. But loose underfur, working its way out through the layers of his guard hair in tatters around his flanks, made him look primordial, wild and unfinished.

Longtusk found himself trembling. He knew he should back down. But some of the other males nearby were watching with a lofty curiosity, and he was reminded sharply of how the Matriarch had watched his humiliation by his infant sister earlier.

If he had no place in the Family, he must find a place here. His Family had taught him how to live as a mammoth; now he must learn to be a Bull. And this was where it would begin.

So he stood his ground.

"Perhaps you have trouble understanding," Rockheart said with an ominous mildness. "You see, this is where I take my water."

"It is not your river alone," Longtusk said at last. He raised his head, and his tusks, long and proud, waved in the face of the great Bull.

Unfortunately one curling tusk caught in a tree root.

Longtusk's head was pulled sideways, making him stagger.

There was a subterranean murmur of amusement.

Rockheart simply stood his ground, unmoving, unblinking, like something which had grown out of this river bank. He said coldly, "I admire your tusks. But you are a calf. You lack prowess in their use."

Longtusk gathered his courage. He raised his tusks again. They were indeed long, but they were like saplings against Rockheart's stained pillars of ivory. "Perhaps you would care to join me in combat, so that you may show me exactly where my deficiencies lie."

And he dragged his head sideways so that his tusks clattered against Rockheart's. He felt a painful jar work its way up to his skull and neck, and the base of his tusks, where they were embedded in his face, ached violently.

Rockheart had not so much as flinched.

Longtusk raised his tusks for another strike.

With a speed that belied his bulk Rockheart stepped sideways, lowered his head and rammed it into Longtusk's midriff.

Longtusk staggered into icy mud, slipped and fell sprawling into the water.

He struggled to his feet. The hairs of his belly and trunk dangled under him in cold clinging masses.

The Bulls on the river bank were watching him, tusks raised, sniggering.

Rockheart took a last trunkful of water, sprayed it languidly over his back, and turned away. His massive feet left giant craters in the sticky mud as he walked off, utterly ignoring Longtusk and his struggles.

And now Longtusk heard a familiar, remote trumpeting . . . "Longtusk! Longtusk! Come here right now! . . ."

"There's your mother calling you," brayed a young

Bull. "Go back to her teat, little one. This is no place for you."

Longtusk, head averted, humiliated, stomped out of the river and through the stand of trees. Where he walked he left a trail of mud and drips of water.

That was the end of Longtusk's first encounter with a bachelor herd.

He could not know it, but it would be a long time before he would see one of his own kind again.

Not caring which way he went, Longtusk lumbered alone over the steppe, head down, ripping at the grass and herbs and grinding their roots with angry twists of his jaw.

He couldn't go back to the herd. And he wasn't going back to his Family. Not after all that had happened today. Not after *this*.

He didn't need his Family—*or* the Bulls who had taunted him. He was Longtusk! The greatest hero in the world!

Why couldn't anybody *see* that?

He walked on, faster and farther, so wrapped up in his troubles he didn't even notice the smoke until his eyes began to hurt.

3

The She-Cat

Startled, he looked up, blinking. Water was streaking down the hairs of his face.

Smoke billowed, acrid and dark; somewhere nearby the dry grass was burning.

Every instinct told him to flee, to get away from the blaze. But which way?

If she were with him, his mother would know what to do. Even a brutal Bull like Rockheart would guide him, for it was the way of mammoths to train and protect their young.

But they weren't here.

Now, through the smoke, he saw running creatures, silhouetted against the glow: thin, lithe, upright. They looked a little like cats. But they ran upright, as no cat did. And they seemed to carry things in their front paws. They darted back and forth, mysterious, purposeful.

Perhaps they weren't real. Perhaps they were signs of his fear.

He felt panic rise in his chest, threatening to choke him.

He turned and faced into the smoke. He thought he could see a glow there, yellow and crimson. It was the fire itself, following the bank of smoke it created, both of them driven by the wind from the south.

Then he should run to the north, away from the fire. That must be the way the other mammoths were fleeing.

But fire—sparked by lightning strikes and driven by the incessant winds—could race across the dry land. Steppe plants grew only shallowly, and were easily and quickly consumed. Mammoths were strong, stocky, round as boulders: built for endurance, not for speed. He knew he could never outrun a steppe firestorm.

What, then?

Through his fear, he felt a pang of indignation. Was he doomed to die here, alone, in a world turned to gray and black by smoke?—he, Longtusk, the center of the universe, the most important mammoth who ever lived?

Well, if he wanted to live, he couldn't wait around for somebody else to tell him what to do. Think, Longtusk!

The smoke seemed to clear a little. Above him, between scudding billows of smoke, the sun showed a spectral, attenuated disc.

He looked down at his feet and found he was standing in a patch of muddy ground, bare of grass and other vegetation. It was a drying river bed, the mud cut by twisted, braided channels. There was nothing to burn here; that must be why the smoke was sparse.

He looked along the line of the river. It ran almost directly south. No grass grew on this sticky, clinging mud—and where the dry driver snaked off into the smoke, the glow of the fire seemed reduced, for there was nothing to burn on this mud.

If he walked *that* way, southward into the face of the smoke, he would be walking toward the fire—but along a channel where the fire could not reach. Soon, surely, he would get through the smoke and the fire, and reach the cleaner air beyond.

He quailed from the idea. It went against every instinct he had—to walk *into* a blazing fire! But if it was the right thing to do, he must overcome his fear.

He raised his trunk at the fire and trumpeted his defiance. And, dropping his head, he began to march stolidly south.

The smoke billowed directly into his face, laced with steppe dust: hot grit that peppered his eyes and scraped in his chest. And now the fire's crackling, rushing noise rose to a roar. He felt he would go mad with fear. But he bent his head and, doggedly, one step at a time, he continued, into the teeth of the blaze.

At last the fire roared around him, and the flames leaped, dazzling white, as they consumed the thin steppe vegetation. Only a few paces away from him grass and low trees were crackling, blackening. Tufts of burning grass and bark scraps fluttered through the air. Some of them stuck to his fur, making it smolder, and he batted them away with his trunk or his tail.

But he had been right. The fire could not reach across the mud of this river bed, and so it could not reach him.

And now there was a change. The sound of the fire seemed diminished, and he found he was breathing a little easier. Blinking, he forced open his eyes and looked down.

He was still standing in his river bed. Its surface had been dried out and cracked by the ferocious heat. To either side the ground was lifeless, marked by the smoldering stumps of ground-covering trees and the blackened remnants of grass and sedge. Near one tree he saw the scorched corpse of some small animal, perhaps a lemming, its small white bones protruding.

The stink of smoke and ash was overwhelming. The steppe, as far as he could see, had turned to a plain of scorched cinders. Smoke still curled overhead . . . but it was a thinning gray layer which no longer covered the sinking sun.

And there was no fire.

He felt a surge of elation. He had done it! Alone, he had worked out how to survive, and had stuck to his resolve in the face of overwhelming danger. Let Rockheart see him now!—for he, Longtusk, alone, had today faced down and beaten a much more savage and ruthless enemy than any Bull mammoth.

. . . *Alone.* The word came back to haunt him, like the distant cry of a ptarmigan, and his elation evaporated.

He turned and faced northward. The fire was a wall across the steppe, from the eastern horizon to the west. Smoke billowed up before it in huge towering heaps, shaped by the wind. It was an awesome sight, and it cut the world in two.

He hammered at the ground with his feet, his stamps calling to the mammoths, his Family. But there was no reply, no rocky echo through the Earth. Of course not; the noise of the fire would overwhelm everything else, and before it all the mammoths must be fleeing—even the greatest of them all, the Matriarch of Matriarchs, fleeing north, even farther from Longtusk.

He would have no chance to gloat of his bravery to Rockheart, or his mother, or anyone else. For everything he knew—the Family, the Clan, the bachelor herd, *everything*—lay on the other side of that wall of fire.

He cried out, a mournful trumpet of desolation and loneliness.

He looked down at himself. He was a sorry sight, his fur laden with mud and heavily charred. And he was hungry and thirsty—in fact he had no clear memory of the last time he'd eaten.

The sun was dipping, reddening. Night would soon be here.

The last of his elation disappeared. He had thought he had won his battle by defeating the fire. But it seemed the battle was only just begun.

There was only one way for him to go: south, away from the fire. He lowered his head and began to walk.

As he marched into deepening darkness, he tried to feed, as mammoths must. But the scorched grass and sage crumbled at his touch.

His thirst was stronger than his hunger, in fact, but he found no free-standing water. He scraped hopefully at the ground with his tusks and feet. But only a little way down, the ground grew hard and cold. This was the permafrost, the deep layer of frozen soil which never thawed, even at the height of summer. He dug his trunk into the soil and sucked hopefully, but there were only drops of moisture to be had, trapped above the ice layer.

He came across a willow. It hugged the ground, low and flat, not rising higher than his knees. He prized it up with his tusks, stripped off its bark and munched the thin, dry stuff, seeking to assuage his thirst.

He knew there were places scattered around the steppe where free-standing water lay close to the surface, even in the depths of winter, and the mammoths could crack through snow and ice to reach it. The adults knew where to find such wells of life, using a deep knowledge of the land passed on from the generations before them—but Longtusk had only begun learning about the land. Now, scraping at the mud, adrift in this blackened landscape where even the trails had been scorched out of existence, he was learning how truly helpless he was.

He walked farther. The trees grew more thickly, short, ancient willows and birches. Soon there were so many of them they covered the ground with a thick matting of branches. He was walking, in fact, on top of a forest. This dry, cold, wind-blasted land was not a place where trees could grow tall.

. . . He heard a hiss, deep and sibilant, somewhere behind him.

Mammoths' necks are short and inflexible, and Longtusk had to turn all the way around—slowly, clumsily, heart hammering.

The cat gazed at him, utterly still, silent.

For an instant he felt overwhelmed, his mind reeling, his courage fragmenting. He was almost irritated. The bachelor herd, the smoke, the fire—wasn't that enough? Must he face this new peril as well?

But he knew he was in deadly danger, and he forced himself to alertness.

The cat was a female, he saw. She seemed huge to Longtusk: not much less than half his own height, rippling muscle under a smooth sheen of brown fur. Her ears were small and forward-pointed, her nose small and black.

And her two saber teeth swept down from her mouth, stained by something dark and crusted. Blood, perhaps. She must already have made a kill, of some prey animal disoriented by the fire. He could smell rotten meat on her breath.

Perhaps she had a family to feed, a brood of brawling sharp-toothed cubs. Cubs hungry for mammoth meat.

The sun, reddened by the smoky air, touched the horizon. Shadows fled across the scorched plains, and ruddy light gleamed deep in the carnivore's eye sockets.

And those eyes were fixed on Longtusk.

He raised his trunk and trumpeted. The sound rolled across the anechoic plains, purposeless.

The cat spread her claws, long and bright, and they sunk into the ground. Her muscles tensed in great sheets.

Fear clamored in his mind, threatening to drown out thought.

He tried to recall fragments of mammoth lore: that few mammoths are targeted by predators; that Bulls, not yet fully grown and yet driven to depart the Family—Bulls like himself—are the most vulnerable to predators like this cat; that the female cat, driven to provide for her family, is deadlier than the male.

But through all this one stark thought rattled around his awareness: *that it is at sunset that the predators hunt.*

She sprang. It was very sudden. Spitting, she soared through the air, a blur of muscle heading straight for his face, claws extended.

Blindly he raised his tusks.

She was knocked sideways, spitting and scratching.

. . . He was bleeding, he realized. There was a series of raked gashes across the front of his trunk, where a paw-swipe had caught him.

Trumpeting, he turned again.

She was crouched low, eyes on him once more, taking step after deliberate step toward him.

The mammoths evolved on open plains, where there is little cover. Under threat from a predator they adopt a ring formation, with the calves and the weak huddled at the center.

But now Longtusk was on his own, with nobody to cover his back, utterly exposed.

He broke away and fled. He couldn't help it.

She will try to slash your trunk. Avoid this. It will cause you agonizing pain and a great loss of blood. Use your tusks. Bring them down on her head to stun her, or stab her with the sharp tips. If she gets in closer, wrap your trunk around her and squeeze until her back breaks. If she gets beneath you, step on her and crush her skull. Never forget she is afraid too: you are bigger and stronger than her, and she knows it . . .

It was a comforting theory, and he recalled how he had played with other calves, mimicking attacks and defenses, swiping miniature tusks back and forth. But the reality, of this spitting, stinking, single-minded cat, was very different.

And now he felt a new sharp warmth on his right hind leg. She had gouged him again. The damage was superficial, but he could feel the blood pumping out of him, weakening him. He kept running, but now he was limping.

It had been a deliberate cut. The cat was trying to shorten the chase.

He ran toward a stand of tall trees, sheltered by an outcrop of rock, their branches green-black in the fading light. Perhaps there would be cover here. He ducked into the shadow of the trees, turned—

Suddenly there was a weight on his back, a mass of spitting, squalling fur, utterly unexpected, and then stabs of sharp pain all across his back: long claws digging through his fur and into his flesh.

He trumpeted in panic. He raised his trunk and tusks, but his neck was short and he could never reach so far. *The trees,* he realized. Their black branches loomed above him. She must have climbed into the branches and dropped down onto him.

On the steppe most trees hugged the ground. Longtusk wasn't used to trees looming over him. He hadn't even considered the possibility that the cat might do such a thing.

He felt, through sharpening stabs of pain, that she was digging her claws deeper into him, and her weight shifted. He knew what she was intending; he had seen the cats at work. She was opening her gaping mouth and raising her down-pointing saber teeth. In a moment she would use them to stab down into his helpless flesh, laying open his spine, or even his skull.

Then the pain would start.

She would not kill him quickly, he knew, for that was not the way of the cats; he would lie in blood and black agony, longing for a release to the aurora, while this cat and her foul cubs tore at his flesh—

He raised his trunk and bellowed defiance. No! He had beaten the fire. He would not be destroyed, in this dismal place, by a carrion-breathed cub of Aglu!

He charged straight at the trees. One branch, black and thick, cut across the sky, only a little above his head height.

As the branch struck her the cat yowled. The pain in his back deepened—her claws raked through his flesh as she tried to cling to him—but suddenly the pain's sharpness eased, and the weight of the cat was gone from his shoulders. Breathing hard, the wounds on his back cold, he whirled around, tusks raised, trunk tucked under his chin for protection.

The cat had vanished.

He trumpeted. His eyes, never strong, helped him little in this fading light. And he could smell nothing— nothing but the metallic stink of his own crusting blood. Probably she had gone downwind of him.

How could she have moved so quickly, so silently? She

was, he realized ruefully, much more expert at hunting than he was at being hunted.

The dark was deepening quickly. His thirst seemed to burn at his throat, a discomfort deeper even than the ache of his wounds. And he longed for shelter.

He recalled the outcrop of rock which had provided cover for these trees to grow. Clumsily, his torn leg and back aching, he lumbered around the trees. He came to a sheer wall of sandstone, perhaps twice as tall as he was, smoothly eroded, its base littered by frost-shattered scree, fallen branches and dead leaves. He moved as close to the rock face as he could, and turned to face the plains beyond.

Perhaps he could last through the night here. He might hear the cat approach if she came across the scree or the leaves. And in the morning—

There was liquid movement to his right. She had been hiding in the mound of broken wood and leaves. Now, gazing at him, she prepared to spring again.

He felt trapped in this dark, glacial moment.

He seemed to have time to study the cat's every detail: the sinuous beauty of her curved, taut muscles, the gaping, bloody maw of her mouth. Blood was crusted on her head, he noticed, a mark of his one minor victory, where he had managed to hurt her by driving her against the tree branch. But her eyes were on him, small and hard, and he could see that she knew she had won. In less than a heartbeat she would reach his soft belly with her claws, and his life would spill out on this lonely rock, far from those who had loved him.

. . . But the cat was hurled sideways and slammed into the rock face.

She fell, limp.

Time flooded over him again, and his heart hammered.

*   *   *

Cautiously, unable to believe he was still breathing, Longtusk crept closer. The cat lay where she had fallen, slumped in the leaves and the scree.

Blood welled from a huge wound in her temple, dark and thick, as if seeking to water the trees that grew here. The stillness of the cat was sudden, startling; this creature of motion and purpose and deadly beauty had become, in a heartbeat, a thing of the rock and the earth, her beautiful muscles slack and useless forever.

He felt no triumph, no relief: only numbness.

Something protruded from her skull.

It was wood, a long, straight branch. It had been stripped of bark, and one end narrowed to a sharp tip. The tip looked blackened, as if it had been in a fire; but it was evidently hard, hard as a tusk—for it had pierced the cat's skull, passing through a neat puncture in her temple and out the other side. The flying stick had knocked her out of her spring; she had probably been dead, he realized, even before she collided with the rock.

There was a rustle a few paces away.

Startled, he reared up and trumpeted.

There was something out there on the darkling plain. Something small, purposeful.

He was surprised to find he still had some fear left inside him, a small bubble of it that rose to the surface of his mind, despite his exhaustion.

But this was no cat. It walked upright, on its hind legs.

It was shorter than Longtusk, but it looked strong, with muscled legs and a broad chest. Its head was large with a wide fleshy nose, and a low brow made of caves of bone from which brown eyes peered suspiciously at Longtusk. Short black hair was matted on the creature's head, and it had fur over its body—*not its own fur,* Longtusk realized with a shock, but scraps of skin from ani-

mals, deer and bison and even fox, somehow joined together.

The two of them stared at each other.

Fragments of lore drifted through Longtusk's mind.
*They walk upright. They wear the skin of other creatures. There
is no fighting them; only flight is possible* . . .

This creature walked upright, like a Firehead. Was it
possible? . . .

But Longtusk felt no fear now. He seemed exhausted,
done with fear.

The strange beast, cautiously, walked forward on its
hind legs toward the cat. Longtusk wondered how it kept
from toppling over. It wrapped its big front paws around
the pointed stick, stepped on the cat's inert head, and
pulled hard. With some reluctance, the stick slid out of
the cat's skull.

Then, watching Longtusk, the creature jabbed with the
stick at the cat's head.

Showing him what it had done.

Slowly Longtusk understood. This creature had
thrown the stick through the air, driven it by sheer
strength and accuracy into the head of the cat—and
thereby saved Longtusk's life.

If this was a Firehead, it meant Longtusk no harm. Perhaps it was not a Firehead, but something else, something like a Firehead, a lesser threat.

Longtusk seemed unable to think it through, to pick
through bits of half-remembered lore.

The creature walked closer to Longtusk. Its head
moved back and forth, side to side, and its eyes were
bright and curious, even though it was obviously nervous of the mammoth's great tusks. It worked its mouth
and a strange complex growl emerged.

Then it reached out with one of its bare front paws,

and, leaning within the radius of the tusks, stroked the long furs on Longtusk's trunk. Longtusk flinched, but he was beyond fear now, and he submitted to the contact. The creature passed its fingers down through Longtusk's matted hair, the motion oddly soothing.

But the paw came away sticky with blood, and the creature looked at Longtusk with renewed concern.

It took its stick and began to walk away. A few paces from Longtusk, it paused and looked back.

Longtusk looked down at the shadowy form of the dead cat. Though the rock would provide him with shelter, he had no desire to stay here. This sinuous corpse, still leaking blood, would surely soon attract more predators, hyenas and foxes and maybe even other cats, before the condors descended on what was left of the carcass.

The light was all but gone, and the wind was rising.

He looked up. The upright creature was still waiting, looking back. And Longtusk had no real choice.

Slowly they walked into the night, the woolly mammoth following the Neanderthal boy.

4
The Dreamers

They came to a shallow river valley, where running water—perhaps a tributary of the dried-out stream that had saved Longtusk from the fire—had cut its way into the hard black rock of the ground.

The upright creature scrambled down a heap of frost-shattered scree. It reached a hole of deeper darkness cut into the hillside. It was a cave, Longtusk realized.

And a glimmer of ruddy light came from within it.

Longtusk was baffled. How could there be light *inside* a cave, a place of shadows?

. . . And now Longtusk's sharp sense of smell detected the tang of smoke, carried on the light evening breeze, and he understood the source of that strange inner glow.

Fire. His upright friend had walked into fire—maybe a nest of true Fireheads!

Longtusk stood there on the river bank, torn by conflicting impulses. Should he flee, or should he rush down the bank and pull out his friend, saving the squat little creature as it had saved him from the she-cat?

But his friend had gone into the cave willingly, with no sign of fear.

The sun had not yet risen since Longtusk had been

separated from his Family. And yet already he had endured a blizzard of new experiences. Perhaps this new vision, of fire within a cave, was simply one more strangeness he must strive to understand.

But none of that mattered. It was almost completely dark now. He was hungry, tired, thirsty— and alone once more.

Using his trunk to feel his way, he worked through the rocks to the edge of the river. He walked farther, following the stream. The river bed shallowed, and he sensed a lake opening out before him: a scent of cold fresh water, a soft sweep of wind across an expansive surface. At the edge of the lake, lying along the shallow beach, he found great linear heaps of feathers left by molting ducks and geese.

When he waded into the water its icy cold struck through the layers of fur on his legs, and he almost cried out from the pain of the wounds inflicted by the cat. But as the water lifted off the caked blood and dirt, the sharp pain turned to a wider ache, and he sensed the start of healing.

He took a trunkful of water and lifted it to his mouth; it was cool and delicious, and he drank again and again, assuaging a thirst he had nursed since the terrible moments of the fire.

He retreated to the tumbled rocks of the shore. He found a gap between two tall rock faces. He nestled there and, trying to ignore the continuing cold ache of his back and legs, waited for sleep to claim him.

In the morning, with the low sun glowing red through the last of yesterday's smoke, he made his way out of his rock cleft and down to the water.

Near the lake, the water and air and land were full of

birds: many species of geese, ducks, even swans on the water, blackbirds and sparrows on the marshy land, and occasional hunters—hawks, kestrels. The short summer was ending, a time when the birds swarmed to breeding grounds like this.

A flock of geese floated on the water, a huge raft of them. They had shed all their flight feathers at once, a great catastrophic molt that had left them temporarily unable to fly, as they put all their energy into breeding and raising young and storing fat for the return journey to their winter lands in the south. All of this had to be completed in just forty or fifty days, before the snow and ice clamped down on the land again.

The rocks were covered by a fine hoar frost, so slippery that even the heavy, wrinkled pads of his feet could not find a firm footing. There was no food to be had here. Nothing grew on these rocks and pebbles and scree, all of it regularly inundated by the flooding lake, save lichen and weed. He knew, gloomily, he would have to travel far today to find the fodder he needed.

But yesterday had depleted him. The wounds on his back ached badly, and he wondered if they were festering. He felt dizzy, oddly hollow, and his eyes were gritty and sore.

Something startled the birds. Ducks and swans rose from the water, a racket of rattling, snapping wings, leaving behind the barking, flightless geese. The birds caught the light, and they seemed to glow against the dull gray of the sky, as if burning from within. There were actually many flocks, he realized, passing to and fro in a great lattice above him, as if he were standing at the bottom of an ocean through which these birds swam.

And he was still utterly, desolately, alone. He wished his Family were here.

. . . There was a splashing sound, a little way out from the lake shore. He turned slowly. He saw motion, a ripple on the water, but his eyes were too poor to make out anything more clearly.

The splashing creature stood up in the water on its two hind legs: upright, ungainly, brushing drops from the hair on its head. It was his friend of yesterday. It had discarded its furs; they lay in a neat pile on the shore. And now Longtusk could clearly see that it—*he*—was a male. His body was coated by a fine light brown hair; wet, it lay flat against the contours of his body. There was an odd patch of discoloration on his face, a jagged line across his cheek like the aurora's subtle curtain. Perhaps it was a birthmark, Longtusk speculated.

He was pushing a twig of some kind—Longtusk thought it was willow—into his mouth and expertly swiveling it around with his paw. Perhaps he was cleaning out his teeth.

Willow, he thought. That's what I will call this odd little creature. Willow.

Longtusk didn't like to admit to himself how pleased he was to see a familiar creature.

Willow let the water drain from his eyes—and he saw Longtusk clearly, standing placidly on the shore only a few paces away.

He yelped in shock, and glanced over at his pile of furs. There was a pointed stick resting there——perhaps the one he had used yesterday against the cat—but it was much too far away to reach.

But of course Longtusk meant him no harm. And when he realized this, after long heartbeats, Willow seemed to relax.

With much splashing, Willow made his way through the water to Longtusk. He reached out to scratch the mammoth's trunk hair as he had the day before. His mouth issued a stream of incomprehensible grunts; his row of teeth shone white in the morning sun.

Willow's face was round, all but bare of the light hair that coated the rest of his muscular body. His skull was long, and black hair dangled from it as from the belly of a mammoth. His nose was broad and deep, and his face seemed to protrude, almost as if it had been pulled forward by his great nostrils. His eyes gleamed like lumps of amber beneath huge bony forehead ridges.

He lifted his willow stick and offered it to Longtusk. For an instant the stubby fingers at the end of Longtusk's trunk touched Willow's palm, and Willow snatched back his paw with a frightened yelp. But then he held the stick forward again, and let Longtusk take it.

Longtusk had never seen Willow's kind before, but now, in the light of day, his mind more clear, he knew what this creature was.

These were not Fireheads, but the cousins of Fireheads. The mammoths called them *Dreamers*.

Dreamers could be found in little pockets of habitation around the landscape, rarely traveling far from their homes. They would sometimes scavenge dead mammoths, but unlike other predators they were little threat.

And there were very few of them. Once—it was said in the Cycle—the Dreamers had covered the world. Now they were rarely encountered.

Willow ran his little paws through the long hairs on Longtusk's flank and back. When he probed at the broken flesh there, Longtusk couldn't help but flinch and growl. Willow stumbled back, his paws coated with blood and dirt.

The Dreamer cupped his paws and began to ladle water over Longtusk's back. As blood and dirt was

41

washed away, the pain was clear and sharp, but Long-tusk made himself stand stock still.

Then Willow bent over and dug. He straightened up with his paws full of black, sticky lake-bottom mud. He began to cake this liberally over Longtusk's wounds. Again this hurt—especially as the little Dreamer couldn't see what he was doing, and frequently poked a finger into a raw wound. But already Longtusk could feel how the thick mud was soothing the ache of his injuries.

There was a guttural shout from the shore. Both Long-tusk and Willow turned.

It was another Dreamer, like Willow. But this one was much taller—presumably an adult, probably a male—and it, he, was dressed in thick heavy furs. There was no hair on the top of his long boulder-shaped head, which was marked with strange stripes of red and yellow.

Stripeskull, Longtusk thought.

Stripeskull had a pointed stick in his paw. This was no skinny sapling as Willow had carried, but a thick wooden shaft, its tip cruelly sharp and blackened by fire—and even Willow's little stick had been enough to bring down a cat, Longtusk recalled. Stripeskull's mus-cles bulged, and Longtusk had no doubt he would be able to hurl that stick hard enough to slice right through Longtusk's thick skin.

But Willow ran out of the lake, dripping glistening water, waving his forelegs in the air. Stripeskull was obvi-ously angry and frightened—but he was hesitating, Long-tusk saw.

The huge adult grabbed Willow's arm in one mighty paw and pulled him away from the lake. Again he raised his stick at Longtusk and jabbered something complex and angry. Then he turned and retreated toward the fire cave, dragging Willow with him.

Willow looked back once. Longtusk wondered if he could read regret, even longing, in the little one's manner.

It didn't matter. For Longtusk, of course, had no place here. Sadly he started to work his way out through the boulders and scree to the higher ground, seeking food.

In the days that followed, Longtusk walked far and wide.

It wasn't particularly surprising that this land was so unfamiliar to him. It was an unpromising, ugly place, all but barren—not a place for mammoths. There seemed to be a sheet of hard black rock that underlay much of the land; here and there the rock broke to the surface, and in those places nothing grew save a few hardy lichen. Even where the rock was buried it had pushed the permafrost closer to the surface, and little could grow in the thin layer of moist soil on top.

Longtusk was a big animal, and he needed to find a great deal of fodder every day. Soon he had to walk far to find a place beyond his own trample marks and decaying spoor.

Still he saw no sign of any other mammoth: no trails, no spoor save his own. He tried trumpeting, rumbling and stamping. His sensitive ears picked up only the distant howl of wolves, the slow grind of the ice sheet to the north, the moan of chill air spilling down from the North Pole.

And winter was drawing in rapidly, the days shriveling and the nights turning into long, cold, star-frosted deserts of darkness. It was a winter Longtusk knew he would be lucky to survive, alone.

Though he roamed far, he was drawn back to the lake and the cave. After all the only being in his world who had shown him any kindness was the Dreamer cub, Willow. It was hard to leave that behind.

There was more than one cave, in fact. There was a whole string of them, right along the river bank and lake shore, gaping mouths in the rock from which the Dreamers would emerge, daily, to do their chores.

Longtusk watched them.

The males would seek out meat. With their long blackened sticks they hunted smaller animals like reindeer and red deer. They generally ignored the larger animals, like horses and aurochs. But they would often scavenge meat from an animal brought down by some more fierce predator, chasing away the hyenas and condors, slicing at the carcass with pieces of stone they held in their paws.

The males ate their meat out in the field, taking little back to the caves. Longtusk realized that like mammoth Bulls they did not provide food or protection for their cubs. That was the job of the females. Slowed by their young, often laden with infants clamped to their breasts, the females did not travel as far as the males, and so did not eat so well. They would hunt with small sticks, seeking out game like rabbits or birds. But their principal foodstuff, plucked from the lake, was aquatic plants like cattails.

The females were as strong and stocky as the males, for they worked even harder in their relentless drive to sustain and protect themselves and their cubs.

As wide as he traveled, Longtusk saw no other groups of Dreamers. This small Clan in their caves seemed utterly isolated, cut off from the rest of their kind. And yet that seemed unimportant to them. They were immersed in their small world, in themselves, in each other; they had no need for a wider web of social contacts like the mammoths' Clans.

All this Longtusk saw in glimpses, as the Moon cycled in the sky. But as a growing mammoth he was not exactly inconspicuous; and whenever the Dreamers saw him they would shout and jab sticks and hurl rocks until he went away. They were not mammoth hunters by habit, but Longtusk knew they could easily kill him if they chose, or if he seemed threatening enough. He recoiled from their weapons, and their hostility—a hostility that seemed shared by all except Willow.

Willow remained with the females and their brood. But he seemed somehow distanced, older than the rest of the infants, often the subject of an irritable cuff from one female or another. Perhaps that was why Willow's behavior was different from the others, why he had been moved to risk his own life to save a mammoth's. Longtusk wondered if Willow, like Longtusk himself, was reaching a cusp, preparing to leave his mother and her sisters and seek out the male hunter groups.

The strange idea that he and Willow might have something in common was obscurely comforting.

As winter drew in, the nights grew long and deep, the days brief.

There was a spate of early snow storms. The air here was sucked dry by the icecap, and there was little fresh snow. But ground blizzards, with old snow picked up by heavy winds, frequently occurred. So, when it snowed, it was usually in the midst of a ferocious wind storm that might persist for days.

Longtusk endured the blizzards. He felt the snow's weight gather on his back, but he knew he was protected. His body generated its own heat by slowly burning the fat reserves he had stored up during the summer. That heat was trapped with remarkable efficiency by his shell of fur and guard hairs—so well, in fact, that snow that fell on his back did not melt.

Still, in the worst of the weather, he could do nothing but stand in his shell of snow and endure. Any movement would have burned up the fat reserves whose primary use was keeping him alive. But even so, despite his hoarding of his reserves, he felt himself being depleted, bit by bit, as the winter drew in.

When the weather relented, Longtusk traveled even farther than before in search of food.

In some places the wind kept patches of sun-cured summer grass free of heavy snow. When he uncovered the ground to feed, he was followed by Arctic hares or ptarmigan, seeking willow buds and insects.

But the land had emptied. The migrant animals like the deer had gone far south to warmer climes, and the Arctic foxes had retreated to sea ice, living exclusively from the remnants of polar bear kills. Some life persisted, nevertheless. There were lemmings that burrowed beneath the snow, ptarmigans that dove into drifts for insulation, even plants that managed to flourish in pockets of warm air beneath the ice.

In these days of darkness and cold and windblown snow, everything was slowed. To extend a trunk tip or open an eye, unprotected by fur, could lead to agonizing pain. Any bit of moisture would turn to crystals, creating an ice fog; when he walked a cloud hung over him, shining with light.

Once he saw a snowy owl gliding silently past, and its breath trailed after it in the air.

One fiercely cold day he walked along the river valley near the Dreamers' caves, seeking water. But he found the river here had run dry.

The river had iced over. But the ice crust had broken

and fallen in, and the valley floor beneath was dry. The river had first frozen over, but then the watershed farther upstream had frozen, and the water beneath the ice crust had stopped flowing. The river had drained away, leaving the unsupported crust above.

Longtusk climbed down to the river bed, the bones of fish crunching beneath his feet, grubbing for water in the cold mud.

He followed the dry bed until he reached the lake, and there, at last, he drank deeply.

But a few days later, the lake froze over.

Longtusk bent to the water's edge and tried to crack the ice with his tusks. The ice splintered and starred as he scraped. But close to the bank, where the ice clung to the muddy bottom, there was too little water beneath to satisfy his thirst. And he knew that if he ventured farther out the ice could crack under him, and he could become trapped in the mud, even drown.

He walked along the shore, seeking a place he knew where the water ran over big chunks of black rock. But even this waterfall had frozen over; great lumps and streamers of white ice clung to the rocks.

He could survive on little food—but he needed water.

He lacked a detailed knowledge of this landscape. He had no idea where he might find frozen-over ponds whose crusts might be thin enough to break with his tusks; nor did he have the skills to discover new water sources for himself.

He was cut off from the wisdom of the Clan. He knew he had much to learn about the land and how to survive—and nobody was here to teach him.

For days, lacking any better idea, he survived on nothing but dribbles of muddy, half-frozen lake bed ooze, and his strength dwindled further.

But then, when he returned hopefully to the lake, he found a wide area of it had been cleared of ice. Without hesitation Longtusk splashed out into the water, ignoring its sharp cold as it soaked into the hair of his legs. He dipped his trunk into the clear liquid and sucked it up gratefully.

The break in the ice was suspiciously neat, a half-disc like a waning Moon. Its inner rim looked chipped and scarred—as if by the paw of a Dreamer.

This cleared pool was not natural; it must be the work of his only friend, the Dreamer cub Willow, who must have seen his distress and decided to help him. Despite the chill of the brief winter day, Longtusk felt warmed.

But soon the winter's cold bit harder.

A savage wind from the north, spilling off the flanks of the ice sheet itself, howled across the battered, exposed land. Dust closed around him, shutting out the brief slivers of daylight. This storm brought little snow, but it drove great billows of dust and sand from the pulverized lands uncovered by the retreating ice.

This was an age of savage weather, dominated by the huge masses of cold air that lingered over the immense polar ice sheets, driven to instability by the accelerating warming of the climate. This hard, dry storm, Longtusk knew, might last for months.

He saw no sign of the Dreamers. They must have been sheltering in their caves.

As for himself, he could only push his body against the rocks of the river bank and try to endure.

The days of the storm wore on. He had nothing to drink but scraps of ice and snow, which anyhow chilled him as much as nourished him; and he couldn't even re-call when he had last found anything to eat.

Frost gathered around his mouth and trunk tip and gummed up his eyes. A deep shivering worked its way into his bones.

It was the wind that did the damage. Still air wouldn't have been so bad, for a thin layer of warm air would have gathered around his body. But the wind, impatient and snatching, stole each scrap of heat his body pro-duced, casting it into the south, gone, useless.

If he was with his Family they would have huddled now, gathered in a group, the youngest calves at the center of the huddle, the adults taking their turns on the outside of the group, facing into the wind. Thanks to the Family, few mammoths would perish in such a storm.

But here, alone, Longtusk had no others to help him and protect him: only these mute, uncaring rocks.

And he knew it wasn't enough.

The shivering went away, and the cold started to pen-etrate deep into the core of his body. When it got there, he would quietly slide into a final sleep, not to wake again until he reached the aurora.

But perhaps that wouldn't be so bad. Perhaps there he would find his mother and his sister and even that bul-lying oaf Rockheart, whom he would now never get a chance to best.

As the cold gathered around his heart, he felt almost peaceful.

. . . There was something warm and soft at the tip of his trunk. It was tugging at him. He tried to open his eyes, but they were shut by ice. He shook his head, rumbling, and forced his eyelids to open with a soft crackle.

Sand and grit immediately dug into his opened eyes. The storm still raged all around him.

Something stood before him, a bundle of fur, upright. Brown eyes peered.

It was Willow. And, with one fur-wrapped paw, the Dreamer cub was tugging at Longtusk's trunk, urging him to follow.

Longtusk had almost reached the blank numbness of death, and it had been comfortable. If he returned to the land of life, he would face all its complexities: choices, hardship, pain. If only Willow let him alone . . . Just a little longer . . .

But you are Longtusk. Surely the greatest hero of them all is destined for a better death than this: alone, ignored, frozen by the mindless wind. Take your chance, Longtusk!

His trunk-fingers slipped into Willow's palm.

It was difficult to walk. His joints had become stiff, so deeply had the cold penetrated them. And when he moved out of the shelter of the rocks, the wind battered him unhindered.

But it wasn't easy for the Dreamer cub either. He felt Willow stagger, but the cub pulled himself upright against Longtusk.

They seemed to walk for a very long time.

At last they reached a place where the wind was diminished. And Longtusk felt a deep warmth radiating over his face and chest.

He was in the mouth of one of the caves. Willow was standing beside him, pulling off his furs in great frosty grit-laden bundles.

The cave was a well of red light and warmth. Flaps of animal skin had been fixed over this cave mouth. Perhaps they were supposed to drape over the entrance, keeping its warmth inside, like the flap of skin over a mammoth's anus.

The warmth came from fire, he realized suddenly: a fire that burned, smokily, in a circle of stones.

He recoiled, instinctive fear rising anew in him. But behind him, the Beringian night howled its fury.

There was no place for him out there. Despite the fire, he forced himself to stay still.

There were many Dreamers here: females, males, infants. They lay on the floor of the cave, fat and sleepy, all of them slabs of muscle. The females clustered together with their infants away from the males, who lay on their backs snoring. Some were naked; others wore light skins around their shoulders and waists. Their bare skin looked greasy, as if it had been coated by the fat of some dead animal—perhaps to keep in their bodies' warmth.

One of the dozing males stirred, perhaps disturbed by the wind that leaked in through the open skins. It was Stripeskull, his red and yellow scalp unmistakable.

His eyes grew large as he saw a mammoth standing in the cave entrance, immense tusk shadows striped over the walls.

With surprising grace Stripeskull rolled to his feet and barked out guttural noises. Other males woke up, blinking and rubbing their eyes; when they saw Longtusk they quickly got to their hind legs, grabbing sticks of wood and sharp stones.

. . . Then the males fell back, making retching noises and waving their paws before their faces.

Longtusk realized that he had just defecated, as mammoths do many times a day, barely conscious of it. He looked back. His dung was a pile of tubular bricks, acrid, immense. He tried to push it outside the cave. But he succeeded only in smearing the hot, sticky stuff over the cave floor.

Willow was going forward to meet Stripeskull. They jabbered at each other in a fast, complex flow; they made gestures too with their heads and paws. It was obviously a language, Longtusk realized, like the mammoths' language of trumpets, growls, stomps and postures. But he had absolutely no idea what they were saying to each other. Perhaps even the frequent cuffs about the head which Stripeskull delivered to Willow were like the mammoths' subtle code of touch and rubbing. But from the way Willow was rubbing his head it was obvious the blows were also meant to hurt.

Lacking any alternative, exhausted, Longtusk stood in the cave mouth and awaited his fate.

At last Willow came to him. He reached out to Longtusk's trunk, and pushed.

Longtusk understood. He let himself be moved back out of the cave. He wasn't welcome here; it had only been a childish impulse of Willow's to bring him here in the first place.

So he must suffer the wind's bony embrace once more. He felt a stab of resentment at the pain he would have to endure before he regained that numb acceptance . . .

But Willow was pulling at his trunk. He looked down. The Dreamer cub was hauling as hard as he could, his feet scraping along the ground, trying to halt the retreating mammoth.

Longtusk stopped. He was out of the cave itself, beyond the curtain of skins, but still inside its mouth. It was enough to shelter him from the wind, and the heat that leaked out of the cave seeped into his bones.

Willow held up a twig of dried wood. Longtusk had

time to grab it before the cub was snatched out of sight by a glaring Stripeskull, who pulled closed the skins, shutting Longtusk out in the dark.

Longtusk munched on the twig, and—standing in the mouth of the cave, on ground imprinted by splayed Dreamer feet, bathed by stray fire warmth—he slipped easily into a deep and dreamless sleep.

5

The Cave

The storm persisted.

Willow brought him water in a sack of skin. Longtusk drank greedily, despite a lingering stink of bison. But a mammoth is a large animal and the load of water—almost too much for Willow to carry—was downed in a couple of heartbeats.

Willow tried bringing him food. At first he produced scraps of meat, dried and salted. The stench was horrifying, and Longtusk shied back.

After that Willow brought him dried grass. There was a lot of grass in the cave; the Dreamers scattered it over the cave floor and pulled it into rough pallets to sleep on. The grass was stale and stank of the Dreamers and their fire, but it rapidly filled up his belly.

After a few days he noticed the Dreamers going out, wrapped in their furs, bringing back loads of his dung. During his brief glimpses through the parted skins, Longtusk saw that they burned the dried dung in their wide, flat hearth—along with grass, wood, bone and even bat guano, scraped from great dry heaps at the back of the cave.

The hearth—a disk of blackened earth, lined with flat

stones—was the centerpiece of the cave. The adults took turns to check on the burning embers, piling on more fuel, or blowing on the glowing lumps of dung and wood and bone. The low fire kept the Dreamers alive, and maintaining it was their single most important activity.

The cave walls were pale rock, and the fire's ruddy light would glimmer from the fleshy stone, casting strange and colorful shadows.

Generally the Dreamers lived as mammoths do, Longtusk observed. The adult males kept to their own society away from the females. The males seemed to spend an inordinate amount of time belching, farting and scratching their testicles. The females grunted at each other continually and watched over their cubs with a sort of irritable affection.

Once a female came into oestrus. She walked provocatively past the indolent males, who rose from their slumbers with growls of interest. A brief contest of shouting and wrestling resolved itself in favor of Stripeskull, and he took the female by the paw and led her to the back of the cave.

The coupling of these two muscle-bound creatures was noisy and spectacular. Afterward the pair of them returned to the hearth, sweating and exhilarated.

Most of the males carried pointed sticks, Longtusk saw. The biggest, strongest males—like Stripeskull—had the proudest sticks. Youngsters like Willow and old, bent, toothless adults had to make do with shorter sticks, some of them broken discards. But even the infants would toddle back and forth waving tiny sharpened branches and yelling.

The sticks were like the tusks of mammoth Bulls, Longtusk realized: not just useful tools, but weapons to be cherished and displayed.

One day Longtusk saw where the sticks came from.

At the back of the cave had been stacked some saplings, slim and straight. Stripeskull took one of these, stripped it of its branches and bark with stone scrapers, and then whittled down one end to a point with more chips of stone. Then he laid the sharpened end into the fire until it charred, and scraped it some more until it was fine and sharp.

He tested it by ramming it into animal carcasses hanging at the back of the cave. The exposure to fire, far from destroying the stick as Longtusk would have expected, had made it harder and more able to penetrate.

He realized now that he owed his life to this strange ingenuity—that and the courage of the cub, Willow.

But the Dreamers were capable of much stranger miracles than merely sharpening sticks.

Longtusk watched as Stripeskull took a nodule of creamy flint. He had gathered it from the river bank, where it had been washed down from chalk deposits upstream. Stripeskull sat near the hearth and laid around him other blocks of stone and bits of bone. Using one of the heavy stones, wrapped in his paw, Stripeskull began to chip at the flint block. Soon he was surrounded by a scattering of fine flakes—but he had turned his rough block of flint into a core shaped like a fat lemming, Longtusk thought, flat on the bottom and rounded on the top. Then he rubbed and ground the rim of the core, flattening it.

What came next seemed to demand great care. He turned the core over, finally selecting a spot. Then he cupped it in one paw, raised the leg bone of a deer in the other, and gave the core a single sharp whack.

When he lifted the flint out of his paw, he left behind a round flake, very fine, its exposed surface smooth as new ice. He inspected it critically, tapped a few flakes off its edge, and tested its sharpness by rubbing it over his leg, shaving off a small patch of fur.

Then he put it to one side, returned to his core, and continued work. When he was done, he had turned a lump of unpromising flint into half a dozen fine stone blades.

He was evidently trying to teach the cub, Willow, how to work the flint. Like a mammoth calf trying to dig out his first waterhole, Willow tried to ape Stripeskull's actions. But his flint nodules just smashed and chipped, and Willow, frustrated, threw away the debris in disgust. The next day Stripeskull would sit with him, patiently, to try again.

After watching all this, Longtusk found a flint nodule just outside the cave mouth. Nearby he saw a scattering of broken flint flakes. He picked up the nodule in his trunk-fingers and turned it over and over. He tried to recall what he had seen, how these objects had been shaped by the ingenuity of Stripeskull. But already the memory of that mysterious magic was slipping from his mind.

Mammoths too could change the world: destroying trees, digging for water, clearing snow. But they would never learn to shape the things around them with the command of these strange, clumsy, upright Dreamers.

The Dreamers put the stones to use in every corner of their cave.

At the back of the cave hung the butchered carcasses of many animals—deer, reindeer, horse and bison—and their skins were stretched out to dry with stones and sticks. Sometimes one of the adults would scrape a skin with a slice of rock, over and over, working the skin to a supple smoothness. Longtusk marveled at the way the

Dreamers' powerful muscles worked, and the stone responded to their huge, dextrous fingers.

And there were even finer uses for the stones. All of the Dreamers used stone flakes to cut the hair that dangled from their heads, or to scrape their faces. Every few days Stripeskull himself would use one of his flint slices to scrape smooth the hair on his head. Then he would splash the raw skin with cold water, and draw lumps of ochre, bits of red and yellow rock, across his scalp to renew his gaudy coloring.

It was obvious from the powerful physique of all the Dreamers, males, females and cubs, that everybody here was expected to work hard throughout their lives. Many of them showed signs of old injury. But the old, the very young, the sick and the frail were cared for.

One small cub, though, was very sickly, much skinnier than others of its height. Longtusk saw how she had trouble feeding herself, despite her mother's increasingly frantic assistance.

There came a day when the cub would not stir from her pallet of grass. Her mother struggled to wake her, and she even tried to suckle the cub, though her breasts were flaccid and empty of milk.

At last the mother gave up. She came to the mouth of the cave. She tipped back her great head on its low, thick neck and raised the limp body of her cub to a stormy sky.

The other females gathered close to the distressed one, comforting her with strokes and caresses. The younger cubs pulled away to the corners of the cave, wide-eyed. The adult males, awkwardly, kept away from the females—all save two of them, who began to dig a deep hole in the ground.

When the hole was done, deep and straight-edged,

Stripeskull clambered into the pit with the body of the female cub. The little one had been washed, her hair shaved and tidied. The grieving mother dropped dried flowers over the body, and Stripeskull sprinkled powdered ochre, a red mist that floated gently down into the pit.

Then the Dreamers began to sing—all of them, adults and all but the smallest cubs—a strange, deep ululation that rolled endlessly like a river, smooth and sad.

Longtusk understood. These Dreamers, in their own way, were Remembering the cub, just as mammoths have always Remembered their own dead.

Longtusk saw that the walls of the grave pit, deep and sheer, were made up of complex layers of debris: rock, flint flakes, blackened ashy dust, bone splinters. Such detritus could only have been laid down by the Dreamers themselves. The Dreamers must have inhabited this cave—on this undistinguished river bank, making their unchanging hearths and tools—for generation upon generation upon generation: an unimaginably long time, reaching into their deepest past. Perhaps there were more bones buried deep here—bones a hundred thousand years deep, likewise scattered with flowers and ochre flakes—here in this trampled ground, where these strange creatures had dreamed away the unchanging millennia.

And still they sang.

Did they sing of a time when their kind had covered the world? Did they sing of their loss, their diminution to dwindling, isolated groups like this?

Did they sing of their future—and their fear?

Longtusk slipped away from the cave mouth and walked off, ignoring the driving dust, until he could hear the Dreamers' song no more.

*　　*　　*

The dust storm passed, and the cold began to ease its grip.

Heavy rain pounded the land, and glacial run-off poured along the river valley, threatening floods. The ground in front of the cave turned into a sink of oozing mud, and the adult Dreamers, slipping and sliding in the mess, complained profusely.

Longtusk knew the time was approaching when he must leave the relative security of this place. Perhaps when the weather was better he could even strike out north, and seek his Family.

So, his winter fur beginning to blow loose in a cloud around him, he took to traveling increasing distances from the cave. He was half-starved, his fat depleted, severely weakened by the harshest winter of his life.

But he still breathed. And, despite the rain and the continuing cold, life was returning to the land. The low, wind-battered trees were sprinkled with buds, full of the optimism of the new season, and the first crocuses and jonquils were showing, bright yellow and purple. Day by day, as he fed on the new growth, his strength returned.

In fact, he found he himself had grown during the bleak cold of winter. His tusks were longer still, heavier, thicker. He flashed them in the air, parrying imaginary opponents, even though there was nobody to see.

One day he found a place where a carpet of new grass, thin green shoots, was pushing through the matted remains of last year's growth. Contentedly he began to graze.

He heard a soft mewling, like a wounded cat, coming from behind a low outcrop of hard black rock.

Pricked by curiosity, he walked over to see.

At first sight he thought it was a Dreamer cub. It was a

female, wearing the ragged remains of cut and shaped skins. She was smaller in height than Willow, so presumably younger. She seemed in distress; she was huddled over on herself, clutching her spindly forelegs to her chest, and she was crying.

He ran his trunk tip over her limbs.

She was like a Dreamer, yes. But she was much thinner, her limbs weaker but more graceful. Even her head was a different shape, with a flat face, a prominent chin, a protruding forehead—no heavy eye ridges—and a compact skull. Her body seemed bare of hair: all except her head, where there was a tangled, dirty mane of fine yellow hair.

She wore something around her neck. He bent to see. Little white objects had been punctured with holes, and then strung together on what looked like a strip of sinew.

They were teeth: tiny mammoth teeth, drawn from a very new calf, perhaps even an unborn.

He rumbled in dismay.

At the noise, the cub's eyes flickered open. They were a startling blue, like steppe melt-pools. When she saw the mountain of muscle and fat and hair over her, tusk shadows looming, she yelped and tried to pull away. But she was weak, and she was trapped by the cleft of rock.

Now he could see quite how ill she was. The fingers on her paws were dead white, and her lips looked blue. But she was not shivering: the cold had penetrated deep into her body, and without help this mite would soon surely die.

He reached down with his trunk, meaning to stroke her, but she wailed feebly, unable to move.

He moved back a few paces. There was a small stand of crocuses glowing in the lee of the rock. With his delicate trunk-fingers, he plucked out a single fat yellow bloom. He carried it to the female, and dropped it on her chest.

She seemed a little less frightened. She tried to close her paw over the flower.

Gently he wrapped his trunk under the cub and lifted her up. She was light as a feather, and her limbs dangled, unresisting. But she had managed to keep hold of her flower. He began to walk, slowly and steadily, toward the cave of the Dreamers.

After a time the cub seemed to lose her fear. She gathered pawfuls of his long trunk hairs and burrowed into them. Soon she was asleep, wrapped in the warm strength of the mammoth's trunk.

The Dreamers reacted with confusion.

This was a stranger—not one of their Clan—not even one of their kind. At first the adults seemed to have difficulty even seeing the limp cub, as if she was a thing a shadows, only half-glimpsed, too strange to comprehend. But the young were fascinated, and they clustered around, lifting aside his trunk fur to see the sleeping cub.

Some of the males came at Longtusk with their pointed, blackened sticks, as they hadn't for some months, as if he had brought them threat in the form of this helpless cub. The females were solicitous. As soon as they realized what distress this strange cub was in, they lifted her away from Longtusk and took her toward the hearth. There they stripped away her ragged skins, rubbed grease into her skin, and huddled around her, sandwiching the cub between their own great bodies.

Willow came up to Longtusk. He rubbed Longtusk's trunk fur affectionately, and Longtusk realized that Willow, at least, thought he had done the right thing—

Somebody screamed.

It was one of the female Dreamers, an old woman, her face twisted by an ancient burn. She was pointing at the three of them: the strange female cub, Willow and Longtusk, over and over, jabbering and growling, frightened.

She sees something, Longtusk realized, chilled. Something about the three of us.

Suddenly the cave walls, solid rock, seemed to melt away, the Dreamers dispersing like smoke, until there was only the three of them, alone, locked together. *She sees the end of my life. She thinks we will die together, we three: the yellow-haired cub, Willow, and me.*

But how can anybody know the future? And what strange fate could make such a thing happen? . . .

The old female stumbled away, scared, shouting.

And there was a howl of outrage.

Blood was pouring down Stripeskull's foreleg, where a stick protruded from his flesh. With a yell of anger and pain he dragged the stick out of his body, ripping the wound wider.

This was no simple stick of sharpened wood, Longtusk realized immediately. It had feathers attached to its base—and it was tipped, not by fire-hardened wood, but by a flake of flint, sharpened to a point much finer than any the Dreamers could manufacture.

And now shadows flitted past the cave, urgent, menacing. Stripeskull threw down the bloody stick and, with a growl of anger, marched to the mouth of the cave.

Longtusk scarcely noticed. He raised his trunk and tested the air, turning it this way and that, questing.

Longtusk was electrified. He could smell mammoth.

6

The Newcomers

He stumbled out of the cave mouth to the open air.

Behind him, from the caves, he heard shouting, raised Dreamer voices. But the noises were small and far away and nothing to do with him. All that mattered was that profound and alluring smell of his own kind: musty fur and dung and even the sharp tang of musth—and, in pulses of deep sound, he thought he could hear huge, heavy strides: many of them, a Family or a bachelor herd, close by.

It was too much to hope that this was *his* Family; he knew he was far from their normal pastures. But these strangers would surely help him find his way back to his own. It was as if he had suddenly recalled who he was. How could he have spent so long, an entire winter, huddled in a mouth of eroded rock?

But the wind was swirling, and it was impossible to tell where the scents were coming from. He crashed deeper into the brush, trunk raised eagerly.

Before long, at the edge of the river, he came to a place where the stink of mammoths was very strong. He searched until he found a small, compact pile of dung.

Mammoth dung . . . perhaps.

He poked at it with his trunk, raised a fragment to his tongue to taste. It was warm and soft, obviously very recent, and its smell was strong and pungent. But its texture was strange—thicker and more fibrous than the dung of his Family—and he could taste a heavy concentration of wood and bark.

Mammoths' diets differ, according to individual taste, and what they eat affects the quality of their dung. But Longtusk knew no mammoth whose diet was quite so skewed as to produce waste like this.

He pushed on.

He found a place where the trees were broken, the branches stripped of their bark and leaf buds, the ground trampled. Another unmistakable sign: mammoths had fed here—more than one, judging by the scale of the damage.

. . . But, like the dung, the pattern of tree damage was odd. Many of the younger saplings' trunks had been pushed aside, as if by animals who were shorter and squatter than he was. And he saw that bark and leaf buds had been taken extensively, even from above head height. Woolly mammoths will take a little bark and foliage in their diet, but they prefer the grasses and herbs of the open steppe.

Still he saw no mammoths: not so much as a silhouette glimpsed through the trees, the swish of a tail, or the curve of a trunk. He rumbled, but there was no reply.

If they were here, whoever they were, why did they not greet him?

He decided to return to the mouth of the Dreamers' cave. From there he would follow the trail that would take him back up to the steppe. Surely there, on the open plain, he would be able to find the strange mammoths.

He reached the edge of the trees, close to the Dreamers'

cave—and, still in the shelter of the trees, he slowed to a halt.

Several of the Dreamers had emerged from their caves. But they were not alone.

Confronting them was a new group of creatures: standing upright like the Dreamers, but spindly, taller, much less robust.

The legs of these others were thin and taut—like those of a horse, meant for running and walking long distances. The newcomers had flat, delicate faces and high bulging skulls. They were covered in skins, like the Dreamers, but Longtusk could see that these garments were much more finely worked than the rough creations of the Dreamers. Their paws were delicate and they held things—pointed sticks and flakes of stone—and other, incomprehensible items, like a length of wood tied up with deer sinew so that it was bent over in an arc.

And they stalked among the Dreamers with arrogance and hostility.

Longtusk spotted Stripeskull. Blood still stained his shoulder where the strange stick had punctured it. But now the big Dreamer was crouching in the dirt. He was roaring defiance, trying to stand using one of his fire-hardened sticks as a prop—but one hind leg was dragging behind him. And Longtusk saw blood pulsing from a broad gash. He was surrounded by five or six of the newcomers, and they held sticks out toward Stripeskull, threatening him.

The Dreamer females and cubs had been brought out of the cave, driven like recalcitrant calves by prods with sticks and stones. The females huddled together in a group, surrounded by the newcomers, with their cubs at the center. They seemed bewildered as much as frightened, and their gaze slid over the newcomers that stalked amongst them—as if they were too strange even to be properly visible, as if the Clan was being overwhelmed by a party of ghosts.

Apart from Stripeskull, Longtusk could see no other Dreamer adult males. Perhaps they were off on one of their scavenging trips—or perhaps they had been driven away, by these cold, calculating others.

Longtusk watched, fascinated, repelled. He knew what he was seeing.

He had never before encountered these creatures, these distorted, hostile cousins of the Dreamers. But many of his kind had—and an understanding of the danger they posed was drummed into every young mammoth.

These were the most ferocious predators of all—more to be feared, despite their frail appearance, than even the great cats—and the only response to encountering them was flight.

For they had mastered fire itself.

And *they* were not content to let embers burn in shallow hearths, like the Dreamers; instead they used fire to drive their way across the land. Perhaps they had even been responsible for the fire which had separated him from his Family. Hadn't he glimpsed slender running forms during his dreadful flight through the smoke?

He had been wrong before, when he had first encountered Willow. About these newcomers there could be no doubt, and black dread settled on his heart.

For these were Fireheads.

One of the newcomers turned and looked directly toward him.

This one was shorter than the others, with a broad, plump belly that glistened with grease. He sniffed loudly, his small, straight nose twitching. He was, thought Longtusk, like a fat, overgrown lemming, walking comically upright on two hind legs.

He knows I'm here, Longtusk thought, hidden as I am among these trees. Or he suspects so, anyhow. He is smarter than the rest.

Now Willow spotted Longtusk too. He called out and lunged forward.

A Firehead tripped him with a stick. Willow sprawled, howling.

One of the females pushed her way out of the group and ran to Willow. Perhaps it was his mother. A Firehead confronted her. She dodged his stick and swung one mighty fist at his long, delicate face. Longtusk heard the unmistakable crack of shattering bone, and the other fell back with a gurgling cry, clutching his face.

But more of the others joined the fray. They wrestled the female to the ground and pinned her there, a male's weight pressing down on each of her mighty limbs.

Now, from the mouth of the cave, another emerged. He was dressed in skins, like the rest, but he wore a crown of what looked like bone—*from which smoke streamed*, as if he carried burning embers cupped in scrapings in the bone. Smoke rose even from his paws, and Longtusk realized he had taken ashes from the precious hearth which the Dreamers had preserved all winter long.

Seemingly oblivious to pain, this grotesque creature raised his paws to the air and howled a cry of thin triumph. He cast the ashes to the ground, scattered them with his feet, and extinguished them in the trampled mud. The others whooped and danced, jabbing their sticks into the air.

The Dreamers looked away, bewildered and defeated.

Burning-head stalked over to the Dreamer female,

who was still pinned to the ground. His teeth showing white, he leaned over her. She bellowed and tried to twist her head away. But he came closer, as if to press his lips against hers.

She hawked and spat at him. He wiped his face and threw strings of greenish phlegm back at her.

Longtusk was baffled. Was this like a fight among mammoth Bulls for access to females? But it made no sense. Even Longtusk could see that the Dreamer female was not in oestrus. Perhaps the other did not want the female, but only to demonstrate his power and dominance.

But now the ugly tableau was disturbed. Another was emerging from the Dreamer cavern: taller even than Burning-head, his head adorned by a cap of yellow-white beads—beads of mammoth ivory, Longtusk realized queasily. This one looked oddly frail, his hair a grizzled white, his skin wrinkled and weather-beaten. But he carried the limp form of the yellow-haired cub in his arms.

The rest, even Burning-head, cringed away from this new one, deferring.

Burning-head was evidently a powerful figure. But it was obvious that this new male was the true power, like the strongest Bull in a bachelor herd.

". . .What fine tusks you have, cousin. And yet they do you little good if you stand facing into the wind."

The voice had come from directly behind Longtusk. He whirled, trumpeting in alarm.

Now the Fireheads knew he was there; they reacted, shouting. But none of that mattered, compared to the massive looming presence suddenly here behind him.

For it was a mammoth . . . and yet it was not.

It, he, was a male. He wasn't as tall as a full-grown mammoth Bull, yet he loomed over Longtusk. He was coated with wiry black-brown hair, shorter and darker than Longtusk's, some of it stained by the gray of age. His back was flat, lacking the fleshy hump of a true mammoth, and he was heavy-set, his chest deep, his limbs and feet broad. And he had broad stubby tusks, heavily chipped and scarred.

Four of them: *four* tusks.

And, strangest of all, Longtusk made out a scar burned into his muscled flank: a strange five-pronged form, burned through the layers of hair and into his flesh, exactly like the outstretched paw of a Dreamer—or a Firehead.

The other opened his great mouth and roared. A gush of warm, fetid air billowed out over Longtusk, stinking of crushed wood and sap. The not-mammoth's teeth were cones of enamel—not flat grinding surfaces like Longtusk's, but sharp, almost like a cat's cruel fangs.

Longtusk staggered back. He crashed out of the trees and into the clearing before the caves, in full view of Fireheads and Dreamers.

There were cries of shock. Panicking, he whirled around.

All but two of the Fireheads had fallen to the ground before him. The two who remained standing—staring at him open-mouthed—were the strong leader and the grotesque Burning-head. The leader put down his cub and picked up an abandoned stick. This was fitted with a blade of something that glittered like ice. He held the stick up, pointing it at Longtusk.

In the Fireheads' distraction, the Dreamers seemed to see their chance. Even the female who had been pinned to the ground was free now. Under her lead, the females gathered their cubs and, quickly, silently, began to slip away up the trail that led to the steppe. Willow pulled

Stripeskull to his feet, then let Stripeskull lean on him so that he hopped forward on his one good hind leg.

Willow cast a single regretful glance back at Longtusk, and then was gone.

But there was no time to reflect.

A powerful trumpet and a slam of broad feet into the ground told Longtusk that the strange not-mammoth was right behind him. Terrified, bewildered, over-whelmed by strangeness, Longtusk turned, trumpeting. The Fireheads cringed anew.

The other's eyes were like pools of tar, embedded in wrinkled sockets of flesh.

"Do you know what that blade is, cousin? It is *quartz*. A kind of rock that's harder and sharper than almost any other. The old fellow may not look so strong, but he could throw that spear so hard that quartz tip will nestle in your heart." The not-mammoth's accent was strange—somehow guttural, primitive—but his language, of rum-bles, trumpets, growls, stamps and posture, was clear to Longtusk.

Longtusk said, "You are not mammoth."

"No. But I am your cousin. Don't you know your Cycle? We are all Calves of Probos. I am better than mammoth. I am *mastodont*."

The two great proboscideans faced each other, chal-lenging, calculating, rumbling: members of hugely an-cient species, separated by evolutionary paths that had diverged twenty-five million years before.

The three Fireheads were engaged in a complex three-way argument.

"We call the leader *Bedrock*," growled the mastodont. "For he is strong and silent as the rock on which the world is built. His cub is called *Crocus*, for the color of her hair. And the Shaman is *Smokehat*—"

71

"What is a Shaman?"

Bedrock had the quartz-tipped spear raised to shoulder height, and it was still pointing at Longtusk's heart. But Crocus was pulling at Bedrock's free foreleg and was jabbering excitedly, pointing at Longtusk.

Meanwhile Smokehat, with his grotesque garb of bone and smoke, was all but dancing with impatience and rage.

"That Shaman wants you killed. Bedrock is prepared to do it. But his cub seems to think you saved her life."

"You can understand them?"

"You pick up a little," the mastodont said wistfully, "if you spend long enough with them. My name is Walks With Thunder."

Longtusk growled. "And mine is Longtusk. Learn it for my Remembering, mastodont, for I am ready to die."

"Oh, that isn't the idea at all."

"What?"

The mastodont reared up, looming over Longtusk and pawing at the air.

Startled, angry, bewildered, Longtusk backed away from this terrifying opponent and plunged into the stand of trees.

He found the trail that led to the open steppe.

He turned back the way he had come and raised his trunk, sniffing the air. There was no sign of pursuit.

But there was a smell of mammoth—no, it was the sharp, wood-ask stink of the animals he must call *mastodont*—and, he realized with mounting alarm, it came from all around him.

He turned again. And there was a mastodont ahead of him.

Like Walks With Thunder, this was a squat, powerfully

built male with four stubby tusks. But he sported a broad scar that ran the length of his face, a scar that all but obliterated the socket of one eye. "Hello, little grazer," he rumbled. "Welcome to the herd."

As Longtusk turned once more, trunk raised, he saw and smelled more mastodonts to his left and right, like a line of stocky, hairy boulders: a row of them, all powerful adult males.

Now, with a drumming of mighty footsteps, the mastodonts marched intently toward him, converging. Every one of them bore the strange scar sported by Walks With Thunder, a Firehead paw burned into hairless flesh. The way they moved together, as if driven by a single mind, was unnerving.

And, strangest of all, there were Fireheads with them. They carried sticks tipped with curved pieces of bone, which they used to tap the mastodonts on the head or ears or flanks. Some of the mastodonts actually had Fireheads sitting astride their backs, with their long, thin hind legs draped over their necks, feet applying sharp kicks to the mastodonts' small ears.

Soon the mastodonts were close enough for him to make out what they were saying in their heavy, strange accent.

". . . Well, well. What have we here? Don't tell me it's a grazer."

"I haven't seen one of those grass-chewers for a long time. I thought they had all died out."

"It must be a Cow. Look at those pretty-pretty tusks. Any self-respecting Bull would be too embarrassed to wear skinny monstrosities like that."

"Hey, little grazer! Can I borrow your tusks? I need a pick to clean out my musth gland, and those spindly things are just the right size . . ."

He saw that the mastodonts had closed the circle around him.

The big scarred Bull facing him was being whipped, severely, by the Firehead with him. The Firehead was shouting, a simple, repetitive sound: *"Agit! Agit!"* It was obvious he was trying to drive the big Bull forward. This Firehead was sapling-thin with a cruel, pinched face.

The scarred Bull, seeming unaware of the multiple wounds being inflicted on him, swiveling his huge, filth-crusted rump and let out a fart of thunderous intensity. A foul brown spray knocked the skinny Firehead backward, and the line of mastodonts reacted with stomps and growls of amusement.

The Bull walked forward nonchalantly out of his dispersing brown cloud, muscles moving under his fat brown-black coat of hair. "Sorry about that. These Fireheads are an irritation at times."

Longtusk stood his ground and raised his tusks. "Come any closer and I'll rip out your other eye."

The mastodont grunted. He reached a stand of low, twisted spruce trees. His trunk flicked out, its pink tip running over one sapling after another. Finally he settled on the biggest, strongest tree of the grove. He wrapped his trunk around its girth and, with a single flick of his huge, low-slung head, ripped the tree out of the ground, roots and all. His mouth gaped, revealing a purple tongue and teeth like miniature mountains, chipped and worn. With a crackling splinter, he bit the tree clean in half, his long jaw bones moving in a powerful up-down motion quite different from the back-and-forth grinding of a mammoth's jaw. Then he stamped on the tree, breaking it up further.

Within a few heartbeats, a healthy tree had been reduced to a few shards.

"My name is Jaw Like Rock," said the mastodont. He opened his huge mouth and belched; a fine spray of spittle and wood chips peppered Longtusk. "I enjoyed that. But you grazers prefer to munch on a few blades of grass, don't you? I suppose if that's all you're strong enough to manage—"

"I'm strong enough to best you," Longtusk said.

Jaw Like Rock looked puzzled. "Oh, yes. It's time for me to get my eye ripped out, isn't it? We'd better get it over with."

Unexpectedly, something barged into Longtusk's backside. Trumpeting, he tried to turn.

Here was Walks With Thunder, his broad brow dipped. "You let me creep up on you downwind again, little grazer. You've a lot to learn."

"I've nothing to learn from you wood-nibblers."

Walks With Thunder's broad head once again rammed his backside, hard. Longtusk stumbled and took two or three steps forward.

Now something wrenched backward on Longtusk's left hind leg. There was a hoop of hide rope knotted around his ankle, over his foot. The rope's other end was tied tightly around the roots of a tree.

He heard a yelp of triumph from his feet.

He looked down. It was the little fat Firehead, the one who had detected his presence before anybody else. He had been crawling on the ground close to Longtusk's feet, and his flabby skin was coated with something dark and pungent.

"Dung," Longtusk said. "Mammoth dung."

"*Your* dung," said Walks With Thunder easily. "That's how Lemming crept up on you. You couldn't smell him. Oldest trick there is, little grazer. And now you're caught."

Longtusk trumpeted his alarm. "Why are you doing this to me? Let me go! In the name of Probos—"

Walks With Thunder exchanged a glance with Jaw Like Rock, and Longtusk thought he detected a brief sadness there.

Walks With Thunder said, "Grazer, this has nothing to do with Probos."

"Don't worry, lad," Jaw said. "We've all been through it."

"Been through what? Let me go." Frustrated, frightened, angry, humiliated, Longtusk tugged with all his strength at the rope. It wouldn't give. Rumbling, enraged, he fell back.

The Fireheads stood around him in a loose circle, letting the drama play itself out.

Jaw Like Rock took a heavy step forward, "Come on then, little grazer. Let's get this over. Give me your best shot."

Longtusk eyed Jaw Like Rock. "There is a stink of Firehead on you," he said. "You have no honor."

Jaw Like Rock stiffened.

Walks With Thunder murmured, "I wouldn't get him angry."

Longtusk cried, "For Probos!" And he roared and lunged with his tusks.

The mastodont sidestepped—but not fast enough; the tip of one mammoth tusk scraped down his flank. "Well done, little grazer," he said, his trunk investigating the wound."You were too fast for me."

Longtusk looked down, and saw a smear of bright crimson at the sharp tip of one curling spiral tusk. He felt a surge of pride. If only Rockheart could see him now! . . .

"Get it over, Jaw," growled Walks With Thunder. "Don't try to make him feel better about it."

Longtusk, straining at the sinew on his leg, said, "What does he mean?"

"Nothing," said Jaw Like Rock, wiping blood off the tip of his trunk on the sparse grass. "He's an old fool. Do your worst, mighty mammoth, calf of Primus!" And he trumpeted and raised his stubby tusks.

Again Longtusk lunged.

But the mastodont was standing at his side. He had moved in a blur of speed, too fast for Longtusk to see. "Forgive me, brave grazer." And he brought his tusks crashing down on Longtusk's head.

It was as if thunder had clapped inside his head. The light was suddenly strange, with everything suffused by a bright golden tinge. To his surprise he found he was kneeling, his trunk dangling on the grass like the discarded skin of a snake.

He tried to lift his tusks, but, oddly, they were scraping on the thin soil of the ground. With every breath he took, the golden light around him intensified.

". . . don't understand it. It's never taken more than a single blow before. That would have felled Kilukpuk herself."

"You aren't used to these woolly grazers, Jaw."

"No. Perhaps all that fur—"

"More likely that wretched dome of bone on the top of his skull. Try it again, Jaw. Just make sure you don't kill him."

A huge face loomed, a gaping jaw, the teeth surrounded by four short, squat tusks. "Try not to move, grazer."

Longtusk felt a wash of fetid breath, a rush of air—and again there was an explosion inside his head.

This time the world fell away, through deepening gold, into darkness.

7

The Taming

The sun was high.

He was standing. He was conscious of hunger, an even more powerful thirst. There was a strong scent of mammoth around him . . . but not quite mammoth.

". . . Milkbreath? Matriarch?"

"They aren't here, lad."

The voice came from directly before him. It was a mammoth—no, a *mastodont*—short and squat, with a long narrow face and an extra pair of tusks. The mastodont seemed to swim into focus, as if ice water were draining out of his eyes.

The mastodont was a Bull, grizzled with age, and his waist and head and legs and tusks were wrapped around with lengths of rope, knotted tight and tied to the stumps of trees. Only his trunk roamed free, its pink tip questing toward Longtusk.

"Walks With Thunder," Longtusk said slowly.

"I'm glad you know me. That oaf Jaw Like Rock is none too gentle; I feared he might have scrambled your brains for good . . . Who's Milkbreath? Your mother?"

Longtusk growled and tried to back away. But he

couldn't move. He could feel ropes wrapped around his legs and torso and head.

"The ropes will tighten if you struggle. They will cut your flesh."

Longtusk pushed hard with one leg. With a creak, the loops tightened just as Walks With Thunder had warned.

He gave up, panting, longing for water. "Who did this?"

"Our keepers. The Fireheads."

"I am mammoth. I have no keeper."

"You do now, little grazer."

"They have tied me up so I will not run away?"

"That's right."

". . . But why you?"

Walks With Thunder emitted a deep snort from his trunk. "To show you it isn't so bad."

Now a Firehead was coming toward them. It was the little fat one Longtusk had called Lemming—the one who had, with stealth, slipped that first loop of rope around Longtusk's leg. He was carrying a skin bag, some dry grass.

Longtusk rumbled and lunged at the little Firehead. All over his body, the ropes creaked and tightened cruelly.

Lemming yelped and staggered backward. He dropped his skin bag, which landed with a thick gurgle.

"Let him feed you," Walks With Thunder urged.

"I feed myself."

"Not any more. Watch . . ."

Lemming retrieved his dropped bag, opened it up and held it out to Walks With Thunder. With a noisy slurp the mastodont sucked up a trunkful of water, draining the bag.

The smell of the water filled Longtusk's head.

Now the little Firehead started stuffing hay into Walks With Thunder's accepting mouth. The mastodont rumbled, "It isn't so bad, Longtusk. Just accept it. You're lucky. Lemming likes you. He's one of the better ones. He goes easy with the goads. Some of the others take it too far. Like Spindle—the one Jaw farted over—"

"I won't give in."

"You're special, are you? Different from us, smarter, stronger?"

"Yes."

"Sniff the air, little grazer."

Longtusk did so—and found he was surrounded by mastodonts: ten, eleven, twelve of them, all males, presumably the same herd who had circled him earlier. Some were pulling branches from the low trees here; but most were feeding on heaps of smashed wood left for them by the Fireheads. One mastodont was wallowing in the mud of a shallow water hole, its fringe crusted with late-winter ice. He was rolling on his side and lifting his squat feet, letting a Firehead scrape mud off his delicate soles with a piece of sharpened stone.

And now a mastodont walked past with a heavy gait. He had a passenger, a skinny Firehead who sat astride the mastodont's neck. His bare feet kicked at the animal's ears, and he struck the mastodont's broad scalp with a stick tipped with sharpened bone.

The mastodont had a broad, ugly scar across his face, eclipsing one eye.

It was Jaw Like Rock. And his rider was the keeper who had beaten him before, Spindle.

"Why does he accept that? He could throw off that creature and crush him in a moment."

"You don't understand. Jaw has no choice. I have no choice. *You* have no choice, but to submit."

"No."

Walks With Thunder's trunk drooped. "I was like you, once. Make it easy on yourself."

"I won't listen to you."

And Longtusk began to push against his ropes once more. They tightened around his neck and legs and belly, but still he struggled, until he was exhausted.

The Firehead keeper came to him again, with water and food; again Longtusk ignored him.

And so it went on, as the sun worked its path around the sky.

Night fell. But it was not dark, not even quiet.

The Fireheads set up huge fires in improvised hearths all around the steppe. Longtusk could feel their uncomfortable heat. The fires sent sparks up into the echoing night, and the Fireheads sat close, their faces shining in the red light, eating and drinking and laughing.

Longtusk—hungry, thirsty, exhausted, his muscles cramped from immobility—now longed for sleep. But sleep was impossible. The Fireheads would come to him and shout in his ears, or whirl pieces of bone on ropes around their heads, making a noise like a howling wind.

Walks With Thunder was still with him. "Give in," he urged. "They won't stop until you do."

"No," mumbled Longtusk.

"Let me tell you a story," Walks With Thunder said. "A story from the Cycle. This is of a time deep in the past— oh, thousands of Great-Years ago, long before the ice came to the earth. In those days there were no mammoths and mastodonts; we were a single kind, and we lived in a land of lush forests, far to the south of here.

"But the Earth cooled. The forests follow the weather, as every mastodont knows. Year by year the land became cooler and drier, and great waves of trees moved north across the Earth—"

"Why are you telling me this?"

"Just listen. Now our Matriarch, the Matriarch of all mastodonts, was called Mammut. She was a descendant of Probos, of course, but she lived long before the mother of the mammoths."

"Ganesha."

"Yes. Now Mammut was wise—"

"They always are in Cycle stories."

Walks With Thunder barked his amusement at that. "Yes. It's always easy after the fact, isn't it? . . . Mammut could see the way the forests were migrating to the north. And she said, 'Just as the forests must follow the weather, so my calves must follow the forests.' And so, under her leadership, her Clan followed the slow march of the forests, seeking out the marshy places beneath the great trees, for that is what mastodonts prefer. And her calves prospered and multiplied, filling the land.

"Now, much later, long after Mammut had gone to the aurora, another forest came marching across the land. A different kind of forest."

"I don't know what you're talking about," Longtusk mumbled.

"It was a forest of Fireheads, little grazer. And the mastodonts fled in panic."

"That is because they were cowards."

Walks With Thunder ignored that. "So the mastodonts called up to the aurora, 'What should we do, great Matriarch?'

"Mammut was wise. She understood.

"As the weather washes over the land, the trees must follow. As the trees wash over the land, the mastodonts must follow. And now, as the Fireheads wash over the land, the mastodonts must follow again. That is what Mammut said. And that is what we accept."

"It isn't much of a story."

"Well, I'm sorry. I was trying to make a point. I left out the fights and the sex scenes."

"Anyway the Fireheads are not trees."

Thunder growled irritably. "The point is that the Fireheads feed us, as the trees do. They even care for us—when they choose. And we cannot be rid of them, little grazer. Any more than the land can rid itself of the trees. Accept them. Accept their food."

Once again, Longtusk saw blearily, the Firehead, Lemming, was before him. He held up a paw, full of grasses and herbs, fragrant, freshly gathered. But Longtusk turned his head away.

It lasted three more days, three more nights.

Walks With Thunder and Jaw Like Rock were both with him.

"Your courage is astonishing, little grazer. Nobody else has ever lasted so long before."

Longtusk, beaten down by hunger and thirst and sleeplessness, could barely see through milky, crusted eyes. "Leave me alone."

Jaw reached out and, with the pink tip of his trunk, smoothed the filth-matted fur of Longtusk's face. "Don't let them kill you," he said softly. "That way they will have won."

Longtusk closed his eyes.

After a time he felt a pressure at the side of his mouth. It was the paw of Lemming, the keeper, once more holding out sweet grasses.

"Take it, grazer. It's no defeat."

"My name is Longtusk."

Walks With Thunder and Jaw Like Rock thumped the ground with their trunks. "Longtusk," they said.

Lemming was staring at him, his eyes round, as if he understood.

Longtusk opened his mouth and took the food.

More days passed. Gradually his strength returned.

His ropes loosened. They had burned and cut him painfully. Lemming treated the wounds with salves of fat and butter, and with water heated in the hearths. He squeezed droplets of milk from an aurochs cow into Longtusk's eyes, soothing their itching.

Five days after he had first accepted the food, more Fireheads came to see him: Bedrock the leader, the Shaman Smokehat with his grotesque headpiece of smoking bone, and the cub, Crocus.

Though Bedrock was cautious and kept hold of her paw, Crocus approached Longtusk. Her necklace of mammoth teeth gleamed in the watery spring sun. She reached past the ropes and ruffled the long hair that dangled from his trunk.

He closed his eyes, recalling how Willow, the male Dreamer cub, used to do the same thing.

He wondered where the Dreamers were now, Stripeskull and Willow and the others. Scattered, he supposed, turned out of the caves they had inhabited for uncounted generations, in the face of the advance of these Fireheads—

Pain lanced into his flank. He trumpeted and reared up, but he was contained by the ropes. There was a stink of burning flesh and hair.

The Shaman, Smokehat, held a piece of stone fixed to the end of a stick. The stone had been chipped and shaped to look like the outspread paw of a Firehead. It glowed red hot.

The mark of the Firehead, the outstretched paw, had been burned into Longtusk's flank.

Like all these others he belonged to the Fireheads, and was forever marked.

He trumpeted his anger and despair.

WARRIOR Two

The Story of Longtusk and the Fireheads

As you know, Icebones (said Silverhair), Longtusk spent most of his years as a young Bull away from other mammoths.

Everywhere he went he won friendship and respect—naturally, since he was the greatest hero of all, and even other creatures could recognize that—and in many instances he was made their leader, and led them to fruitfulness and success before passing on to continue his adventures.

And so it came to pass that Longtusk came to live with the Fireheads, and to rule them.

Now the Fireheads are the strangest creatures in all the Cycle: weak yet strong, smart yet stupid. In the summer heat they had difficulty finding the food and drink they needed, and in the winter cold they suffered because they had no winter coat.

So Longtusk decided to teach them how to live.

When they were cold, he took them to the west, where Rhino lived.

Now Rhino was a magnificent beast with a coat as thick as a mammoth's and great horns like upturned tusks (yes, she really existed, Icebones, have patience!). And Longtusk said to the Fireheads, "You need coats like Rhino's to fend off the cold. See how warm and comfortable she is? When the wintertime is over she sheds her hair, and you may take it to make your own coats. Isn't that right, Rhino?"

And Rhino replied, "Yes, Longtusk"—for all the creatures of the world knew Longtusk—"my hair will be all your friends need, and they may have it."

And the Fireheads muttered and calculated, for that is their way.

And when Longtusk's back was turned, they attacked poor Rhino, and robbed her of her fine coat, and even took her magnificent horns.

When he found out what had happened, Longtusk berated the Fireheads for their greed and impatience. "You could have taken all you needed, if only you had waited!"

And the Fireheads said they were sorry. But in their hearts they were not.

When it rained, Longtusk took the Fireheads to the east, where Dreamer lived.

Now Dreamer was a little like the Fireheads, but she was placid and kind and accepting, and she had lived for many years in caves hollowed out of the rock of a hillside. And, of course, the caves kept the rain from her head.

And Longtusk said to the Fireheads, "You need a cave like Dreamer's to fend off the rain. See how warm and comfortable she is? There are many caves in this hillside, and you may take them for your own shelter. Isn't that right, Dreamer?"

And Dreamer replied, "Yes, Longtusk"—for all the creatures of the world knew Longtusk—"the caves will be all your friends need, and they may have them."

And the Fireheads muttered and calculated, for that is their way.

And when Longtusk's back was turned, they attacked poor Dreamer, and robbed her of her fine cave, and threw her out into the rain.

When he found out what had happened, Longtusk berated the Fireheads for their greed and impatience. "You could have taken all you needed without stealing Dreamer's home!"

And the Fireheads said they were sorry. But in their hearts they were not.

Then the Fireheads became thirsty.

So Longtusk took them to the north, where the mammoths lived.

He brought them to a place where the mammoths, in their wisdom, knew that water seeped from deep in the ground. They were digging there with tusks and feet, bringing the water to the surface.

And Longtusk said to the Fireheads, "You must dig for water as the mammoths do. See how much water there is? And when you have learned what the mammoths have to teach you, you can find water of your own. Isn't that right, Matriarch?"

And the Matriarch of the mammoth Family said, "Yes, Longtusk"—for all the mammoths knew Longtusk—"in the ground there is all the water your friends need, and we will teach them how to find it."

And the Fireheads muttered and calculated, for that is their way.

And when Longtusk's back was turned, they attacked the poor mammoths, and drove them away, and robbed them of their water.

When he found out what had happened, Longtusk berated the Fireheads. "You could have found your own water without robbing the mammoths—oh, you are impossible!"

And the Fireheads said they were sorry. But in their hearts they were not.

By now Longtusk knew that all his teaching was wasted on such creatures. He had decided besides that he had spent enough time away from his Clan.

So he turned his back on the Fireheads and walked away,

leaving them to fend for themselves. They called to him plaintively, begging him to return, but he would not.

And so Longtusk returned to the mammoths, and became their Patriarch, and . . .

But that's another story. Perhaps the greatest of them all.

What happened to the Fireheads without Longtusk's wisdom, driven only by their own foolishness, cold and wet and thirsty? Nobody knows.

Some say they quickly died out.

And some say they became monsters.

1

The Bone Pit

All around Longtusk, sleeping mastodonts lay like immense boulders. In the summer they preferred to sleep on their backs, exposing their bare feet and bellies to the cool air. From time to time one of them, startled by a noise, would rise smoothly and silently to his feet, like some hairy ghost, before settling back.

But Longtusk could not sleep—even after the months he had been kept here in the Firehead settlement.

He could hear small Firehead footsteps as they pattered across the hard ground, their thin Firehead voices as they came and went on their strange, incomprehensible business. Sometimes he even heard the clear voice of the female cub, Crocus, who—in another life that was long ago and far away—he had saved from freezing.

And, worst of all, he could smell the meat they hung up on frames of wood to dry: rags of brown and purple, laced here and there by pale fat or strings of tendon, some of it even clinging to shards of white bone. Most of the meat came from deer and horse and smaller animals, but there were some larger chunks, great knobbly pieces of bone he couldn't recognize.

And he could smell the meat that burned, slowly, in

the great stone-lined pits in the ground, the billowing greasy black smoke that lingered in the air.

At least he had put aside the panic he had felt continually when he had first been brought here to the Firehead settlement, as every instinct drove him to flee the smoke from the fires. But he would never grow used to that dreadful meat stink. It seemed to have seeped into his very fur, so that he was never free of it.

So Longtusk endured, waiting for morning.

The keepers came in the gray light of dawn. They talked softly and cleared their throats to alert the mastodonts of their approach. The mastodonts stirred, rumbling, and there was a rustle of leathery skin against the hobbles that bound their legs.

Most of the mastodonts were Bulls—not really a bachelor herd, for the tree-browsing mastodonts were more solitary than mammoths, Longtusk had found. But there were Families here too, Cows and calves.

The keepers approached their animals, one by one, talking softly. The mastodonts rumbled and whooshed in response, reaching out with their trunks to search the Fireheads' layers of fur for tidbits of food. It was a display of affection and submission that never failed to embarrass Longtusk.

This morning the fat little keeper the mastodonts called Lemming approached Longtusk, holding out a juicy strip of bark. And, as he always did, Longtusk rumbled threateningly, curled his trunk and backed away as far as the hobbles knotted tightly around his legs would let him.

Lemming wore trousers and leggings of deer skin, moccasins and a broad hat of a tougher leather, and his clothing was stuffed with dry grass to keep him warm.

Bits of grass stuck out around his wide, greasy face as he studied Longtusk, peering into the mammoth's ears and eyes and mouth.

Jaw Like Rock, his hobbles already loosened, came loping over. With a deft movement he snatched the bark from Lemming's paw and tucked it into his mouth. "Waste of good food," he rumbled as he munched.

"It comes from the paw of a Firehead," Longtusk said.

"So what? Food is food."

"I'm not like you."

"He wasn't intending you any harm, you know. He was checking your eyes and ears for infection. And he wanted to see your tongue, too." Jaw opened his mouth and unrolled his own tongue, a leathery black sheet of muscle that dripped with saliva. "The keepers know that a healthy mastodont has a nice pink tongue umblemished by black spots, brown eyes without a trace of white, the right number of toenails, strong and sturdy joints, a full face and broad forehead . . . You have all of that; if you were a mastodont you'd be a prize."

Longtusk growled, impatient with advice.

"You're the only mammoth we have here, Longtusk. The keepers don't know what to make of you. Some of them think you can't be tamed and trained, that you're too wild. And the Shaman, Smokehat, is jealous of you."

"Jealous? Why?"

"Because the Fireheads used to believe that mammoths were gods. Some of them seem to think *you're* a god. And that takes away from the Shaman's power. Having you around gives even little Lemming a higher status. Don't you understand any of this, grazer?"

"No," said Longtusk bluntly.

"All I'm saying is that if you give him an excuse, the Shaman will have you destroyed. Lemming is fond of you. But you're going to have to help him, to give him some sign that you'll cooperate, or else—"

But now, as if to disprove Jaw's comforting growl, his own keeper approached: Spindle, thin, ugly and brutal. He lashed at Jaw with his stick, apparently punishing the mastodont for his minor theft of the food.

Jaw didn't so much as flinch.

"Of course," he rumbled sourly, "not everything's wonderful here. But there are ways to make life bearable."

And he lifted his fat, scarred trunk and sneezed noisily. A gust of looping snot and bark chips sprayed over Spindle, who fell over backward, yelling.

Jaw Like Rock farted contentedly and loped away.

The mastodonts were prepared for another working day. Their hobbles were removed—or merely loosened, in the case of Longtusk and a few others, mastodonts in musth and so prone to irritability. Longtusk was a special case, of course, and he wore his hobbles with a defiant pride. As they worked the keepers were careful to keep away from his tusks, so much more large and powerful than the strongest mastodont's.

Ten mastodonts, plus Longtusk, were formed up into a loose line. Walks With Thunder was at the head. Lemming sat neatly on the great mastodont's neck, his fat legs sticking out on either side of Thunder's broad head.

Lemming tapped Thunder's scalp and called out, *"Agit!"*

Walks With Thunder loped forward, trumpeting to the others to follow him.

The mastodonts obeyed. They were prompted by cries from the keepers—*Chai ghoom! Chi! Dhuth!*, Right! Left! Stop!—and they were directed by gentle taps of the keepers' goads: gentle, yes, but Longtusk had learned by hard experience that the keepers also knew exactly where to strike him to inflict a sharp burst of pain, brief and leaving no scar.

Half the mastodonts bore riders. Most of the others carried the equipment the working party would need during the day. Those without riders were led by loose harnesses of rope tied around their heads.

Longtusk, of course, had no rider, and his harness was kept tighter than the rest. Not only that, his trunk was tied to Walks With Thunder's broad tail, so that he was led along the path like an infant with his mother.

Then they walked slowly out of the Firehead settlement.

The Fireheads had spread far, reshaping the steppe, and they were still building. They had made themselves shelters—like the caves of the Dreamers—but of wood and rock and turf and animal skin. They built huge pits in the ground into which they hurled meat ripped from the carcasses of the creatures they hunted. And the Fireheads had built a great stockade of wood and rock, within which the mastodonts were confined. To Longtusk it was a place of distortion and strangeness, and he was habitually oppressed, crushed by a feeling of confinement and helplessness and bafflement.

But for now they were out of the stockade, and with relief Longtusk found himself on the open steppe. As the sun climbed into a cloud-dusted sky, they soon left behind the noise and stink of the settlement, and walked on steadily south.

The air was misty and full of light. Longtusk saw that it was a mist of life: vast clouds of insects, mosquitoes and blackflies and warble flies and botflies, that rose from the lakes to plague the great herbivores—including himself—and a dreamier cloud of ballooning spiders and wind-borne larvae, riding the breezes to a new land.

Through this dense air the mastodonts walked steadily, their fat low-slung rumps swaying gracefully, their tails swishing and their trunks shooting out from side to side in search of branches and leaves from the few low trees which grew here. After walking for a time they started to defecate together, a long synchronized symphony of dung-making.

Much of the land was bare, a desert of gravel and soils and a few far-flung plants. Here and there he noticed thicker tussocks of grass, speckled with wild flowers, fed by the detritus at the entrances to the dens of the Arctic foxes, and on the slight rises where owls and jaegers devoured their prey, watering the soil with blood. Steppe melt-ponds stood out boldly, bright blue against the tan and green of the plain. In the center of the larger ponds Longtusk could see the gleam of aquamarine, cores of ice still unmelted at the height of summer.

His footsteps crunched on dead leaves, bits of flowers, fragments of twig, a thick layer of it. Some of this material might be years old. And later he came across the carcass of a wolf-killed deer. It had been lightly consumed, and now its meat had hardened, its skin turned glassy. He knew it might lie here for three or four years before being reduced to bones.

On the steppe, away from the Fireheads' frantic rhythms, time pooled, dense and slow; even decomposition worked slowly here.

He came across a golden plover, sitting on her nest on the ground. She stared back at him, defiant. The birds of the steppe had to build their nests on the ground, as there were no tall trees. Some of them—like buntings and longspurs—even lined their nests with bits of mammoth wool. This plover's nest was made of woven grass, and it contained pale, darkly speckled eggs. As the mastodonts walked by, the plover got off its nest and ran back and forth, feigning a broken wing, trying to distract these possible predators from the nest itself.

Walks With Thunder, as he often did, tried to explain life to Longtusk.

". . . The Fireheads are strange, but there is a logic to everything they do. Almost everything, anyhow. They are predators, like the wolves and foxes. So they must hunt."

"I know that. Deer and aurochs—"

"Yes. But such animals pass by this way only infrequently, as they follow their own migrations in search of their fodder for summer or winter. And so the Fireheads must store the meat they will eat during the winter. That is the purpose of the pits—even if all those dead carcasses are repellent to us. And it explains the way they salt their meat and hang it up to dry in strips, or soak it in sour milk, and—"

"But," Longtusk complained, "why do they not follow the herds they prey on, as the wolves do? All their problems come from this peculiar determination to stay in one place."

Walks With Thunder growled, "But not every animal is like the mastodont—or the mammoth. *We* don't mind where we roam; we go where the food is. But many animals prefer a single place to live. Like the rhinos."

"But these Fireheads have nothing—no fat layers, hardly any hair, no way of keeping warm in the winter or digging out their food."

"But they have their fire. They have their tools. And," Walks With Thunder said with a trace of sadness, "they have us."

"Not me," rumbled Longtusk. "They have me trapped. But they don't have *me*."

To that, Walks With Thunder would say nothing.

Longtusk disturbed a carpet of big yellow butterflies that burst into the air, startling him. One of the butterflies landed on the pink tip of his trunk, tickling him. He swished his trunk to and fro, but couldn't shake the butterfly free; finally, the mocking brays of the mastodonts sounding in his ears, he blew it away with a large sneeze.

They came to a river which meandered slowly between gently sloping hummocks. Vegetation grew thickly, down to the water's edge: grass, herbs and a stand of spruce forest almost tall enough to reach Longtusk's shoulders. Farther downstream there were thickets of birch and even azalea, with lingering pink leaves from their spring bloom. In the longer grass wild flowers added splashes of color: vetch, iris, primroses, mauve and blue and purple and yellow.

The mastodonts were allowed to rest. They spread out, moving through the sparse trees with a rustle of branches, tearing off foliage and shoving it into their mouths greedily. Some of them walked into the water, sucking up trunkfuls of the clear, cold liquid and spraying it over their heads and backs.

Longtusk was still hobbled. He moved a little away from the rest, seeking the grass and steppe vegetation he preferred.

He had never been here before. It seemed a congenial place—for mastodonts anyhow. But Longtusk, clad in his thick fur, was already too hot, and mosquitoes buzzed, large and voracious. He looped his trunk into his mouth, extracted a mixture of spit and water, and blew it in a fine spray over his face and head and belly.

He wondered what the Fireheads wanted from this place. Stone, perhaps. The Fireheads liked big flat slabs of stones to put inside their huts and storage pits—but he could see no rock of that kind here. Perhaps they would bring back wood; the mastodonts were strong enough to knock over and splinter as many trees as required.

The keepers came to round up the mastodonts, calling softly and tapping their scalps and flanks with their bone-tipped goads. The mastodonts cooperated with only routine rumbles of complaint.

All the mastodonts had worked here many times before, and they appeared to know what to do. The most skillful and trusted, led by Walks With Thunder, walked down toward the river. They came to a place where the grass had been worn away by deep round mastodont footprints. They began to scrape at the muddy river bank with their tusks and feet, and clouds of mosquitoes rose up around them as they toiled.

Longtusk could see that they were uncovering something: objects that gleamed white in the low sun. He wondered what they were.

. . . There was a sudden, sharp stench, a stink of death and decay, making Longtusk flinch. Some of the mastodonts trumpeted and rumbled in protest, but, under the calm, watchful eye of Walks With Thunder, they continued to work. Perhaps something had died here: a bison or rhino, its carcass washed along the river.

Soon, with the supervision of the keepers, they were dragging the large white objects from the mud. Walks With Thunder dug his tusks under one of the objects and wrapped his trunk over the top; he rammed his feet against the ground and hauled, until the clinging, cold mud gave way with a loud sucking noise, and he stumbled back.

The thing's shape was complex, full of holes. It was mostly white, but something dark brown clung to it here and there, around which mosquitoes and flies buzzed angrily.

It might have been a rock.

Jaw Like Rock stood alongside Longtusk, swishing his tail vigorously. "I can stand the work," the squat Bull muttered. "It's these wretched mosquitoes that drive me to distraction."

Longtusk asked, "Are those rocks heavy?"

Jaw turned to look at him quizzically. "What rocks?"

"The rocks they are pulling out of the river bank."

Jaw hesitated. He said carefully, "Nobody has told you what we're doing here? Thunder hasn't explained?"

"No. Aren't they rocks?"

Jaw fell silent, seeming troubled.

Longtusk found, at his feet, a patch of what looked like mammoth dung. He poked at it and it crumbled. It was dried out, stale, half frozen, obviously old. Regretfully he lifted a few crumbs to his mouth; their flavor was thin.

Since the day he had been separated from his Family by the fire storm—despite the way the Fireheads had him undertake these jaunts across the countryside—he had never seen a single one of his own kind.

But the expeditions always headed south.

He asked Jaw about this.

"Sometimes there are expeditions to the north, Longtusk," Jaw rumbled. "But—"

"But what?"

Jaw Like Rock hesitated, uncomfortable. "Ask Walks With Thunder."

Longtusk growled, "I'm asking you."

"It is difficult to work there. It is poor land. The ice is retreating northward and uncovering the land; but the new land is a rocky desert. To the south, plants and animals have lived for many generations, and the soil is rich . . ."

He's keeping something from me, Longtusk thought. Something about the northern lands, and what the Fireheads do there.

"If the south is so comfortable, why do the Fireheads live where they do? Why not stay where life is easy?"

Jaw sneezed as pollen itched at his trunk. He slid his trunk over one tusk and began to scratch, scooping out lumps of snot. "Because to the south there are already too many Fireheads. They have burned the trees and eaten the animals, and now they fight each other for what remains. Fireheads are not like us, Longtusk. A Firehead Clan will not share its range with another.

"Bedrock tried to take the land belonging to another Clan. There was a battle. Bedrock lost. So he has come north, as far as he can, so that his Clan can carve out a new place to live."

Longtusk tried to understand what all this meant.

He imagined a line that stretched, to east and west, right across the continent, dividing it into two utterly different zones. To the south there was little but Fireheads, mobs of them, fighting and breeding and dying. To the north the land was as it had been before, empty of Fireheads.

And that line of demarcation was sweeping north, as Firehead leaders like Bedrock sought new, empty places to live, burning across the land like the billowing line of fire which had separated him from his Family.

It was to the north that Longtusk knew he must return one day, when the chance arose. For it was to the north—where there were no Fireheads, in the corridor of silent steppe which still encircled the planet below the ice—*that* was where the mammoth herds roamed.

The keepers approached Longtusk now. It was time to don his pack gear, he realized gloomily. He was not yet trusted with complex tasks like digging, but he was regarded as capable of carrying heavy weights.

The pack gear was substantial.

First the keepers laid over him a soft quilted pad. It extended from his withers to his rump and halfway down his sides. On top of this came a saddle of stout sacking stuffed with straw. It had a split along the back to relieve the pressure on his spine; most of the weight he had to carry would rest on his broad rib cage. And then came a platform, a flat plate of cut wood with four posts in the corners, with ropes slung between the posts to prevent his load from falling off.

The whole assembly was strapped to him by one length of thick plaited rope which went around his head and girth and up under his tail. To prevent chafing the rope was passed through lengths of hollow bone that rubbed smoothly against his chest.

And now Walks With Thunder was approaching with his mysterious, complex load, and the stench of decay grew stronger.

Longtusk became fearful.

He could see that Thunder's cargo was rounded, with two gaping sockets at the front. It seemed to have tooth marks, as if some scavenger had worked on it. The brown stuff that clung to it looked like flesh, heavily decayed and gnawed by the scavenger. There was rough skin over the scraps of flesh, and lanks of hair clung, brown and muddy.

It was bone, Longtusk realized with horror. A bone, to which decaying meat still clung.

"What's going on here, Jaw? What *is* that thing?"

"Listen to me," said Jaw Like Rock urgently. "It isn't

what it seems . . ." He laid his trunk over Longtusk's head, trying to soothe him, but Longtusk shook it off.

The keepers began to look alarmed.

The bone thing had the stump of a tusk, broken and gnawed, sticking out of its front. A mammoth tusk.

"Nobody was killed here," Jaw was saying. "This wasn't the fault of the Fireheads, or anybody else. It just happened, a very long time ago . . ."

Longtusk looked again at the river bank. He saw that the white objects were not rocks, not one of them. They were all bones: thick leg bones and vertebrae and ribs and shoulder blades and skulls, sticking out of the mud, many of them still coated with flesh and broken and chewed by scavengers.

It was a field of corpses: the corpses of mammoths.

And here was Walks With Thunder, about to load the great vacant skull onto Longtusk's back.

Longtusk swept his tusks, knocked the skull from the grasp of an astonished Walks With Thunder, and smashed it to pieces underfoot.

He recalled little after that.

They got him under control, and brought him through the long march back to the Fireheads' settlement.

As the day wound to its close, their work done, the mastodonts were allowed to find food and water, and to mingle with the Family of Cows and calves.

Longtusk did not expect such freedom tonight.

He hadn't injured any of the Fireheads. But, despite Thunder's apologies and urging, he hadn't allowed the keepers to remount his pack gear or to place any of their grisly load on his back. The other mastodonts, some grumbling, had had to accept his share of the load. As a result he was expecting punishment.

But now the little keeper, Lemming, faced him. To Longtusk's surprise, Lemming came close, easily within range of the mammoth's great tusks. He seemed to trust Longtusk.

Lemming reached out with one small paw and touched the long hairs that grew from the center of Longtusk's face, between his eyes. Tiny fingers pulled gently at the hairs, combing out small knots, and the Firehead spoke steadily in his thin, incomprehensible voice. He seemed regretful, as if he understood.

Now Lemming reached down and loosened the hobbles around Longtusk's ankles. Then, with the gentlest of taps from his goad, he encouraged Longtusk to wander off toward his feeding ground.

Longtusk—confused, dismayed, baffled by kindness—moved away from the trees in search of steppe grass.

The Moon was high and dazzling bright—a wintry Moon, brilliant with the reflected light of ice-laden Earth. It was Longtusk's only companion.

Even when he ate, he had to do it alone. He needed the coarse grass and herbs of the steppe, and could tolerate little of the lush leaves and bark the mastodonts preferred. Tonight, though, he could have used a little company.

Walks With Thunder had apologized for not warning him, and tried to explain to him about the bones in the river bank. It wasn't a place of slaughter. It wasn't even the place where all those decomposing mammoths had died.

Mammoths had been drawn to the river's water over a long period of time—generations, perhaps even a significant part of a Great-Year. But a river bank could be a hazardous place. Mammoths became stuck in clinging mud and starved, or fell through thin ice and drowned. Their bodies were washed down the river, coming to rest in a meander or backwater.

Again and again this happened, the corpses washing downstream from all along the river bank, and coming to rest in the same natural trap, until a huge deposit of bodies had built up.

Sometimes the river would rise, immersing the bodies and embedding them in mud and silt, and fishes might nibble at the meat. And in dry seasons the water would drop, exposing the bodies to the air. The stench of their rot would attract flies, and larvae would burrow through the rotting flesh. Predators would come, wolverines or foxes or wolves, to gnaw on the exposed bones.

At last the bodies were buried by silt and peat, and vegetation grew over them.

But then the river's path had changed. The water began to cut away at the great natural pit of bones, exposing the corpses to the air once more . . .

"You see?" Thunder had said. "Nobody killed those mammoths. Why, they might have died centuries ago, their bodies lying unremarked in the silt layers until now. What's left behind is just bone and rotting flesh and hair. The Fireheads imagine they have a use for all those old bones—and what harm does it do? The mammoths have gone, their spirits flown to the aurora. Strange, yes, are the ways of the Fireheads, but you'll learn to live with them. *I* have . . ."

Yes, thought Longtusk angrily, and he ripped tufts of grass roughly from the ground as he stomped along alone, all but blinded by his teeming thoughts. Yes, Thunder, you've grown used to all this. It doesn't matter what happens to my bones when I've flown to the aurora; you're right.

But you have forgotten you are a Calf of Kilukpuk. You

have forgotten how we Remember those who go to the aurora before us.

I will not forget, no matter how long I live, how long I am kept here. *I* will never forget that I am mammoth.

". . . Are you in musth?"

The contact rumble was light, shallow. Close.

Preoccupied, he looked up. A small mastodont was facing him. A calf? No, a Cow—not quite fully grown, perhaps about his own age. She was chewing on a mouthful of leaves. Her jaw was delicate and neatly symmetrical, along with the rest of her skull, and that chewing, unmammoth-like motion didn't seem as ugly and unnatural when she did it as when a big ugly Bull like Jaw Like Rock took whole branches in his maw of a mouth and—

"You're staring at me," she said.

"What? . . . I'm sorry. What do you want?"

"I want to feed in peace," she growled. Her four tusks were short, Moon white, and she raised them defiantly. "And I want you to answer my question."

"I'm not in musth."

"The Matriarch says I must keep away from Bulls in musth. I'm not ready for oestrus yet. And even if I was—"

"I said, I'm not in musth," he snapped, rumbling angrily.

"You act as if you are."

"That's because—" He tried to calm down. "It's not your fault."

She stepped closer, cautiously. "You're the mammoth, aren't you? The calf of Primus. I heard them talking about you. I never met a mammoth before."

Longtusk felt confused.

What should he say to her? In his short life he had had little contact with Cows outside his immediately Family.

106

If this was a Bull he'd know what to do; he'd just start a fight.

He snorted and lifted his head. "What do you think of my tusks?"

She evaded his tusks, apparently unimpressed, and reached out with her slender trunk. She placed its warm, pink tip inside his mouth, startling him. Then she stepped back and lowered her trunk.

She sneezed. "Ugh. Saxifrage."

"I like saxifrage. Where I come from, we all eat saxifrage."

She curled her trunk contemptuously. She turned and ambled away, her hips swaying with liquid grace, and she tore at the grass as she passed.

Good riddance, thought Longtusk.

". . . Wait," he called. "What's your name?"

She raised her trunk, as if sniffing the air, and trumpeted her disdain. "Neck Like Spruce."

"My name is—"

"I know already," she said. And she walked off into moonlight.

2

The Rider

All too soon the short Arctic summer was gone, and winter closed in once more.

During the day Longtusk, seeking food, would scrape aside the snow and frost to find thin grass and herbs, dead and frozen. Sometimes Fireheads would follow him and chop turf and twigs from the exposed ground, fuel to burn in their great hearths.

The mastodonts, less well adapted to the cold, needed leaves and bark from the trees. But soon all the trees close to the Firehead settlement were stripped or destroyed, and they had to travel far to find sustenance.

This became impossible as the winter closed in, and the Firehead keepers would come out of their huts to bring feed, bales of yellowed hay gathered in the summer months. Longtusk watched with contempt as the mastodonts—even strong, intelligent males like Walks With Thunder and Jaw Like Rock— clustered around the bales, tearing into them greedily with their tusks and trunks.

The Fireheads regularly checked the mastodonts' trunks, eyes, ears and feet. Frostbite of the mastodonts' ears was common, and the Fireheads treated it with salves of fat and butter.

During the long nights, the mastodonts would huddle together for warmth, grumbling and complaining as one or another was bumped by a careless hip or prodded by a tusk. And they would regale each other with tales from their own, peculiarly distorted, version of the Cycle: legends of the heroic Mammut and her calves as they romped through the impossibly rich forests of the far south, where the sun never set and the trees grew taller than a hundred mastodonts stacked up on top of each other.

Longtusk tried to join in with tales of the heroes of mammoth legend, like Ganesha the Wise. But he'd been very young when he had heard these stories, and his memory was poor. When he jumbled up the stories the mastodonts would trumpet and rumble their amusement, nudging him and scratching his scalp with their trunks, until he stalked off in anger.

But as they talked and listened the younger mastodonts—and Longtusk—were soaking up the wisdom of their elders, embedded in such legends: how to find water in dry seasons or frozen winters, where to find salt licks, and particularly rich stands of trees.

Longtusk had left his Family at a very young age, and he found he had much to learn, even about the simple things of life.

There was a time when the toes of both his forelegs and hind legs gave him trouble, the skin cracking and becoming prone to infection.

Finally Walks With Thunder noticed and took him to one side. "This is what you must do," he said. The mastodont rummaged among his winter-dry fodder and selected a suitable branch. Holding it in his trunk he stripped the leaves away and peeled back the bark, munching it efficiently. Then he took the branch, broke it into four lengths and laid them out in front of him. He selected one piece and, with brisk motions, sharpened it to a point against a rock.

Then, satisfied with the shape, he began to clean methodically between his toenails, digging out the dirt, and wiping the stick clean.

"You never saw this before?" he said as he worked.

"No," Longtusk said, embarrassed.

"Longtusk, you sweat between your toes. You must keep your toes clean or the glands will clog, causing the problems you are suffering now. It is even more important to keep your musth glands clean." He picked up a shard of stick and, with a practiced motion, dug it into one of the temporal glands in the side of his face. "But you must be careful to use a suitable stick: one that is strong and straight and not likely to break. If it snaps and jams up your gland, it cannot discharge and it will drive you crazy." He eyed Longtusk. "You don't want to end up like that fool Jaw Like Rock, do you? . . ."

When the nails were clean the mastodont blew spittle on them with his trunk and polished them until they gleamed.

And so, as he grew, month on month, Longtusk's education continued, the orphan mammoth under the brusque, tender supervision of the older mastodonts.

In the worst of it, when the snow fell heavily or the wind howled, there was nothing to do but endure. Longtusk did not measure time as a human did, packaging it into regular intervals. Even in summer, time dissolved into a single glowing afternoon, speckled by moments of life and love, laughter and death. And in the long reaches of winter—when sometimes it wasn't possible even to risk moving for fear of dissipating his body's carefully hoarded heat—time slid away, featureless, meaningless, driven by the great rhythms of the world around him, and by the deep blood-red urges of his own body.

Longtusk secretly enjoyed these unmarked times, when he could stand with the others in the dark stillness and feel the shape of the turning world.

Longtusk's deep senses revealed the world beyond the horizon: in the hiss of a gale over a distant stretch of steppe, the boom of ocean breakers on a shore, the crack of ice on melting steppe ponds. And, in the deepest stillness of night, he could sense the thinness of this land bridge between the continents, with the frozen ocean to the north, the pressing seas to the south: surrounded by such immense forces, the land seemed fragile indeed.

Longtusk was learning the land on a level deeper than any human. He had to know how to use it to keep him alive, as if it was an extension of his own body, as if body and land merged into a single organism, pulsing with blood and seasons. As he matured, he would come to know Earth with a careless intimacy a human could never imagine.

Once, Longtusk woke from a heavy slumber and raised his head from a snowdrift.

Snow lay heavily, blanketing the ground. But the sky was clear, glittering with stars. The mastodonts were mounds of white. Here and there, as a mastodont stirred, snow fell away, revealing a swatch of red-black hair, a questing trunk or a peering eye.

And the aurora bloomed in the sky, an immense flat sheet of light thrown there by the wind from the sun.

It started with a gush of brightness that resolved itself into a transparent curtain, green and soft pink. Slowly its rays became more apparent, and it started to surge to east and west, like the guard hairs of some immense mammoth, developing deep folds.

It appeared at different places in the sky. When the light sheet was directly above, so that Longtusk was looking up at it, he saw rays converging on a point high above his head. And when he saw it edge-on it looked like smoke, rising from the Earth. Its huge slow movements were entrancing, endlessly fascinating, and Longtusk felt a great tenderness when he gazed at it.

Mammoths—and mastodonts—believed that their spirits flew to the aurora on death, to play in the steppes of light there. He wondered how many of his ancestors were looking down on him now—and he wondered how many of his Family, scattered and lost over the curve of the Earth, were staring up at the aurora, entranced just as he was.

The aurora moved steadily north, breaking up into isolated luminous patches, like clouds.

At last the days began to lengthen, and the pale ruddy sun seemed to leak a little warmth, as if grudgingly.

Life returned to the steppe.

The top layers of the frozen ground melted, and fast-growing grasses sprouted, along with sedges, small shrubs like Arctic sagebrush, and types of pea, daisy and buttercup. The grasses grew quickly and dried out, forming a kind of natural hay, swathes of it that would be sufficient to sustain, over the summer months, the herds of giant grazing herbivores that lived there.

Early in the season a herd of bison passed, not far away. Longtusk saw a cloud of soft dust thrown high into the air, and in the midst of it the great black shapes crowded together, with their humpback shoulders and enormous black horns; their stink of sweat and dung assailed Longtusk's acute sense of smell. And there were herds of steppe horses—their winter coats fraying, stripes of color on their flanks—skittish and nervous, running together like flocks of startled birds.

In this abundance of life, death was never far away. There were wolves and the even more ferocious dholes, lynxes, tigers and leopards: carnivores to exploit the herbivores, the moving mountains of meat. Once, near an outcrop of rock, Longtusk glimpsed the greatest predator of them all—twice the size of its nearest competitor—a mighty cave cat.

And—serving as a further sign of the relentless shortness of life—condors and other carrion eaters wheeled overhead, waiting for the death of others, their huge outfolded wings black stripes against the blue sky.

Work began again. The mastodonts were put to digging and lifting and carrying for the Fireheads.

Longtusk was still restricted to crude carrying. Those who had shared his chores last season were now, by and large, tamed and trained and trusted, and had moved on to more significant work. Of last year's bearers, only Longtusk remained as a pack animal.

What was worse, during the winter he had grown. Towering over the immature, restless calves he had to work with—his mighty tusks curling before him, useless—he endured his work, and the taunts of his fellows. But a cloud of humiliation and depression gathered around him.

Longtusk realized, with shock, that he was another year older, and he had withstood yet another cycle of seasons away from his Family. But compared to the heavy brutal reality of the mastodonts around him, his Family seemed like a dream receding into the depths of his memory.

He was surrounded by restraints, he was coming to realize, and the hobbles and goads of the keepers were only the most obvious. These mastodonts had lived in captivity for generations. None of them even knew what it was to be free, to live as the Cycle taught. And his own memories—half-formed, for he had been but a calf when taken—were fading with each passing month.

And besides, he didn't want to be alone, an outsider, a rogue, a rebel. He wanted to belong. And these complacent, tamed mastodonts were the only community available to him. The keepers knew all this—the smarter ones—and used subtle ploys to reinforce the invisible barriers that restrained the mastodonts more effectively than rope or wood: pain for misbehavior, yes, but rewards and welcoming strokes when he accepted his place.

If he could no longer imagine freedom, a life different from this, how could he ever aspire to it?

So it was that when Walks With Thunder came to him and said that the keeper, Lemming, was going to make an attempt to teach him to accept a rider, Longtusk knew the time had come to defy his instincts.

Lemming snapped, *"Baitho! Baitho!"*

Walks With Thunder murmured, "He's saying, *Down.* Lower your trunk, you idiot. Like this." And Thunder dipped his trunk gently, so it pooled on the ground.

Longtusk could see that all over the stockade mastodonts were turning toward him. Some of the Fireheads were pausing in their tasks to look at him, their spindly forelegs akimbo; he even spotted the blonde head of the little cub, Crocus, watching him curiously.

Longtusk growled. "They want to see the mammoth beaten at last."

"Ignore them," Walks With Thunder hissed. "They don't matter."

The Firehead raised his stick and tapped Longtusk on the root of his trunk.

Longtusk rapped his trunk on the ground, and as the air was forced out of the trunk it emitted a deep, terrifying roar.

Lemming fell back, startled.

"Try again," Thunder urged.

I have to do this, Longtusk thought. I *can* do this.

He lowered his head and let his trunk reach the ground, as Thunder had done.

"Good lad," said Thunder. "It's harder to submit than to defy. Hang onto that. You're stronger than any of us, little grazer. Now you must prove it."

The Firehead stepped onto Longtusk's trunk. Then he reached out and grabbed Longtusk's ears, his tipped stick still clutched in his paw.

Longtusk, looking forward, found he was staring straight into the Firehead's small, complex face.

This, he realized, is going to take a great deal of forbearance indeed.

"*Utha! Utha!*" cried Lemming.

"Now what?"

"He's telling you to lift him up."

"Are you sure?"

"Just do it."

And Longtusk pushed up with his trunk, lifting smoothly.

With a thin wail the Firehead went sailing clean over his rump.

Walks With Thunder groaned. "Oh, Longtusk . . ."

The Firehead came bustling round in front of him. He was covered in mastodont dung, and he was jumping up and down furiously.

"At least he had a soft landing," Longtusk murmured.

"Baitho!"

"He wants to try again," Walks With Thunder said. "Go ahead, lower your trunk. That's it. Let him climb on. Now take it easy, Longtusk. Don't throw him—*lift* him, smoothly and gently."

Longtusk made a determined effort to keep the motions of his trunk even and steady.

But this time Lemming was thrown backward. He completed a neat back-flip and landed on his belly in the dirt.

Other Fireheads ran forward. They lifted him up and started slapping at his furs, making great clouds of dust billow around him. They were flashing their small teeth and making the harsh noise he had come to recognize as *laughing*: not kind, perhaps, but not threatening.

But now the other keeper, Spindle, came forward. His goad, tipped with sharp bone, was long and cruel, and he walked back and forth before Longtusk, eyeing him. He was saying something, his small, cruel mouth working.

"Take it easy, Longtusk," Walks With Thunder warned.

"What does he want?"

"If Lemming can't tame you, then Spindle will do it. *His* way—"

Suddenly Spindle's thin arm lashed out toward Longtusk. His goad fizzed through the air and cut cruelly into the soft flesh of Longtusk's cheek.

Longtusk trumpeted in anger and reared up, as high as his hobbles would allow him. He could crush Spindle with a single stamp, or run him through with a tusk. How *dare* this ugly little creature attack *him*?

But the Firehead wasn't even backing away. He was standing before Longtusk, forelegs extended, paws tucked over as if beckoning.

"Don't, Longtusk," Walks With Thunder rumbled urgently. "It's what he wants. Don't you see? If you so much as scratch Spindle, they will destroy you in an instant. *It's what he wants . . .*"

Longtusk knew Thunder was right. He growled and lowered his tusks, glaring at Spindle.

The Firehead, tiny teeth gleaming, lashed out once more, and again Longtusk felt the goad cut deep into his flesh.

But suddenly it ceased.

Longtusk looked down. The girl-cub, Crocus, was standing before him. She seemed angry, distressed; tears ran down her small face. She was tugging at Spindle's foreleg, making him stop. Her father, Bedrock, and the Shaman Smokehat were standing behind her.

Spindle was hesitating, his blood-tipped goad still raised to Longtusk.

At last Bedrock gestured to Spindle. With a snort of disgust the keeper threw his goad in the dirt and stalked away.

Now Crocus stood before Longtusk, gazing up at him. She was growing taller, just as he was, and an elaborate cap of ivory beads adorned her long blonde hair, replacing the simple tooth necklace circle she had worn when younger. She seemed afraid, he saw, but she was evidently determined to master her fear.

"*Baitho*," she said, her voice small and clear. Down, down.

And Longtusk, the warm blood still welling from his face, obeyed.

She stepped onto his trunk, reached forward, and grabbed hold of his ears.

He raised his trunk, gingerly, carefully.

Thunder was very quiet and still, as if he scarcely dared breathe. "Right. Lower her onto your back. Gently!

Recall how fragile she is . . . imagine she's a flower blossom, and you don't want to disturb a single petal."

Rumbling, working by feel, Longtusk did his best. He felt the cub's skinny legs slide around his neck.

"How's that?"

Walks With Thunder surveyed him critically. "Not bad. Except she's the wrong way around. She's facing your backside, Longtusk. Try again. Let her off."

Longtusk lowered his hind legs. Crocus skidded down his back, landing with a squeal in the dirt.

"By Kilukpuk's hairy navel," Walks With Thunder groaned, and Bedrock stepped forward, anxious.

But Crocus, though a little dusty, was unharmed. She trotted around to Longtusk's head once more. She pulled her face in the gesture he was coming to recognize as a *smile*, and she patted the blood-matted hair of his cheek. "*Baitho*," she said quietly.

Again he lowered his trunk for her.

This time he got her the right way around. Her legs wrapped around his neck, and he felt her little paws grasping at the long hairs on top of his head. She was a small warm bundle, delicate, so light he could scarcely feel her.

Rumbling, constrained by his hobbles, Longtusk took a cautious step forward. He felt the cub's fingers digging deeper into his fur, and she squealed with alarm. He stopped, but she kicked at his flanks with her tiny feet, and called out, "*Agit!*"

"It's all right," Walks With Thunder said. "She's safe up there. Go forward. Just take it easy, Longtusk."

So he stepped forward again.

Crocus laughed with pleasure. Keepers ran alongside him—as did Bedrock, still wary, but grinning. The watching mastodonts raised their trunks and trumpeted in salute.

But the Shaman, ignored by the Fireheads and their leader, was glaring, quietly furious.

It was all a question of practice, of course.

By the end of that first day Longtusk could lift the little Firehead onto his back, delivering her the right way around, almost without effort. And by the end of the second day he was starting to learn what Crocus wanted. A gentle kick to the left ear—maybe accompanied by a thin cry of *Chi!*—meant he should go left. *Chai Ghoom!* and a kick to the right ear meant go right. *Agit!* meant go forward; *Dhuth!* meant stop. And so on.

By the end of the third day, Longtusk was starting to learn subtler commands, transmitted to him through the cub's body movements. If Crocus stiffened her limbs and leaned back he knew he was supposed to stop. If she leaned forward and pushed his head downward he should kneel or stoop.

Crocus never used a goad on him.

It wasn't all easy. Once he spied an exceptionally rich clump of herbs, glimpsed through the branches of a tree. He forgot what he was doing and went that way, regardless of the little creature on his back—who yelped as the branches swept her to the ground. Alternatively if Longtusk thought the path he was being told to select was uncomfortable or even dangerous—for instance, if it was littered with sharp scree that might cut his footpads—he simply wouldn't go that way, regardless of the protests of the cub.

After many days of this the keeper, Spindle, came to him, early in the morning.

Spindle raised his goad. *"Baitho! Baitho!"*

Longtusk simply glared at him, chewing his feed, refusing to comply.

The beating started then, as intense as before, and Longtusk felt old wounds opening on his cheek. But still he would not bow to Spindle.

Nobody else, he thought. Only the girl-cub Crocus.

At last Crocus came running with the other keepers. With sharp words she dismissed Spindle. Then, with Lemming's help, she applied a thick, soothing salve to the cuts Spindle had inflicted on Longtusk's cheek and thighs.

Without waiting for the command, Longtusk lowered his trunk and allowed her to climb onto his back once more.

Although Longtusk's workload didn't change, he became accustomed to meeting Crocus at the beginning or end of each day. She would ride him around the mastodont stockade, and Longtusk learned to ignore the mocking, somewhat envious jeers of the mastodonts. As she approached he would coil and uncoil his trunk with pleasure. Sometimes she brought him tidbits of food, which he chewed as she talked to him steadily in her incomprehensible, complex tongue.

She seemed fascinated by his fur. Longtusk had a dense underfur of fine woolly hair that covered almost all his skin. His rump, belly, flanks, throat and trunk were covered as well by a dense layer of long, coarse guard hair that dangled to the ground, skirt-like. The guard hair melded across his shoulders with a layer of thick but less coarse hairs that came up over his shoulders from low on the neck.

Crocus spent a great deal of time examining all this, lifting his guard hairs and teasing apart its layers. As for Longtusk, he would touch Crocus's sweet face with the wet tip of his trunk, and then rest against her warmth, eyes closed.

Eventually Crocus's visits became a highlight of his day—almost as welcome as, and rather less baffling than, his occasional meetings with the young mastodont Cow, Neck Like Spruce.

Once he took Crocus for a long ride across the bare steppe. They found a rock pool, and Longtusk wallowed there while Crocus played and swam. The sun was still high and warm, and he stretched out on the ground. She climbed onto his hairy belly and lay on top of him, soothed by the rumble of his stomach, plucking his hair and singing.

Even though he knew he remained a captive—even though her affection was that of an owner to the owned—and even though the growing affection between them was only a more subtle kind of trap, harder to break than any hobbles—still, he felt as content as he had been since he had been separated from his Family.

But he was aware of the jealous glares of Spindle and Smokehat.

Longtusk grew impatient with all these obscure mental games, the strange obsessions of the Fireheads. But Thunder counseled caution.

"Be wary," he would say, as the mastodonts gathered after a day's work. "You have a friend now. She recalls you once saved her life. And that's good. But you're also acquiring enemies. The Shaman is jealous. It is only the power of her father, Bedrock, which is protecting you. Life is more complicated than you think, little grazer. Only death is simple . . ."

3

The Settlement

The Fireheads' numbers were growing, with many young being born, and they worked hard to feed themselves.

As spring wore into summer, Firehead hunters began making journeys into the surrounding steppe. The hunters looked for tracks and droppings. What they sought, Longtusk was told, was the spoor of wolves, for that told them that there was a migrant herd somewhere nearby, tracked by the carnivores.

And at last the first of the migrants returned: deer, some of them giants, their heads bowed under the weight of their immense spreads of antlers.

The deer trekked enormous distances between their winter range in the far south, on the fringe of the lands where trees grew thickly, and their calving grounds on the northern steppe. The calving grounds were often dismal places of fog and marshy land and bare rock. But they had the great advantage that most predators, seeking places to den themselves, would fall away long before the calving grounds were reached. And when the calves were born the deer would form into vast herds in preparation for the migration back to the south: enormous numbers of them, so many a single herd might stretch from horizon to horizon, blackening the land.

To Longtusk these great migrations, of animals and birds, seemed like breathing, a great inhalation of life.

And the Fireheads waited for the migrant animals to pass, movements as predictable as the seasons themselves, and prepared to hunt.

One day, late in the summer, Crocus walked with her father and the Shaman to the bone stockpile, a short distance from the mastodont stockade.

Longtusk, still not fully trusted, wasn't allowed anywhere near this grisly heap of flensed bones, gleaming in the low afternoon sun.

Crocus walked around the pile, one finger in her small mouth. She ran her paws over clutches of vertebrae, and huge shoulder blades, and bare leg bones almost as tall as she was. At last she stopped before a great skull with sweeping tusks. As the skull's long-vacant eye sockets gaped at her, the cub rubbed the flat surfaces of the mammoth's worn yellow teeth.

Longtusk wondered absently what that long-dead tusker would have made of this.

Crocus looked up at her father and the Shaman, talking rapidly and jumping up and down with excitement. This skull was evidently her choice. Bedrock and Smokehat reached down and, hauling together, dragged the skull from the heap. It was too heavy for them to lift.

Then, his absurd headdress smoking, the Shaman sang and danced around the ancient bones, sprinkling them with water and dust. Longtusk had seen this kind of behavior before. It seemed that the Shaman was making the skull special, as if it was a living thing he could train to protect the little cub who had chosen it.

When the Shaman was done, Bedrock gestured to the mastodont trainers. Lemming and the others walked through the stockade and selected Jaw Like Rock and another strong Bull. Evidently they were to carry the skull off.

But Crocus seemed angry. She ran into the stockade herself, shouting, *"Baitho! Baitho!"*

Longtusk lowered his trunk to the ground and bent his head. With the confidence of long practice she wriggled past his tusks, grabbed his ears and in a moment was sitting in her comfortable place at his neck. Then, with a sharp slap on his scalp, she urged him forward. *"Agit!"*

She was, he realized, driving him directly toward the pile of bones.

As he neared the pile an instinctive dread of those grisly remains built up in him. The other Fireheads seemed to sense his tension.

He kept walking, crossing the muddy, trampled ground, one broad step at a time.

He reached the great gaping skull where it lay on the ground. There was a lingering smell of dead mammoth about it, and it seemed to glare at him in disapproval.

Crocus tapped his head. *"A dhur! A dhur!"* She wanted him to pick it up.

I can't, he thought.

He heard a high-pitched growl around him. The hunters were approaching him with spears raised to their shoulders, all pointing at his heart.

The Shaman watched, eyes glittering like quartz pebbles.

From out of nowhere, a storm cloud of danger was gathering around Longtusk. He felt himself quiver, and in response Crocus's fingers tightened their grip on his fur.

Longtusk stared into the vacant eyes of the long-dead mammoth. What, he wondered, would *you* have me do?

It was as if a voice sounded deep in his belly. *Remember me*, it said. *That's all. Remember me.*

He understood.

He touched the vacant skull with his trunk, lifted it, let it fall back to the dirt. Then he turned.

He faced a wall of Firehead hunters. One of them actually jabbed his chest with a quartz spear tip, hard enough to break the skin. But Longtusk, descending into the slow rhythms of his kind, ignored these fluttering Fireheads, even the spark of pain at his chest.

He gathered twigs and soil and cast them on the ancient bones, and then turned backward and touched the bones with the sensitive pads of his back feet. Longtusk was trying to Remember the spirit which had once occupied this pale bone, this Bull with no name.

The Fireheads watched with evident confusion—and the Shaman with rage, at this ceremony so much older and deeper than his own posturing. Farther away, the mastodonts rumbled their approval.

The Firehead cub slid to the ground, waving back the spears of the hunters. Slowly, hesitantly, Crocus joined in. She slipped off her moccasins and touched the skull with her own small feet, and bent to scoop more dirt over the cold bones. She was copying Longtusk, trying to Remember too—or, at least, showing him she understood.

At last, Longtusk felt he was done. Now the skull was indeed just a piece of bone, discarded.

Crocus stepped up to him, rubbed the fur between his eyes, and climbed briskly onto his back. She said gently, *"A dhur."*

Clumsily, but without hesitation, he slid his tusks

under the skull and wrapped his trunk firmly over the top of it. Then he straightened his neck and lifted.

The skull wasn't as heavy as it looked; mammoth bone was porous, to make it light despite its great bulk and strength. He cradled it carefully.

Then—under the guidance of Crocus, and with Bedrock, the Shaman, and assorted keepers and spear-laden hunters following him like wolves trailing migrant deer—he carried the skull toward the Firehead settlement.

Ahead of him, smoke curled into the air from a dozen fires.

The trail to the settlement was well beaten, a rut dug into the steppe by the feet of Fireheads and mastodonts. But Longtusk had not been this way before.

He passed storage pits. Their walls were scoured by the tusks of the mastodonts who had dug out these pits, and they were lined with slabs of smooth rock. Longtusk could see the pits were half-filled with hunks of dried and salted meat, or with dried grasses to provide feed for the mastodonts; winter seemed remote, but already these clever, difficult Fireheads were planning for its rigors.

Farther in toward the center of the settlement there were many hearths: out in the open air, blackened circles on the ground everywhere, many of them smoldering with dayfires. Chunks of meat broiled on spits, filling the air with acrid smoke.

There was, in fact, a *lot* of meat in the settlement.

Some of it dangled from wooden frames, varying in condition from dry and curled to fresh, some even dripping blood. There were a few small animals, lemmings and rabbits and even a young fox, hung up with their necks lolling, obviously dead.

And, most of all, there were Fireheads everywhere: not the few keepers and hunters the mastodonts encountered in their stockade and during the course of their work, but many more, more than he could count. There were males and females, old ones with yellowed, gappy teeth and frost-white hair, young ones who ran, excited, even infants in their mothers' arms. They all wore thick clothing of fur and skin, stuffed with grasses and wool; all but the smallest cubs wore thick, warming moccasins.

Some of the Fireheads worked at the hearths, turning spitted meat. One female had a piece of skin staked out over the ground and she was scraping it with a sharpened stone, removing fat and clinging flesh and sinew, leaving the surface smooth and shining. He saw a male making deerskin into rope, cutting strips crosswise for strength. They seemed, in fact, to use every part of the animals they hunted: tendons were twisted into strands of sinew, and bladders, stomach and intestines were used to hold water.

They made paint, of ground-up rock mixed with animal fat, or lichen soaked in aurochs' urine. Many of them had marked their skins with stripes and circles of the red and yellow coloring, and they wore strings of beads made of pretty, pierced stones or chipped bones.

Many of the Fireheads were fascinated by Longtusk. They broke off what they were doing and followed, the adults staring, the cubs dancing and laughing.

Here was one small group of Fireheads—perhaps a family—having a meal, gathered around a sputtering fire. They had bones that had been broiled on their fire, and they cracked the bones on rocks and sucked out the soft, greasy marrow within. Longtusk wondered absently what animals the bones had come from.

As he passed—a great woolly mammoth bearing a huge skull and with the daughter of the chief clinging proudly to his back—the Fireheads stopped eating, stared, and joined the slow, gathering procession that trailed after Longtusk.

. . . Now, surrounded by Fireheads, he was aware of discomfort, a sharp prodding at his rump.

He turned. He saw the Shaman, Smokehat, bearing one of the hunters' big game spears. The quartz tip was red with blood: Longtusk's blood.

He saw calculation in the Shaman's small, pinched face. Sensing his tension, Smokehat was deliberately prodding him, trying to make him respond—perhaps by growing angry, throwing off Crocus. If that happened, if he went rogue here at the heart of the Firehead settlement, Longtusk would surely be killed.

Longtusk snorted in disgust, turned his back and continued to walk.

But the next time he felt the tell-tale prod at his rump he swished his tail, as if brushing away flies. He heard a thin mewl of complaint.

Smokehat was clutching his cheek, and blood leaked around his fingers. Longtusk's tail hairs had brushed the Firehead's face, splitting it open like a piece of old fruit. With murder in his sharp eyes, the Shaman was led away for treatment; and Longtusk, with quiet contentment, continued his steady plod.

He heard a trumpeted greeting. He slowed, startled.

There were mastodonts here: a small Family, a few adult Cows, calves holding onto their mothers' tails with their spindly little trunks. They wandered freely through the settlement, without hobbles or restraints, mingling with the Fireheads.

One of the Cows was Neck Like Spruce.

"Well, well," she said. "Quite a spectacle. Life getting dull out in the stockade, was it?"

When he replied, his voice was tight, his rumbles shallow. "If you haven't anything useful to say, leave me alone."

She sensed his tension, and glanced now at the hunters who followed him, spears still ready to fly. "Just stay calm," she said seriously. "They are used to us. In fact they feel safer if we are here. Where there are mastodonts, the cats and wolves will not attack . . . Where are you going?"

He growled. "Do I look as if I have the faintest idea?"

She trumpeted her amusement, and broke away from her Family to walk alongside him.

At last the motley procession approached the very heart of the Firehead settlement, and Longtusk slowed, uncertain.

There were larger structures here—perhaps a dozen of them, arranged in an uneven circle. They were rough domes of gray-green and white. The largest of all, and the most incomplete, was at the very center.

Crocus slid easily to the ground. She took the tip of Longtusk's trunk in her small paw and led him into the circle of huts.

He stopped by one of the huts. It was made of turf and stretched skin and rock, piled up high. On the expanses of bare animal skin, there were strange markings, streaks and whirls of ochre and other dyes, and there and there the skin was marked with the unmistakable imprint of a Firehead paw, marked out as a silhouette in red-brown coloring. The dome-shaped hut had a hole cut in its top, from which smoke curled up to the sky.

There were white objects arrayed around the base of the hut. White, complex shapes.

Mammoth bones.

Big skulls had been pushed into the ground by their

tusk sockets, all around the hut. Curving bones, shoulder blades and pelvises, had been layered along the lower wall of the hut. There were heavier bones, femurs and bits of skulls, tied to the turf roof. And two great curving tusks had been shoved into the ground and their sharp points tied together to form an arch over a skin-flap doorway.

Some of the bones were chipped and showed signs of where they had been gnawed by predators, perhaps as they had emerged from the remote river bank where they had been mined.

Now the flap of skin parted at the front of the hut, and a woman pushed out into the colder air. She gaped at the woolly mammoth standing before her, and clutched her squealing infant tighter to her chest.

Longtusk, baffled, was filled with dread and horror. "By Kilukpuk's last breath, what *is* this?"

"This is how the Fireheads live, Longtusk," said Neck Like Spruce. "The turf and rock keeps in the warmth of their fires . . ."

"But, Spruce, *the bones*. Why. . . ?"

She trumpeted her irritation at him. "This is a cold and windy place, if you hadn't noticed, Longtusk. The Fireheads have to make their huts sturdy. They prefer wood, but there is little wood on this steppe, and what there was they have mostly burned. But there are plenty of bones."

"Mammoth bones."

"Yes. Longtusk, your kind have lived here for a *long* time, and the ground is full of their bones. In some ways bone is better than wood, because it is immune to frost and damp and insects. These huts are built to last a long time, Longtusk, many seasons . . . And it does no harm," she said softly.

"I know." For, he realized, these mammoths had long

gone to the aurora, and had no use for these discarded scraps.

There was a gentle tugging at his trunk. He glanced down. It was Crocus; she was trying to get him to come closer to the big central hut.

He rumbled and followed her.

This hut would eventually be the biggest of them all—a fitting home for Bedrock and his family, including little Crocus—but it was incomplete, without a roof.

A ring of mammoth femurs had been thrust into the ground in a circle at the base, and an elaborate pattern of shoulder blades had been piled up around the perimeter of the hut, overlapping neatly like the scales of some immense fish.

The floor had been dug away, making a shallow pit. Flat stones had been set in a circle at the center of the hut to make a hearth. And there was a small cup of carved stone, filled with sticky animal fat, within which a length of plaited mastodont fur burned slowly, giving off a greasy smoke. With a flash of intuition he saw that it would be dark inside the hut when the roof had been completed; perhaps sputtering flames like these would give the illusion of day, even in darkness.

Under Crocus's urging, he laid down the skull he carried, just outside the circle of leg bones. Crocus jumped on it, excited, and made big swooping gestures with her skinny forelegs. Perhaps this skull would be built into the hut. Its glaring eye sockets and sweeping tusks would make an imposing entrance.

Now Crocus ran into the incomplete hut, picked up a bundle wrapped in skin, and held it up to Longtusk. When the skin wrapping fell away Longtusk saw that it was a slab of sandstone, and strange loops and whorls had been cut into its surface.

"Touch it," called Neck Like Spruce.

Cautiously Longtusk reached forward with his trunk's fragile pink tip, and explored the surface of the rock.

". . . It's *warm*."

"They put the rocks in the fires to make them hot, then clutch them to their bellies in the night."

Now Crocus was jabbering, pointing to the markings on the skin walls, streaks and whorls and lines, daubed there by Firehead fingers. The cub seemed excited.

He traced his trunk tip over the patterns, but could taste or smell nothing but ochre and animal fat. He growled, baffled.

"It's another Firehead habit," Spruce said testily. "Each pattern means something. Look again, Longtusk. The Fireheads aren't like us; they have poor smell and hearing, and rely on their eyes. Don't touch it or smell it. Try to look through Firehead eyes. Imagine it isn't just a sheet of skin, but a—a hole in the wall. Imagine you aren't looking at markings just in front of your face, but forms that are far away. Look with your eyes, Longtusk, just your eyes. *Now*—now what do you see?"

After a time, with Crocus chattering constantly in his ear, he managed it.

Here was a curving outline, with a smooth sheen of ochre across its interior, that became a bison, strong and proud. Here was a row of curved lines, one after the other, that was a line of deer, heads up and running. Here was a horse, dipping its head and stamping its small foot. Here was a strange creature that was half leaping stag and half Firehead, glaring out at him.

He looked around the settlement with new eyes— and he saw that there were makings *everywhere*, on every available surface: the walls of the huts, the faces of the Fireheads, the shafts of the hunters' spears, even

Crocus's heated stone. And all of the markings *meant* something, showing Fireheads and animals, mountains and flowers.

The illusions were transient and flat. These "animals" had no scent, no voices, no weight to set the Earth ringing. They were just shadows of color and line.

Nevertheless they were here. And everywhere he looked, they danced.

The settlement was alive, transformed by the minds and paws of the Fireheads, made vibrant and rich—as if the land itself had become conscious, full of reflections of itself. It was a transformation that could not even have been imagined by any mammoth or mastodont who ever lived. He trembled at its thin, strange beauty.

How could any creatures be capable of such wonder— and, at the same time, such cruelty? These Fireheads were strange and complex beings indeed.

Now Crocus dragged his face back to the wall of her own hut. Here was a row of stocky, flat-backed shapes, with curving tusks before them.

Mastodonts. It was a line of mastodonts, their tusks, drawn with simple, confident sweeps, proud and strong.

But Crocus was pointing especially at a figure at the front of the line. It was crudely drawn, as if by a cub—by Crocus herself, he realized.

It looked like a mastodont, but its back sloped down from a hump at its neck. Its tusks were long and curved before its high head, and long hairs draped down from its trunk and belly.

He growled, confused, distressed.

"Longtusk?" Neck Like Spruce called. *"That's you,* Longtusk. Crocus made you on the wall. You see? She was trying to honor you."

"I understand. It's just—"

"What?"

"I haven't seen a mammoth since I was separated from my Family. Neck Like Spruce, I think I've forgotten what I look like."

"Oh, Longtusk . . ."

Crocus came to him, perceiving his sudden distress. She wrapped her arms around his trunk, buried her face in his hair, and murmured soothing noises.

4

The Hunt

Winter succeeded summer, frost following fire.

Sometimes, Longtusk dreamed:

Yellow plain, blue sky, a landscape huge, flat, elemental, dominated by the unending grind and crack of ice. And mammoths sweeping over the land like clouds—

He would wake with a start.

All around him was order: the mastodont stockade, the spreading Firehead settlement, the smoke spiraling to the sky. *This* was the reality of his life, not that increasingly remote plain, the mammoth herds that covered the land. *That* had been no more than the start of his journey—a journey that had ended here.

Hadn't it?

After all, what else was there? Where else could he go? What else was there to do with his life, but serve the Fireheads?

Troubled, he returned to sleep.

And five years wore away.

The hunting party of Fireheads and mastodonts—and one woolly mammoth—marched proudly across the landscape. The high summer cast short shadows of

Longtusk and his rider: Crocus, of course, now fully grown, long-legged and elegant, and as strong and brave as any of the male Firehead hunters. She was equipped for the hunt. She carried a quartz-tipped spear, and wore a broad belt slung over her shoulder, laden with stone knives and hammers, and—most prized of all—an atlatl, a dart thrower made of sculpted deer bone.

". . . Ah," Walks With Thunder said now, and he paused. "*Look.*"

Longtusk looked down at the ground. At first he saw nothing but an unremarkable patch of steppe grass, with a little purple saxifrage. Then he made out scattered pellets of dung.

Walks With Thunder poked at the pellets with his trunk tip. "See the short bitten-off twigs in there? Not like mastodonts; we leave long twisted bits of fiber in our dung. And we produce neat piles too; *they* kick it around the place as it emerges . . ." He brought a piece of dung into his mouth. "Warm. Fresh. *They* are close. Softly, now."

Alert, evidently excited, he trotted on, and the party followed.

Over the years Longtusk had been involved in many of the Fireheads' hunts. Most of them targeted the smaller herbivores. The Fireheads would follow a herd of deer or horse and pick off a vulnerable animal—a cow slowed by pregnancy, or a juvenile, or the old or lame—and finish it quickly. Then they would butcher it with their sharpened stones and have the mastodonts carry back the dripping meat, skin and bones.

The hunts were usually brief, efficient, routine events, and only rarely would the hunters take on an animal the size of, say, a giant deer. The hunters were after all seeking food, and they tried to make their success as certain as possible, minimizing the risks they took.

But today's hunt was different. Today they were going after the largest prey of all. And only the strongest and most able hunters, including Bedrock himself, had been included in the party.

Though Crocus had joined in hunts before—the only female Firehead to do so—and had become skillful with spear and stone knife, this was the first time she had been allowed by her father to take part in such an event. And so—because Longtusk still refused to allow any other rider on his back but Crocus—it was the first time for him, too.

They were heading west, and they came to a strange land.

There were pools here, but they were small and misshapen and filled with icy, cloudy, sour water. Trees, mostly spruce, struggled to grow, but they were stunted and leaned at drunken angles. The ground was broken and hummocky, and Longtusk had to step carefully. Here and there, in fact, the turf was no more than a thin crust over a deeper hollow. With his deeper senses he could hear the peculiar echoes the crusty ground returned, but still an incautious footstep could lead to a stumble or worse.

Walks With Thunder, with Bedrock proudly borne on his back, loped alongside Longtusk. "The ice is retreating to its northern fastness. But this is a place where a remnant of ice was covered over by wind-blown silt and soil before it could melt. The earth is thin; the trees can establish only shallow roots, so they grow badly. And the ice is still there, beneath us . . . Look."

They came to a low ridge, half Longtusk's height. Under a lip of grass, he could see ice protruding above the ground, dirty, glistening with meltwater.

"The stagnant ice is slowly melting away. As it does so it leaves hollows and caverns under a crust of unsupported earth. But sometimes the rain and meltwater will work away at the ice, turning it into a honeycomb. So watch your step, little grazer, for you don't want to snap a tusk or an ankle. And you *don't* want to dump your rider on her behind."

So Longtusk stepped carefully.

When the sun was at its highest the party paused to rest. The mastodonts were freed of their packs, hobbled loosely and allowed to wander off in search of food.

Later some of them, Longtusk included, underwent some refresher training in preparation for the hunt, along with their riders. Jaw Like Rock, ridden by the cruel Spindle, led them.

Jaw trotted back and forth across the broken ground, and Spindle, riding Jaw's back, got cautiously to his feet. His feet were bare to improve his grip, and he kept his balance by holding out his forelegs.

Jaw kept up a commentary for the mastodonts. "You can see he can hold his place up there. The hunters stand so they get a better leverage when they hurl their spears and darts.

"But you have to realize it isn't natural. He isn't stable. I can feel he's on the brink of falling over. He can shift his feet and hind legs to adjust his balance, and I have to try to keep my back steady as I move. See? It gets a lot harder when you're racing over this crusty ground alongside the prey . . . And if you stop working at it even for a moment—"

He stopped dead.

Spindle tried to keep his balance, waving his forelegs in the air. But without Jaw's assistance, he was helpless. With a wail, he tumbled to the ground, landing hard.

Longtusk heard his own rider, Crocus, break into peals of laughter. The mastodonts trumpeted and slapped the ground with their trunks.

Spindle was predictably furious. He got to his feet, brushing off dirt and grass blades. He picked up his goad and began to lash at Jaw's face and rump.

The other keepers turned away, as if disgusted, and the mastodonts rumbled their disapproval.

Longtusk said grimly, "I don't know how you put up with that."

Jaw eyed him, stolidly enduring his punishment. "It's worth it. Anyway, nothing lasts forever—"

A contact rumble washed over the steppe. "Silence," Walks With Thunder called. "*Silence*. Rhinos . . ."

There were three of them, Longtusk counted: two adults and a calf.

They were at the edge of a milk-white pond. One of the adults—perhaps a female—was in the water, which lapped around the fur fringing her belly. Her calf was in the pond beside her, almost afloat, sometimes putting her head under the water and paddling around her mother.

The other adult, probably a male, stood on the shore of the pond. He was grazing, trampling the grass flat and then using his big forelip to scoop it into his mouth.

They were woolly rhinos.

They were broad, fat tubes of muscle and fat. Their skin was heavy and wrinkled. On massive necks were set squat, low-slung heads with small ears and tiny black eyes. Their bodies were coated with dark brown fur, short on top but dangling in long fringes from their bellies. They had high humps over their shoulders, short tails and, strangest of all, each had two long curving horns protruding up from their noses. The bull's nasal horn in particular was long and glinting and sharp.

Small birds clustered on the bull's back, pecking, searching for mosquitoes and grubs.

Now the cow climbed out of the water, ponderous and slow, followed by her calf. Dripping, she grunted, shifted her hind legs, and emitted a spray of urine, horizontal and powerful, that splashed into the pond water and over the nearby shore. The urine came in gargantuan proportions. Longtusk saw, bemused, a series of powerful blasts, until it dwindled to a trickle down the long hairs of the cow's hind legs.

The bull, rumbling in response, immediately emptied his own bladder in a spray that covered the cow's. Then he rubbed his hind feet in the wet soil.

Thunder grunted. "The rhinos talk through their urine and dung. When other rhinos come this way, they will be able to tell that the cow over there is in oestrus, ready to mate. But the bull has covered her marker, telling the other bulls that she is *his* . . ."

They were almost like mammoths, Longtusk thought, wondering: short, squat, deformed—nevertheless built to survive the harshness of winter.

The party of mastodonts and Fireheads began to pad softly forward.

"They haven't sensed us yet," said Thunder. "See the way the Bull's ears are up, his tail is low? He's at his ease. Let's hope he stays that way."

The rhino calf was the first to notice them.

She (or he, it was impossible to tell) was prizing up dead wood with her tiny bump of a horn, apparently seeking termites. Then she seemed to scent the mastodonts. She flattened her ears and lifted her tail.

She ran around her mother, prodding her with her

horn. At first the mother, dozing, took no notice. But the calf put both her front feet on the mother's face and blew in her ear. The cow got to her feet, shaking her head, and rumbled a warning to the male.

The rhinos began to lumber away from the pond, in the direction of open ground. The small birds which had been working on the backs of the rhinos flew off in a brief burst of startled motion.

The mastodonts and their riders pursued, rapidly picking up speed. Those animals heavy with pack were left behind, while others lightly laden for the chase hurtled after the rhinos: they included Thunder, bearing Bedrock, Jaw with Spindle—and Longtusk, carrying Crocus, who clung to his hair, whooping her excitement as the steppe grass flew past.

"This is it," said Thunder, tense and excited. "We're going after the bull."

Longtusk said, "Why not the cow? She is slowed by the calf."

"But she is not such a prize. See the way the bull's back is flat and straight, the cow's sagging? That shows she is old and weak. This hunt is a thing of prestige. Today these hunters are chasing honor, not the easiest meat. We go for the male."

Soon they passed the cow and her calf. The cow flattened her ears, wrinkled her nose and half-opened her mouth, as if she was about to charge. But the mastodonts and their riders ignored her, flying onward over the steppe in pursuit of the greater quarry.

They drew alongside the male rhino. He ran almost elegantly, Longtusk thought: like a horse, his tail high, his feet lifting over the broken ground. Even as he ran he bellowed his protest and swung his powerful horns this way and that, trying to reach the mastodonts.

With practiced ease Bedrock slid to his feet on the broad back of Walks With Thunder and prepared his at-latl. He raised a dart—it was almost as long as Bedrock was tall, and its tip, pure quartz crystal, glinted cruelly—and he fitted a notch in the base of the dart to the thrower. The thrower, perhaps a third the length of the dart, was carved from the femur of a giant deer.

Longtusk could feel Crocus clambering to her feet on his back. She was unsteady, and he sensed her leaning forward, ready to grab at his hairs if she felt herself falling. Nevertheless she hefted her own dart.

And she threw first.

She hurled hard and well—but not accurately enough; the dart's tip glanced off the rhino's back, scraping through his hair, and slid onward toward the ground.

Now her father raised his dart. He held it flat, with the thrower resting on his shoulder, his hand just behind his ear. Then, with savage force, his entire lean body whipping forward, he thrust at the dart. Longtusk saw the thin shaft bow into a curve, and then spring away from Bedrock, as if it was a live thing, hissing through the air.

The hard quartz tip shone like a falling star as it flew at the rhino. The dart hit beneath the rhino's rib cage—exactly where it could do most damage.

The dart point had been designed and made by master craftsmen for its purpose. It was long, sharp and did not split off or shatter on first impact. Instead it drove itself through the rhino's hair and layers of hide and fat, embedding itself in the soft, warm organs within.

The rhino screeched, his voice strangely high for such an immense animal. Longtusk could smell the sharp metallic tang of the blood which spurted crimson from the wound, and black fluid oozed from the rhino's lips.

But still, with awesome willpower, the rhino ran on. The pain must have been agonizing as the dangling, twisting spear ripped at the wound, widening it further and deepening the internal injury.

Now another mastodont bearing a young, keen-eyed hunter called Bareface drew alongside the rhino. The hunter took careful aim and hurled his dart—not at the rhino's injured torso, but at his hind legs.

The dark sliced through fur and flesh. The rhino fell flat on the ground and rolled over, snapping off the dart that protruded from his side.

Still defiant, the rhino tried to rise. But his hind leg dangled uselessly, pumping blood, and he fell again in dirt already soaked with his own blood. Urine and dung gushed, liquid, adding to the mess in the dirt.

The mastodonts halted. The Fireheads jumped down, approaching the rhino warily.

The rhino thrashed in the dirt and bellowed his rage, slashing the air with his long horn. But he was already mortally wounded; a spray of red-black liquid shot from his mouth.

Defying the swings of that cruel horn, Bedrock leaped nimbly onto the rhino's broad back, grabbing great pawfuls of fur. With grim determination, already covered in dirt and blood, Bedrock crawled forward until he reached the base of the rhino's neck. Then he pulled from his belt a long, sharp chisel of rock. Defying the thrashings of the rhino, he stabbed the chisel into the creature's flesh, at the top of his spine. Then he produced a hammer rock from his belt.

Under Bedrock's single blow, the stone blade slid easily through the rhino's hide.

As his spine was severed the rhino's eyes widened, startled, almost curious. Then he slumped flat against the blood-stained dirt, his magnificent body reduced to a flaccid, quivering mound.

He raised his head to face Longtusk. He breathed in short sharp gasps, *whoosh, whoosh, whoosh.*

Walks With Thunder said grimly, "He's trying to speak to you. *Who are you? Why are you doing this?"*

"How can you understand him?"

"We are all Hotbloods, grazer."

Then, mercifully, Bedrock drove another blade into the rhino's spine.

The rhino's head slumped to the ground. His body rumbled and shuddered as its huge, complex processes closed down.

When life was gone, panting mastodonts and blood-spattered Fireheads stood away from the corpse. They seemed united by the vivid moment, stilled, as if the world pivoted on the death of this huge, defiant animal.

Then Bedrock climbed onto the rhino's back, his furs stained with blood. He raised his paws in the air and hollered his triumph, and his hunters yelled in response. They sound like wolves, Longtusk thought; it is the feral cry of the predator.

And I have run with them. For an instant an image of his mother came into his mind, her smell and warmth and touch, as clearly as if she was standing before him. Oh, Milkbreath, I have come on a long journey since I last saw you!

Bedrock jumped down and walked to the rhino's slumped head. He gripped his hammer rock and swung it against the base of that huge horn. With a sharp crack, the horn split away from a shallow depression in the rhino's face. Bedrock raised the horn to the sky, then tucked it into his belt.

The hunters gathered around the rhino, producing

their knives of stone, and began to slice through skin and fur.

Longtusk said, "Now what? It will take a while to butcher this huge animal."

"Oh, they aren't going to butcher it," said Jaw Like Rock. "It's too big a beast to haul across the steppe, too much meat to eat and store. They will dig out the liver and consume that. And, of course, Bedrock has his horn . . ."

"The horn?"

Walks With Thunder rumbled, "Bedrock has a dozen horns already. He will take this one and have it shaped into a dagger or a drinking cup, and he will treasure it forever, a token of his bravery. This wasn't about gathering meat. Today the Fireheads have proved, you see, what brave hunters they are . . . Look up there."

Condors wheeled overhead, their wings stretched out, cold and black.

"*They* know," said Thunder. "They have seen this before, and—"

A Firehead cried out.

It was Bedrock. He stood upright, but a look of puzzlement clouded his face. And his body was quivering.

A thin, small spear protruded from his skull.

Then his eyes rolled back in his head, blood gushed from his mouth, and he collapsed as if his bones had dissolved.

Crocus rushed forward and began to keen, her voice high and thin.

Walks With Thunder said grimly, "Circle."

Longtusk immediately obeyed, taking his place with the others in a rough protective ring around the fallen Firehead. It was an ancient command, millions of years old, so old it was common to both mastodonts and mammoths.

Now Longtusk could smell and hear the assailants who had so suddenly struck down Bedrock. They were Fireheads, of course—but not from the settlement. They were some way away, and they danced and stamped their delight. The skin of their small faces was coated with a fine white powder—perhaps rock flour, sieved from the shallow pools of this strange landscape—a powder that stank sharply of salt.

The young hunter, Bareface, his shaven-smooth visage twisted into an unrecognizable snarl, whipped his foreleg with suppleness and speed.

A boomerang went flying. It spun, whistling, as it soared through the thin air. It was a piece of mammoth ivory carved smooth and curved like a bird's wing, with one side preserving the convex surface of the original tusk, the other polished almost flat.

The strange Fireheads didn't even seem to see it coming—they scattered as it flew among them, like mice disturbed by an owl— but the boomerang flew unerringly to the temple of one of them, knocking him to the ground.

Jaw growled his approval. "The one who struck down Bedrock. *He* will not live out the day . . ."

"*Whiteskins,*" Thunder muttered. "I never thought I'd see their ugly, capering forms again."

Longtusk said, "You've met them before?"

"Oh, yes. Many times. But never so far north."

Now Crocus came running to Longtusk. Her face was contorted with rage, and her blonde hair blew around her. She held the stone chisel which Bedrock had driven into the rhino's spine. "*Baitho! Baitho!*" He lowered his head and trunk, and she grabbed his ears and scrambled onto his back. "*Agit!*"

Her intention was unmistakable.

Without thought—despite rumbles of warning from the mastodonts, cries of alarm from the hunters—Longtusk charged toward the Whiteskins.

Longtusk expected the Whiteskins to flee. But they held their ground. They dropped to their knees and raised weapons of some kind.

Suddenly there were more small spears of the type that had felled Bedrock flying through the air around him, fast and straight.

"They are not spears," puffed Thunder as he ran after the mammoth, "but *arrows.* The Whiteskins have bows—never mind, grazer! Just keep your head high when you run. *You* can take an arrow or two—but not your rider."

And, as if in response to Thunder's warning, a small flint-tipped spear—no, an *arrow*—plunged out of nowhere into Longtusk's cheek. The pain was sharp and intense; the small blade had reached as far as his tongue.

Without breaking stride, he curled his trunk and plucked the arrow out of his cheek. Blood sprayed, but immediately the pain lessened.

Jaw Like Rock was charging past him, the keeper Spindle clinging to Jaw's hair as if for life itself, his mouth drawn back in a rictus of terror. Jaw called, "Had a mosquito bite, grazer?"

"Something like that."

The big tusker trumpeted his exhilaration and charged forward.

Still the strange Fireheads did not break and run.

An arrow lodged in the foreleg of Jaw Like Rock. Longtusk could smell the sharp, coppery stink of fresh blood. Jaw screamed and pulled up, despite repeated beatings from Spindle on his back. Jaw knelt down, snapping away the arrow. Then, bellowing with rage and pain, he plunged on.

Still Spindle continued to beat him and scream in his ear.

Now they were on the Whiteskins. Mastodonts, Whiteskins and Fireheads flew at each other in a crude, unco-ordinated mêlée, and trumpets, yells and screams broke the dust-laden air.

Longtusk lunged at the Whiteskins around him with his tusks and trunk. But, nimble and light on their feet, they stayed out of his reach. They jabbed at him with their spears and rocks, aiming to slash at his trunk or belly, or trying for his legs.

Calmly, Thunder called to Longtusk: "Watch out for those knives. These brutes have fought us before. They are trying for your hamstrings. Recall that rhino, grazer. I've no intention of carrying you back to the stockade."

Longtusk growled his gratitude.

Jaw Like Rock, enraged by pain, feinted at a fat Whiteskin. The Firehead, evading the lunge of those tusks, got close to Jaw with his spear. But Jaw swung his tusks sideways and knocked the Whiteskin to the ground. Then, with a single ruthless motion, he placed his foot on the head of the scrambling Whiteskin.

Jaw pressed hard, and the head burst like an overripe fruit, and the Whiteskin was limp.

Through all of this Spindle clung to Jaw's back, white-eyed, obviously terrified.

But for Longtusk there was no time for reflection, or horror; for now one of the Whiteskins came directly at him, jabbing with a long spear. He was a big buck, shaven-headed and stripped to the waist, and the whole of his upper body was coated with the acrid white paste.

He had a wound on his temple, a broad cut sliced deep into the greasy flesh there—as if made by a boomerang.

Crocus, on his back, yelled her anger. With a screech like a she-cat, her blonde hair flying around her, she leaped off Longtusk's back. She landed on the big Firehead, knocking him flat. She raked her nails down his bare back, leaving red gouges. The Whiteskin howled and twisted—and, despite Crocus's anger and determination, he soon began to prevail, for Crocus's strength and weight were no match for this big male.

Walks With Thunder, surrounded by his own circle of assailants, called breathlessly, "Protect her, Longtusk. She's important now. More than you know . . ."

Longtusk had every intention of doing just that, but while the two Fireheads flailed in the dirt, he could easily harm Crocus as much as her opponent. He stood over them, trumpeting, waiting for an opportunity.

At last the Whiteskin wrestled Crocus flat on her back. He straddled her, sitting astride her belly, raising his fists to strike.

Now was Longtusk's chance.

The mammoth reached out with his trunk, meaning to grab the Whiteskin around his neck . . .

The Whiteskin jerked upright, suddenly. His paws fluttered in the air around his face, like birds, out of his control. Then he fell backward, twitched once, and was still.

Longtusk reached down and pulled the corpse off Crocus.

He saw immediately how the Whiteskin had died. The chisel that had destroyed the rhino—still stained by the great beast's blood—had been driven upward into the Whiteskin's face, through the soft bones in the roof of his mouth, and into his brain.

The girl got to her feet. She stared down at the creature she had killed. Then she anchored one foot on the White-skin's ugly, twisted face, and yanked the chisel out of his skull. The last of his blood gushed feebly.

She stepped on his chest and emitted a howl of victory—just as her father had on bringing down the rhino.

Then she fell to her knees and buried her face in her paws.

Longtusk reached out his trunk to her. She curled up, pulling the long hairs close around her, as she had as a cub, lost and alone on the steppe.

The Whiteskins were fleeing. The mastodonts trumpeted after them, and the Firehead hunters hurled their last spears and darts.

In all, four Whiteskins had fallen. Under the watchful, contemptuous eyes of Jaw Like Rock—whose leg wound still leaked blood—the trainer, Spindle, walked from one Whiteskin corpse to the next, jabbing his spear into their defenseless cooling bodies.

Walks With Thunder came up to Longtusk. He was dusty, blood-spattered, breathing hard. "I'm getting too old for this. Bedrock came north to find a place to live without war . . . But the world is filling up, it seems.

"Now we must attend to business. We must collect Bedrock's body. And we will walk back the way we came and retrieve the spears that were thrown. Then we will return to the settlement. Now, everything will be differ-ent . . . *Jaw!*"

Longtusk looked up in time to see it happen.

He had heard of this before. A mastodont, cruelly treated by a Firehead keeper, would not lash out in anger. Instead he would bide his time, enduring the insults and punishment, waiting for the right opportunity.

Now here was Spindle, without his goad, dancing on the bodies of already dead Whiteskins; and here was Jaw Like Rock, calmly watching him, unrestrained, not even hobbled.

In the very last instant Spindle seemed to understand the mistake he had made. He raised his paws, as if pleading.

Jaw lunged forward with a single clean, strong motion, a thrust born of experience and training, and his tusk punctured Spindle's heart.

5

The Remembering

The hunting party returned to the Firehead settlement, subdued, all but silent. They moved slowly, for Jaw Like Rock was forced to walk hobbled, armed Firehead hunters shadowing his every step.

Walks With Thunder, meanwhile, moving with slow dignity, bore the bodies of Bedrock and Spindle, wrapped in fur blankets. The long nasal horn of the rhino, Bedrock's last trophy, was laid on top of his body, still caked with dried blood.

Crocus walked beside Thunder, clutching her father's cold paw.

"*War*," growled Thunder, and he raised his trunk suddenly, as if sniffing the winds of vanished past. "You've been lucky to see so little of it, little grazer. Brutal and bloody it is, for Fireheads and mastodonts. They teach us special commands, and put us through mock battles to ensure we will not panic at the furious noise, the stink of blood. And they feed us drinks of fermented grass seed, a powerful potion that drives sanity from the mind, replacing it with a mist of blood . . .

"And then comes the battle.

"It can be magnificent, Longtusk! We charge into the

ranks of the enemy, all but invulnerable to their arrows and axes, and scatter their ranks. We stab with our tusks and crush with our feet. If the enemy has never seen mastodonts before they are terrified, awed out of their wits.

"But it never lasts.

"As warriors we are clumsy beasts, Longtusk. The Firehead fighters learn to step aside and assail us from the sides, encircling us and separating us, striking with arrows and spears, slashing our trunks and hamstrings, killing our riders.

"And sometimes—despite the training, despite the intoxicating brews—we recall who we are. Then we panic and retreat, even trampling our own warriors." He closed his small eyes, deep in their pits of wrinkled skin. "I thought I had put it all behind me. Now it is coming again."

When they reached the Firehead settlement, Bedrock's body was immediately claimed by the Shaman, Smokehat, who had it brought into his own hut of bone and turf. The Shaman berated the Firehead hunters who had been with Bedrock when he died, and even Longtusk and the mastodonts.

As for Crocus, she retreated into Bedrock's hut—hers, now—carrying the rhino horn.

As the days wore on, Crocus was forced to receive a string of visitors: older males of the Firehead tribe, there to consult, Thunder told Longtusk, about the meaning of the sudden appearance of these other Fireheads, the Whiteskins, on the steppe. But she did not emerge from her hut, refusing even to see Longtusk.

Longtusk felt bereft. He hadn't realized how much he had come to rely on Crocus's companionship, which seemed to fill a need not satisfied even by the mastodonts.

He threw his great muscles into the work of heavy lifting and hauling, and his companions treated him with a bluff respect. And when he wasn't working he spent much of his time in the Firehead settlement.

It was unusual for Bull mastodonts to be allowed to wander without keepers through the Firehead community, but after his long association with Crocus—during which time not a hair on her head had been harmed—Longtusk seemed to be regarded as a special case.

But he remained the only mammoth in the captive herd, and adults gaped at him or cowered from his immense tusks, and he was constantly followed around by a small herd of goggling Firehead cubs. They collected the hair he shed, and used it to stuff their moccasins and hats and pillows. He learned to endure the perpetual tugs and strokes of the cubs, and he took great care not to step on one of those stick-thin limbs or eggshell skulls.

Work went on for Fireheads and mastodonts: hunting game for food, building and rebuilding the huts, extending and filling the storage pits for meat and hay—for the cycle of the seasons was not slowed even by death, and the inevitable approach of winter was never far from the thoughts of anybody in the community.

He watched them butcher a deer. They took its flesh to eat and its skin to make clothing. They even used the tough skin of its forelegs for boot uppers and mittens. They made tools and weapons from its bones and antlers. They used the deer's fat and marrow for fuel for their lamps, and its blood for glue, and its sinews for bindings, lashings and thread. Gradually the deer was reduced to smaller and smaller pieces, until it was scattered around the settlement.

Longtusk saw a mother use her hair to wipe feces from the backside of a cub.

He saw a male take the lower jawbone of a young deer, from which small sharp teeth protruded like pebbles. He sawed off the teeth at their roots, producing a series of beads almost identical in shape, size and texture, and held together by a strip of dried gum. It was a necklace.

He saw an old male pinch the tiny hearts of captive gulls, seeking to kill them without spoiling their feathers. He skinned the birds, turned the empty skins inside out, and wore the intact skins on his feet—feathers inside—within his boots.

Endless detail, endless strangeness—endless horror.

But the Fireheads went about their tasks without joy or enthusiasm. Even the cubs, when they tried to run and play, were snapped at and cuffed. The settlement had become a bowl of subdued quiet, of slow footsteps.

And Longtusk felt increasingly agitated.

It was natural, he told himself. Bedrock had been the most important of the Fireheads; his death brought finality and change. Who wouldn't be disturbed?

. . . But he couldn't help feeling that his inner turmoil was something beyond that. He was aware that his mood showed in the way he walked, ripped his fodder from the ground, snarled at the Firehead cubs who got in his way or tugged too hard at his belly hairs.

At length, he came to understand what he was going through. He felt oddly ashamed, and he kept it to himself.

Still, Walks With Thunder—as so often—seemed more aware of Longtusk's moods and difficulties than anybody else. And he came to Longtusk, engaging him in a rumbling conversation as they walked, fed, defecated.

". . . It's interesting to see how differently they treat you," Thunder said, as he watched Firehead cubs, wide-eyed, trot after Longtusk. "Differently from us, I mean.

You have to understand that you mammoths were once worshipped as gods by these creatures."

"Worshipped?"

"Remember when we found you at the Dreamer caves, how they threw themselves on the ground? There is little wood here. Trees struggle to grow on land freshly exposed by the ice. And so the Fireheads rely on the mammoths—especially your long-dead ancestors—for bones and skin and fur, material to build their huts and make their clothing and burn on their hearths. Without the resources of the mammoths, it's possible they couldn't survive here at all."

Longtusk reminded Thunder of the Dreamers, who had lived so modestly in their rocky caves.

"Ah, but the Fireheads are not like the Dreamers," said Thunder. "*They* would not be content with eking out unchanging lives like pike basking in a pool. And it is this lack of contentment that drives them on . . . to greatness and to horror alike.

"They've discarded those old beliefs, I think; now, a mammoth is just another animal to them. But still you hairy beasts seem to be admired in a way they have never admired *us*, despite our long association with them. Of course that doesn't stop them from going north and—" He stopped abruptly.

The north: the old mystery, Longtusk thought, a mystery that had eluded him for years, despite his quizzing of Jaw Like Rock and other mastodonts; it was as if they had been instructed—perhaps by Thunder—to tell him nothing.

"Going north for what?" he asked now. "*What* do they seek in the north, Thunder?"

"I shouldn't have spoken . . . What's this?" Suddenly Thunder's trunk reached out to Longtusk's ear.

Longtusk couldn't help but flinch as Thunder's trunk, strong and wiry, probed in his fur until its tip emerged coated in a black, viscous liquid.

"By Kilukpuk's mighty dugs," Thunder said. "I thought I could smell it. The way you've been dribbling urine . . . You're in musth. Musth!"

Musth—a state of agitation associated with stress or rut; musth, in which this foul-smelling liquid would ooze from a mammoth's temporal gland; musth—when a mammoth's body was temporarily not under his full control.

"No wonder you're so agitated. And it's not the first time either, I'll wager."

Longtusk pulled away, trumpeting his irritation. "I'm an adult now, Thunder, a Bull. I don't need—"

"It's one thing to know what musth is and quite another to control it. And you've picked a terrible time to start oozing the black stuff. In a few days you'll play perhaps the most important role of your life."

"What role? I don't understand."

"With Crocus, of course. It will be tiring, difficult, stressful—even frightening. Through it all you must maintain absolute control—for all our sakes. And you decide *now* is the time to go into musth . . . *Oh.* Neck Like Spruce."

Longtusk felt his trunk curl up. "Who?"

"You can't fool me, grazer. That's the name of the pretty little Cow you've been courting, isn't it?"

"Courting? I don't know what you're talking about."

"Perhaps you don't. We don't always understand ourselves very well. It's true, nevertheless—and now this." Thunder rumbled sadly. "Longtusk, I'm just an old fool of a mastodont. I'm not even one of your kind. And I know I've filled your head with far too much advice over the years."

Longtusk was embarrassed. "I appreciate your help. I always have—"

"Never mind that," said Thunder testily. "Just listen to me, one last time. You and I—we look alike, but we're very different. Our kinds were separated, and started to grow apart, more than a thousand Great-Years ago. And that is a long, long time, ten times longer than the ice has been prowling the world."

"Why are you telling me this?"

"While you're in musth—now and in the future—*stay away from Neck Like Spruce*. Otherwise you'll both be hurt, terribly hurt."

"I don't understand, Thunder . . ."

But Thunder would say no more. Rumbling sadly, he walked slowly away, in search of fresh forage.

Soon the settlement, without throwing off its pall of gloom, began to bustle with activity. Longtusk learned that the Fireheads were preparing for their own form of Remembering ceremony for their fallen leader.

Everything was being rebuilt; everything was changing. It was obvious the Remembering of Bedrock would mark a great change in the affairs of the settlement—and therefore, surely, in Longtusk's own life as well, a change whose outcome was impossible to predict.

Every surface, of rock and treated skin, was scraped bare and painted with new, vibrant images. And everywhere the Fireheads made their characteristic mark, the outstretched paw. The artist would lay a bare paw, fingers open, against the rock, then suck paint into the mouth and spray it through a small tube and over the paw to make a silhouette.

The most busy Firehead, at this strange time, was the old male the mastodonts called Flamefingers. He was the manufacturer of the finest tools and ornaments of bone, ivory and stone. Flamefingers was fat and comfortable. The skills of his nimble paws had won him a long and comfortable life, insulated from the dangers of the hunt or the hard graft of the storage pits.

Flamefingers had an apprentice. This wretched male cub had to bring his master food and drink, cloths for the old Firehead to blow his cavernous nose, and even hollowed-out bison skulls, pots for the great artisan to urinate in without having to take the trouble to stand up.

Longtusk watched in fascination as the young apprentice wrestled to turn an ancient mammoth tusk—an immense spiral twice his height—into ivory strips and pieces, useful for the artisan to work.

At the tusk's narrow, sharp end, he simply chopped off pieces with a stone axe. Where the tusk was too wide for that, he chiseled a deep groove all around the tusk until only a fine neck remained, and then split it with a sharp hammer blow.

To obtain long, thin strips of ivory the apprentice had to cut channels in the tusk and then prize out the strips with chisels. Often the strips would splinter and break—an outcome which invariably won the apprentice abuse and mild beatings from his impatient master.

But the apprentice could even bend ivory, making bracelets small enough to fit around the slim wrists of Fireheads. First he soaked a section of the tusk in a pit of foul-smelling urine. Then he wrapped the softened tusk in a fresh animal skin, soaked with water, and placed it in the hot ashes of a hearth. The skin charred and fell away in flakes. But the ivory—on extraction from the hearth with tongs made of giant deer antlers—was flexible enough to bend into loops tied off with thongs.

Flamefingers, meanwhile, made a bewildering variety of artifacts from the ivory pieces.

He made tools, whittling suitable sections into chisels, spatulas, knives, daggers and small spears. He engraved the handles of these devices with crosshatched cuts to ensure a firm grip when the tools were held in the paw, and returned the tools to the apprentice for arduous polishing with strips of leather.

But Flamefingers also made many artifacts with no obvious purpose save decoration: for example thin disks, cross-sections from the fatter end of the tusks, with elaborate carvings, pierced through the center to take a rope of sinew or skin.

But the most remarkable artifacts of all were the figurines, of Fireheads and animals.

Flamefingers started with a raw, crudely broken lump of ivory that had been soaked for days. But despite this softening the ivory was difficult to work—easy to engrave along the grain, but not across it—and the artisan patiently scraped away at the surface with stone chisels, removing finer and finer flakes.

And, slowly, like the sun emerging from a cloud, a form emerged from the raw tusk, small and compact, coated in hairs that were elaborately etched into the grain.

Longtusk could only watch, bewildered. The artisan seemed able to see the object within the tusk before he had made it—as if the figure had always been there, embedded in this chunk of ancient ivory, needing only the artisan's careful fingers to release it.

The artisan held up the finished piece on his paw, blew away dust and spat on it, polishing it against his clothing.

Then he looked up at Longtusk standing over him,

with the usual gaggle of Firehead cubs clutching his belly hairs.

Flamefingers smiled. He held up the figure so Longtusk could see it.

Longtusk, drawn by curiosity, reached out with the pink tip of his trunk and explored the carving. Flamefingers watched him, blue eyes gleaming, fascinated by the reaction of the woolly mammoth to the toy.

It was a mammoth, exquisitely carved.

But, though it was delicate and fine, there was a faint, lingering smell of the long-dead mammoth who had owned this tusk, overlaid by the sharp stink of the spit and sweat of Firehead.

Longtusk, intrigued but subtly repelled, rumbled softly and stepped away.

On the day of Bedrock's Remembering, Crocus at last emerged from her hut. Her bare skin was pale from her lengthy confinement. But her golden hair blazed in the light of the low sun.

All the Fireheads—even the Shaman—bowed before her. She turned and surveyed them coldly.

Today the Fireheads would do more than Remember Bedrock. Today, Longtusk had learned, the Fireheads would accept their new leader: this slim young female, Crocus, the only cub of Bedrock, and now the Matriarch of the Fireheads.

Crocus stepped forward to Longtusk. She walked confidently, as a new Matriarch should. But Longtusk could see how fragile she was from the tenseness of her lips, the softness of her eyes.

"*Baitho,*" she said softly.

Obediently he dipped his head and lowered his trunk to the ground. She climbed on his back with practiced ease. He straightened up, feeling invigorated by her gentle presence at his neck once more.

He raised his trunk and trumpeted; the noise echoed from the silent steppe.

He turned and, with as much grandeur as he could muster, he began to walk toward the grave. The Fireheads and mastodonts formed up into a loose procession behind him.

And now, at a gesture from the Shaman, the music began.

They had flutes made of bird bones, hollowed out and pierced. They had bull-roarers, ovals of carved ivory which they spun around their heads on long ropes. They had instruments made of mammoth bones: drums of skulls and shoulder blades to strike and scrape, jawbones which rattled loudly, ribs which emitted a range of notes when struck with a length of femur. And they sang, raising their small mouths and ululating like wolves.

In all this noise, Longtusk and his passenger were an island of silence, towering over the rest. Her fingers twined tightly in his fur, as they had when she was a small and nervous cub just learning to ride him, and he knew that this day was extraordinarily difficult for her.

The grave was on the outskirts of the settlement, a simple straight-sided pit dug into the ground by Walks With Thunder.

Crocus slid to the ground and stood at the lip of the grave, paws folded. Longtusk stood silently beside her, the wind whipping the hair on his back.

The body of Bedrock already lay at the bottom of the pit, a small and fragile bundle wrapped in rhino hide. Bedrock's artifacts were set out around him: spears and knives and chisels and boomerangs, the tools of a homebuilder and hunter, many of them made of mammoth ivory. And mammoth vertebrae and foot bones had been set out in a circle around him, as if protecting him.

But now the Shaman was here in his ridiculous smoking hat, his skin painted with gaudy designs. He leapt into the pit and began to caper and shout. He had rattles of bone and wood that he shook over Bedrock's inert form, and he scattered flower petals and sprinkled water, raising his face and howling like a hyena.

As Crocus watched this performance she started to tremble—not from distress, Longtusk realized, but from anger. It was a rage that matched Longtusk's own musth-fueled turmoil.

At last, it seemed, she could stand it no more. She tugged Longtusk's trunk. "*A dhur,*" she said. Pick up that thing.

Longtusk snorted in acquiescence. He knelt down, reached into the pit with his trunk, and plucked the Shaman out of the grave, burning hat and all. He set the Firehead down unharmed by the side of the pit.

Smokehat was furious. He capered and jabbered, slapping with his small paws at Longtusk's trunk.

Crocus stepped forward, eyes alight, and she screamed at the Shaman.

His defiance seemed to melt before her anger, and he withdrew, eyes glittering.

There was silence now. Crocus stepped up to the grave once more. She sat down, legs dangling over the edge of the pit.

Longtusk reached down to help her. But she pushed his trunk away; this was, it seemed, something she must do herself.

She scrambled to the pit floor. She brushed away the dirt and petals that the Shaman had scattered over her father.

She dug an object out of her clothing and laid it on top of the body. It was the rhino horn, the trophy of the last hunt—still stained with the creature's blood, as raw and unworked as when it had been smashed from the rhino's skull. Then she stroked the hide covering her father, and she picked up earth and sprinkled it over the body.

She was Remembering him, Longtusk realized. Her simple, tender actions, unrehearsed and personal, were—compared to the foolish ritualistic capering of the Shaman—unbearably moving.

Bedrock had been leader of the Fireheads from the moment Longtusk had first encountered these strange, complex, bewildering creatures. But here he lay, slain and silent, destroyed by a single arrow fired by a white-painted Firehead who had never known Bedrock's name, had known nothing of the complex web of power and relationships which had tangled up his life. As he gazed on the limp, passive form in the pit, Longtusk was struck by the awful simplicity of death, the conclusion to every story.

At last Crocus stood up. The Fireheads reached into the pit and lowered down bones. They were mammoth shoulder blades and pelvises. Crocus used the huge flat sheets of bone to cover the body of Bedrock. Even in death he would be protected by the strength of the mammoths, which, through their own deaths, had sustained his kind in this hostile land.

Crocus reached up to Longtusk. This time she accepted his help, and he lifted her out of the grave and set her neatly on his back. Then he began to kick at the low piles of earth which had been scooped out of the ground.

When it was done, Longtusk made his way back to the hut Crocus had shared with her father, but now inhabited alone. She slid to the ground, ruffled the fur on his trunk with absent affection, and entered her hut, tying the skin flaps closed behind her.

When she was gone, Longtusk felt a great relief, for he thought this longest and most painful of days was at last done.

But he was wrong.

The Fireheads, having completed their mourning of their lost leader, began to celebrate the ascension of their new Matriarch. And it was soon obvious that the celebrations were to be loud and long.

As the sun dipped toward the horizon the Fireheads opened up a pit in the ground. Here, the butchered remains of several giant deer had been smoking since the previous day. They gathered around and ripped away pieces of the meat with their bare paws, and chewed on it until their bellies were distended and the fat ran down their chins.

Then, as the cubs and females danced and sang, the males produced great pots of foul-smelling liquid, thick and fermented, which they pumped down their throats. Before long many of them were slumping over in sleep, or regurgitating the contents of their stomachs in great noxious floods. But then they would revive to begin ingesting more food and liquid, growing more raucous and uncoordinated as the evening wore on.

The mastodonts watched this, bemused.

At last, under the benevolent guidance of Walks With Thunder, the Cows gathered their calves and quietly made their way to the calm of the stockade, where all but the most trusted of the Bulls were kept.

Longtusk, his emotions still muddled and raging, followed them.

Lemming was here, bringing bales of hay from one of

the storage pits. *"Lay, lay,"* he said. Eat, eat. Longtusk had noticed before that this little fat Firehead seemed happier in the company of the mastodonts than his own kind, and he felt a surge of affection.

All the mastodonts were in the stockade.

. . . All save Jaw Like Rock.

Agitated, disturbed by the throbbing noise and meat smells wafting from the Firehead settlement, Longtusk roamed the stockade. But he couldn't find the great Bull. When he asked after Jaw, he was met with blank stares.

Then—as the night approached its darkest hour, and the drumming and shouting of the Fireheads reached a climax—he heard a single, agonized trumpeting from the depths of the settlement.

It was Jaw Like Rock.

Longtusk bellowed out a contact rumble, but there was no reply.

He sought out Walks With Thunder.

"Didn't you hear that? Jaw Like Rock called out."

"No," said Thunder bleakly. "You're mistaken."

"But I heard him—"

Thunder wrapped his trunk around Longtusk's. "Jaw is dead. Accept it. It is the way."

Again that trumpeting came, thin and clear and full of pain.

Longtusk, confused, distressed, blundered away from the stockade and headed into the Firehead settlement.

Tonight it had become a place of bewildering noise and stink and confusion. The Fireheads ran back and forth, full of fermented liquid and rich food—or they slept where they had fallen, curled up by the hearths in the open air. He saw one male and female coupling, energetically but clumsily, in the half-shadow of a hut wall.

Few Fireheads even seemed aware of Longtusk; he had to be careful, in fact, not to step on sleeping faces.

He persisted, pushing through the noise and mess and confusion, until he found Jaw Like Rock.

They had put him in a shallow pit, scraped roughly out of the ground and surrounded by stakes and ropes. Fire burned brightly in lamps all around the pit, making the scene as bright as day, but filling the air with stinking, greasy smoke.

It was a feeble confinement from which a great tusker like Jaw Like Rock could have escaped immediately.

But Jaw was no longer in full health.

Jaw was dragging both his hind legs. It seemed his hamstrings or tendons had been cut, so he could no longer bolt or charge. And there were darts sticking out of his flesh, over his belly and behind his ears. His skin was discolored around the punctures, as if the darts had delivered a poison. He was wheezing, and great loops of spittle hung from his dangling tongue.

There were Fireheads all around the pit, all male, and they were stamping, clapping and hammering their drums of bone and skin. One of them was creeping into Jaw's pit, carrying a long spear. It was Bareface, Longtusk saw, the young hunter who had distinguished himself on the fatal rhino hunt. He was naked, coated in red and yellow paint.

Longtusk trumpeted. "Jaw! Jaw Like Rock!'

Jaw's answering rumble was faint, and punctuated by gasps for breath. "Is that you, grass chewer? Come to see the dead Bull?"

"Get out of there!"

". . . No. It's over for me. It was over the moment I tusked that spawn of Aglu. I planned it, after all, waited for my moment . . . But it was worth it. At least Spindle will torture no more mastodonts. Or mammoths."

"You aren't dead! You breathe, you hurt—"

"I'm dead as poor Bedrock in his hole in the ground. Don't you see? *We belong to the Fireheads*. They tend our wounds, and order our lives, and feed us. But we live and die by their whim. It is—a contract. And here, at the climax of this night of celebration, this one who creeps toward me on his belly, Bareface, will prove his courage by dispatching me to the aurora."

"But they've already crippled you! Where is the courage in that?"

"The ways of the Fireheads are impossible to understand . . . But, yes, you're right, Longtusk. We must see some courage tonight." Jaw raised himself on his crippled legs and trumpeted his defiance. "Remember me, calf of Primus! Remember!"

And with a roar that shook the ground, he hurled himself forward toward Bareface.

The hunter, with lightning-fast reflexes, jammed the shaft of his spear into the ground.

Jaw's great body impaled itself. Longtusk heard flesh rip, and smelled the sour stink of Jaw's guts as they spilled, dark and steaming, to the ground.

The Fireheads roared their triumph. Longtusk trumpeted and fled.

He was in a stand of young trees in the new, growing forest that bordered the Firehead settlement. It was still deep night, dark and cloudy.

He couldn't recall where he had run, how he had got here.

But *she* was here—he could sense it through his rage, his grief and confusion, the musth that burned through his body—*she*, Neck Like Spruce, no calf now but a warm and musty presence, solid and massive as the

Earth itself, here in the dark, as if she had been waiting for him.

He searched out, sensing and hearing her, and found her. Her secretions were damp on the tip of his trunk. Tasting them, he knew that she, too, was ready: in oestrus, bearing the egg that might grow into their calf.

He heard her urinate, a warm dark stream, and then she turned to face him. He found her trunk, and intertwined it with his, tugging gently, seeking its tip; the soft fingers of her trunk, so unlike his own, explored the long hairs that dangled from his belly.

For a last instant he recalled the warnings of Walks With Thunder: *stay away from Neck Like Spruce. Stay away . . .*

Then his mouth found hers, warm tongues flickering, and the time for thinking was over.

6

The Cleansing

Winter and summer, winter and summer . . .

As she approached the second anniversary of her father's death and her own accession to power, Crocus assembled a great war party of mastodonts and Firehead hunters. It was a time of preparation, and gathering determination—and dread.

The artisans had worked all winter, manufacturing, repairing and sharpening knives and spear points and atlatls. And every time the weather cleared sufficiently the hunters had gone out to hurl spears and boomerangs at rocks and painted animal figures—and, when they spotted them, live targets, the animals of the winter like the Arctic foxes. There were days when the settlement seemed to bristle with the Fireheads and their weapons, spears, darts and knives as dense as the spiky fur of a mastodont. But all the weapons were small and light—not designed for big game, like the giant deer or the rhino, but to pierce the flimsy hides of other Fireheads: weapons of war, not hunting.

When the preparations were complete, Crocus called for a final feast.

The Firehead hunters gorged themselves on food and

drink. Longtusk watched cubs crack open big animal bones to suck out the thick marrow within, the bones returned by hunting parties that roamed north. Not for the first time Longtusk wondered what animal provided those giant snacks.

Longtusk spent his time with Neck Like Spruce, who was now heavy with calf—*his* calf.

It was unusual for a Bull, mammoth or mastodont, to remain close to his mate so long after the mating; usually a Bull would stay around just long enough to ensure conception by his seed had taken place. But Neck Like Spruce's case was different.

The calf was already overdue. Like mammoths, the oestrus cycle of these mastodonts was timed so that the calves would be born in early spring, maximizing the time available for them to feed and grow strong before the calves faced the rigors of their first winter.

And throughout it had been a difficult pregnancy, despite the best attention of Lemming, the keeper, and his array of incomprehensible medicines: salves of water and hot butter for wounds, blood-red deer meat to treat inflammations, drops of milk for sore eyes . . . Spruce had become a gaunt, bony shadow, and her hair had fallen out in clumps.

It disturbed Longtusk that there was absolutely nothing he could do—and it disturbed him even more that Lemming, the undisputed Firehead expert on mastodonts and their illnesses, was at this crucial time preparing to leave, accompanying the Bulls on their northern march.

Through that last night, Longtusk stayed with Neck Like Spruce. She slept briefly. He could see the calf in her belly struggle fitfully, pushing at the skin that contained it.

*   *   *

The next morning, the Fireheads nursing sore heads and crammed bellies, the party assembled in a great column and began its sweep to the north. With Crocus on his back, Longtusk led the slow advance.

Since that first encounter with the Whiteskins two years before there had been several skirmishes with other bands of Fireheads. Crocus's tribe, settled for several years in their township of mammoth-bone huts, were well-fed, healthy and strong, and were able to fend off the attacks—mounted mostly by bands of desperate refugees, forced north from the overcrowded southern lands.

But this wouldn't last forever, predicted Walks With Thunder.

"There is no limit to the number of Fireheads who might take it into their heads to come bubbling up from the south. We can defend ourselves and this settlement as long as the numbers are right. But eventually they will overrun us."

"And then?" said Longtusk.

"And then we will have to flee—go north once again, as we have done before, and find a new and empty land. And this is what Crocus, in her wisdom, knows she must plan for; it is surely going to come in her time as Matriarch."

So it was that Crocus was remaking herself. Still young, already skilled in hunting techniques, she had learned to use the tribe's weapons with as much skill and daring as any of the buck male warriors. And she had learned to command, to force her tribe to accept the harshest of realities.

But Longtusk thought he detected a growing hardness in her—a hardness that, when he thought of the affectionate cub who had befriended him, saddened him.

As for himself, Longtusk was now bigger and stronger than any of the mastodonts. He was no longer the butt of jokes and taunts in the stockade; no longer did the mastodonts call constant attention to his differences, his dense brown hair and strange grinding teeth. Now he was Longtusk, warrior Bull, and his immense tusks, scarred by use, were the envy of the herd.

Only Walks With Thunder still called him "little grazer"—but Longtusk didn't mind that.

And, such was Crocus's skill in riding Longtusk—and so potent was the mammoth's own intelligence and courage—that the stunning, unexpected combination of warrior-queen and woolly mammoth leading the column could, said Walks With Thunder, prove to be the Fireheads' most important weapon of all.

During the long march, Longtusk's days were arduous. He was the first to break the new ground, and he had to be constantly on the alert for danger—not just from potential foes, but also the natural traps of the changing landscape. He paid careful attention to the deep wash of sound which echoed through the Earth in response to the mastodonts' heavy footsteps, and avoided the worst of the difficulties.

And, of course, he had to seek out food as he traveled. Firehead Matriarch on his back or not, he still needed to cram the steppe grasses and herbs into his mouth for most of every day. But the mastodonts preferred trees and shrubs, and if he found a particularly fine stand of trees he would trumpet to alert the others.

A few days out of the settlement a great storm swept down on them. The wind swirled and gusted, carrying sand from the frozen deserts at the fringe of the icecap, hundreds of days' walk away, to lash at the mastodonts' eyes and mouths, as if mocking their puny progress. Crocus walked beside Longtusk, blinded and buffeted, clinging to his long belly hairs.

At last the storm blew itself out, and they emerged into calmness under an eerie blue sky.

They found a stand of young trees that had been utterly demolished by the winds' ferocity. The mastodonts browsed the fallen branches and tumbled trunks, welcoming this unexpected bounty.

Walks With Thunder, his mouth crammed with green leaves, came to Longtusk. "Look over there. To the east."

Longtusk turned and squinted. It was unusual for a mastodont to tell another to "look," so poor was their eyesight compared to other senses.

The sun, low in the south, cast long shadows across the empty land. At length Longtusk made out something: a blur of motion, white on blue, against the huge sky.

"Birds?"

"Yes. Geese, judging from their honking. But the important thing is where they come from."

"The northeast," Longtusk said. "But that's impossible. There is only ice there, and nothing lives."

"Not quite." Walks With Thunder absently tucked leaves deeper into his mouth. "This is a neck of land, lying between great continents to west and east. In the eastern lands, it is said, the ice has pushed much farther south than in the west. But there are legends of places, called *nunataks*—refuges—islands in the ice, where living things can survive."

"The ice would cover them over. Everything would freeze and die."

"Possibly," said Thunder placidly. "But in that case, how do you explain those geese?"

"It is just a legend," Longtusk protested.

Thunder curled his trunk over Longtusk's scalp affectionately. "The world is a big place, and it contains many mysteries. Who knows what fragment of rumor will save our lives in the future?" He saw Crocus approaching. "And the biggest mystery of all," he grumbled wearily, "is how I can persuade these old bones to plod on for another day. Lead on, Longtusk; lead on . . ."

The geese flew overhead, squawking. They were molting, and when they had passed, white fathers fell from the sky all around Longtusk, like snowflakes.

As the days wore on they traveled farther and farther from the settlement.

Longtusk hadn't been this far north since he had first been captured by the Fireheads. That had been many years ago, and back then he had been little more than a confused calf.

But he was sure that the land had changed.

There were many more stands of trees than he recalled: spruce and pine and fir, growing taller than any of the dwarf willows and birches that had once inhabited this windswept plain. And the steppe's complex mosaic of vegetation had been replaced by longer grass—great dull swathes of it that rippled in the wind, grass that had crowded out many of the herbs and low trees and flowers which had once illuminated the landscape. It was grass that the mastodonts consumed with relish. But for Longtusk the grass was thin, greasy stuff that clogged his bowels and made his dung slippery and smelly.

And it was warmer—much warmer. It seemed he couldn't shed his winter coat quickly enough, and Crocus grumbled at the hair which flew into her face. But she did not complain when he sought out the snow that still lingered in shaded hollows and scooped it into his mouth to cool himself.

The world seemed a huge place, massive, imperturbable; it was hard to believe that—just as the Matriarchs had foreseen, at his Clan's Gathering so long ago—such dramatic changes could happen so quickly. And yet it must be true, for even he, young as he was, recalled a time when the land had been different.

It was an uneasy thought.

He had been separated from his Family before they had a chance to teach him about the landscape—where to find water in the winter, how to dig out the best salt licks. He had had to rely on the mastodonts for such instruction.

But such wisdom, passed from generation to generation, was acquired by long experience. And if the land was changing so quickly—so dramatically within the lifetime of a mammoth—what use was the wisdom of the years?

And in that case, what might have become of his Family?

He shuddered and rumbled, and he felt Crocus pat him, aware of his unease.

After several more days Crocus guided Longtusk down a sharp incline toward lower ground. He found himself in a valley through which a fat, strong glacial river gushed, its waters curdled white with rock flour. The column of mastodonts crept cautiously after him, avoiding the sharp gravel patches and slippery mud slopes he pointed out.

After a time the valley opened, and the river decanted into a lake, gray and glimmering.

The place seemed familiar.

Had he been here before, as a lost calf? But so much had changed! The lake water was surely much higher than it had once been, and the long grass and even the trees grew so thickly now, even down to the water's edge, that every smell and taste and sound was different.

. . . Yet there was much that nagged at his memory: the shape of a hillside here, a rock abutment there.

When he saw a row of cave mouths, black holes eroded into soft exposed rock, he knew that he had not been mistaken.

Crocus called a halt.

She and her warriors dismounted, and on all fours they crept through the thickening vegetation closer to the caves. They inspected footprints in the dirt—they were wide and splayed, Longtusk saw, more like a huge bird's than a Firehead's narrow tracks—and they rummaged through dirt and rubble.

At last, with a hiss of triumph, the hunter called Bareface picked up a shaped rock. It was obviously an axe, made and wielded by clever fingers—and it was stained with fresh blood.

And now there was a cry: a voice not quite like a Firehead's, more guttural, cruder. The mastodonts raised their trunks and sniffed the air.

A figure had come out of the nearest cave: walking upright, but limping heavily. He stood glaring in the direction of the intruders, who still cowered in the vegetation. He was short and stocky, with wide shoulders and a deep barrel chest. His clothing was heavy and coarse. His forehead sloped backward, and an enormous bony ridge dominated his brow. His legs were short and bowed, and his feet were flat and very wide, with short stubby toes, so that he left those broad splayed footprints.

He was obviously old, his back bent, his small face a mask of wrinkles that seemed to lap around cavernous nostrils like waves around rocks. And his head was shaven bare of hair, with a broad red stripe painted down its crown.

Not a Firehead, not quite. This was the Fireheads' close cousin: a Dreamer. And Longtusk recognized him.

"He is called Stripeskull," Longtusk rumbled to Thunder. "I have been here before."

"As have I. This is where we found you."

Walks With Thunder described how, when the Fireheads had first moved north, they had sent scouting parties ahead, seeking opportunities and threats. Bedrock himself had led an expedition to this umpromising place—and Crocus had been, briefly, lost.

"The Dreamers saved her from the cold," said Longtusk.

Thunder grunted. "That's as maybe. We drove the Dreamers from their caves. But the land was too harsh, and we abandoned it and retreated farther south."

"And the Dreamers returned to their caves?"

"They are creatures of habit. And, back then, the Fireheads did not covet their land."

"But now?"

"See for yourself. The land has changed. Now the Fireheads want this place . . ."

Longtusk said, "It was so long ago."

"For you, perhaps," Thunder said dryly. "For me, it seems like yesterday."

"How did Stripeskull get so *old*?"

"Dreamers don't live long," growled Thunder. "And I fear this one will not grow much older."

"What do you mean?"

But now Stripeskull seemed to have spotted the intruders. He was shouting and gesturing. He had a short burned-wood spear at his side, and he tried to heft it, but his foreleg would not rise above the shoulder.

A spear flew at him. It neatly pierced Stripeskull's heart.

Longtusk, shocked, trumpeted and blundered forward.

Stripeskull was on the ground, and blood seeped red-black around him, viscous and slow as musth. His great head rocked forward, and ruddy spittle looped his mouth. He looked up and saw the mammoth, and his eyes widened with wonder and recognition. Then he fell back, his strength gone.

Longtusk rumbled mournfully, and touched the body with the sole of his foot. He was gone, as quickly destroyed as a pine needle on a burning tree. How could a life be destroyed so suddenly, so arbitrarily? This was Stripeskull, who had grudgingly spared his own Family's resources to save Longtusk's life; Stripeskull, with long memories of his own stretching back beyond his Family to a remote, frosty childhood—Stripeskull, gone in an instant and never to return, no matter how long the world turned.

But even while Stripeskull's body continued to spill its blood on the trampled dust, the Fireheads were moving onward, driven, busy, eager to progress.

Crocus beckoned to Longtusk. She led him to the dark mouth of the cave. *"Bowl, bowl!"* Speak . . .

With a growing feeling of unease, he raised his trunk and trumpeted. The noise echoed within the cramped rock walls of the cave, where it must have been terrifying.

A Dreamer came running out—a female, Longtusk saw, young, comparatively slim, long brown hair flying after her. She saw the mammoth, skidded to a halt and screamed.

She did not know him. The Dreamers grew quickly, as Thunder had said; perhaps this one had been an infant, or not even born, during his time here.

She tried to retreat—but the Shaman, grinning, had

moved behind her, blocking her from the cave. Her eyes widened, and for a brief moment Longtusk saw the Shaman through her eyes: ridiculously tall, with a forehead that bulged to smoothness, willow-thin legs, a nose as small and thin as a spring icicle . . .

Firehead warriors threw a net of hide rope over the female, as if she was a baby rhino, and they wrestled her to the ground. But she was strong, and was soon ripping her way through the net. So they tied more rope around her, leaving her squirming in the dirt.

The hunters fell back, panting hard; one of them was missing a chunk of his ear, bitten off by the Dreamer female. They seemed to be studying her body as she writhed and struggled.

"Perhaps they will mate with her," Longtusk said.

"If they do it will be for pleasure only," said Walks With Thunder. "*Their* pleasure, not hers. Something else you need to know, Longtusk. Firehead cannot seed Dreamer with cub. They are alike, you see, cousins."

"Like mastodonts and mammoths."

Thunder growled, oddly. "But their blood does not mix. And so they compete, like—like two different species of gulls, seeking to nest on the same cliff face. To the Fireheads, the Dreamers are just an obstacle, something to be cleared out of the way."

"Then what will become of the Dreamers?"

"Though they are strong, they are no match for the cunning Fireheads. If they are lucky, the other Dreamers will have seen what happened here, and scattered."

"And if not?"

Thunder snorted. "The Fireheads are not noted for their mercy to their kin. The Dreamers will be butchered, the survivors enslaved and taken to the settlement where they will work until they die."

Now there was a howl from the cave.

Another Dreamer emerged—this time a male. He was young and strong, and he had a stone knife in his free paw—crude, but sharp and potent. And he had taken a captive. It was Lemming, the mastodont keeper. The Dreamer's foreleg was tight around Lemming's neck. Lemming was whimpering, and blood dripped from a wound in his upper foreleg.

The Dreamer's small eyes, glinting in their caves of bone, swiveled this way and that. He seemed to be trying to get to the female on the ground. Perhaps that was his sister, even his mate.

Crocus stepped forward. She was obviously concerned for Lemming. She held out her paws and said something in her high, liquid tongue.

The Dreamer, not understanding, jabbered back and slashed with his knife.

Longtusk acted without thinking. He slid his trunk around the Dreamer's neck and yanked so hard the Dreamer lost his grip on Lemming, and he fell back into the dirt at Longtusk's feet. The mammoth pinned him there with a tusk at the throat.

Lemming fell to the ground, limp. Crocus ran to him and called the others for help.

The Shaman stalked toward the fallen Dreamer. *"Maar thode,"* he snapped at Longtusk. *"Maar thode!"*

Break. Kill.

Longtusk leaned forward, increasing the pressure on the Dreamer's throat.

But the Dreamer was saying something too, calling in a language that was guttural and harsh, yet seemed strangely familiar.

On the Dreamer's face, under a crudely shaved veneer of stubble, there was a mark, bright red, jagged like a lightning bolt. It had faded since this Dreamer was a cub, but it was still there.

Willow, thought Longtusk. The first Dreamer I found, grown from a cub to an adult buck.

And he recognizes me.

Crocus was close by.

Once again the three of us are united, Longtusk thought, and he felt a deep apprehension, as if the world itself was shaking beneath him. He had long forgotten the raving of the strange old Dreamer female when he had first brought Crocus here, her terror at the sight of the three of them together . . . Now that terror returned to him, a chill memory.

The Shaman hammered Longtusk's scalp with his goad, cutting into his skin. *"Maar thode!"*

Longtusk stepped back, lifting his tusk from the Dreamer's throat. Willow lay at his feet, as if stunned.

With a hasty gesture, Crocus ordered other hunters forward. They quickly bound Willow with strips of hide rope. He did not resist, though his massive muscles bulged.

The Shaman glared at Longtusk with impotent fury.

Now Crocus, accompanied by more hunters, made her way into the cave. There seemed to be no more Dreamers present, and with impunity the hunters kicked apart the crude central hearth. Under Crocus's orders, two of the hunters began to dig a pit in the ground.

"It seems we will stay here tonight," Walks With Thunder growled. "The cave will provide shelter. And see how the hunters are making a better hearth, one which will allow the air to blow beneath and—"

"The Dreamers have lived here for generations," Longtusk said sharply. "I saw it, the layers of tools and bones in the ground. Even the hearth may have been a Great-

Year old. Think of that! And now, in an instant, it is gone, vanished like a snowflake on the tongue, demolished by the Fireheads."

"Demolished and remade," growled Thunder. "But that is their genius. These Dreamers lived here, as you say, for generation on generation, and it never occurred to a single one of them that there might be a different way to build a hearth."

"But the Dreamers didn't *need* a different hearth. The one they had was sufficient."

"But that doesn't matter, little grazer," Thunder said. "You and I must take the world as it is. *They* imagine how it might be different. Whether it's *better* is beside the point; to the Fireheads, change is all that matters . . ."

The two Dreamer captives, Willow and the female, huddled together on the ground, bound so tightly they couldn't even embrace. They seemed to be crying.

If Crocus recalled how the Dreamers had saved her life, Longtusk thought, she had driven it from her mind, now and forever.

That night, when Crocus came to feed him, as she had since she was a cub, Longtusk turned away. He was distressed, angered, wanting only to be with his mate and calf in the calm of the steppe.

Crocus left him, baffled and upset.

That night—at the Shaman's insistence, because of his defiance over Willow—Longtusk was hobbled, for the first time in years.

The Fireheads stayed close to the caves for several days. Crocus sent patrols to the north, east and west, seeking Dreamers. They wished to be sure this land they coveted was cleansed of their ancient cousins before they brought any more of their own kind north.

Lemming became very ill. His wound turned swollen and shiny. The Shaman, who administered medicine to the Fireheads, applied hot cloths in an effort to draw out the poison. But the wound festered badly.

At last the bulk of the column formed up for the long journey back to the settlement. They left behind three hunters and one of the mastodonts. The captive Dreamers had to walk behind the mastodonts, their paws bound and tied to a mastodont's tail.

The hunters were heavily armed, but there had been no sign of more Dreamers since that first encounter. Perhaps, like the mammoths, the Dreamers had learned that the Fireheads could not be fought: the only recourse was flight, leaving them to take whatever they wanted.

"Since you refused to kill the Dreamer buck," growled Thunder as they walked, "the Shaman has declared you untrustworthy."

"He has always hated me," said Longtusk indifferently.

"Yes," said Thunder. "He is jealous of your closeness to Crocus. And that jealousy may yet cause you great harm, Longtusk. I think you will have to prove your loyalty and trustworthiness. The Shaman is demonstrating, even now, what he does to his enemies."

"What do you mean?"

"Lemming. The Shaman is letting him rot. His wound has festered and turned green, like the rest of his foreleg and shoulder. That is his way. The Shaman does not kill; he lets his enemies destroy themselves. Still, they die."

"But why?"

Thunder snorted. "Because Lemming is a favorite of Crocus's—and so he is an obstacle to the Shaman. And any such obstacle is, simply, to be removed, as the Fireheads remove the Dreamers from the land they covet.

The Fireheads are vicious, calculating predators," the old mastodont said. "Never forget that. *The wolf's first bite is his responsibility. His second is yours* . . . Quiet."

All the mastodonts stopped dead and fell silent. The Fireheads stared at them, puzzled.

"A contact rumble," Walks With Thunder said at last. "From the settlement."

Longtusk strained to hear the fat, heavy sound waves pulsing through the very rocks of the Earth, a chthonic sound that resonated in his chest and the spaces in his skull.

"The calf," Thunder said. "The Cows have sung the birth chorus. Longtusk—Neck Like Spruce has dropped her calf."

Longtusk felt his heart hammer. "And? Is it healthy?"

". . . I don't think so. And Spruce—"

Longtusk, distressed, trumpeted his terror. "I'm so far away! So far!"

Thunder tried to comfort him. "If you were there, what could you do? This is a time for the Cows, Longtusk. Neck Like Spruce has her sisters and mother. And the keepers know what to do."

"The best keeper is Lemming, and he is here, with us, bleeding in the dirt! Oh, Thunder, you were right. A mammoth should not mate a mastodont. We are too different—the mixed blood—like Fireheads and Dreamers."

"Any calf of yours will be strong, Longtusk. A fighter. And Neck Like Spruce is a tough nut herself. They'll come through. You'll see."

But Longtusk refused to be comforted.

Lemming was dead before they reached the settlement. His body, stinking with corruption, was buried under a heap of stones by a river.

And when they arrived at the settlement, Longtusk learned he was alone once more.

Neck Like Spruce had not survived the rigors of her birth. The calf, an impossible, attenuated mix of mammoth and mastodont, had not lasted long without his mother's milk.

The Remembering of mother and calf was a wash of sound and smell and touch, as if the world had dissolved around Longtusk.

When he came out of his grief, though, he felt cleansed.

He had lost a Family before, after all. If it was his destiny to be alone, then so be it. He would be strong and independent, yielding to none.

He allowed Crocus to ride him. But she sensed his change. Her affection for him dried, like a glacial river in winter.

Thus it went for the rest of that summer, and the winter thereafter.

7

The Test

In the spring, seeking to feed the growing population of the settlement, the Fireheads organized a huge hunting drive.

It took some days' preparation.

Trackers spotted a herd of horses on the steppe. Taking pains not to disturb the animals at their placid grazing, they erected drive lines, rows of cairns made of stone and bone fragments. The mastodonts were used to carry the raw materials for these lines, spanning distances it took a day to cross. The cairns were topped by torches of brush soaked in fat.

Then came the drive.

As the horses grazed their way quietly across the steppe, still oblivious of danger, the hunters ran along the drive lines, lighting the torches. The mastodonts waited, in growing anticipation. It fell to Longtusk to keep the others in order as they scented the horses' peculiar, pungent stink, heard the light clopping of their hooves and their high whinnying.

The horses drifted into view.

Like other steppe creatures, the horses were well adapted to the cold. They were short and squat. Their bellies were coated with light hair, while their backs sprouted long, thick fur that they shed in the summer, and the two kinds of hair met in a jagged line along each beast's flank. Long manes draped over their necks and eyes, and their tails dangled to the ground.

The horses could look graceful, Longtusk supposed, and they showed some skill at using their hooves to dig out fodder even from the deepest snow. But they were foolish creatures and would panic quickly, and so were easily hunted en masse.

At last the order came: *"Agit!"*

Longtusk raised his trunk and trumpeted loudly. The mastodonts charged, roaring and trumpeting, with tusks flashing and trunks raised.

The horses—confused, neighing—stampeded away from the awesome sight. But here came Firehead hunters, whirling noise-makers and yelling, running at the horses from either side.

All of this was designed to make the empty-headed horses run the way the hunters wanted them to go.

The horses, panicking, jostling, soon found themselves in a narrowing channel marked out by the cairns of stone. If they tried to break out of the drive lines they were met by noise-makers, spear thrusts or boomerang strikes.

The drive ended at a sharp-walled ridge, hidden from the horses by a crude blind of dry bush. The lead horses crashed through the flimsy blind and tumbled into the rocky defile. They screamed as they fell to earth, their limbs snapped and ribs crushed. Others, following, shied back, whinnying in panic. But the pressure of their fellows, pushing from behind, drove them, too, over the edge.

So, impelled by their own flight, the horses tumbled to

their deaths, the herd dripping into the defile like some overflowing viscous liquid.

When the hunters decided they had culled enough, they ordered the mastodonts back, letting the depleted herd scatter and flee to safety. Then the hunters stalked among their victims, many of them still screaming and struggling to rise, and they speared hearts and slit throats.

Later would come the hard work of butchery, and the mastodonts would be employed to carry meat and hide back to the settlement. It would be hard, dull work, and the stink of the meat was repulsive to the mastodonts' finely tuned senses. But they did it anyhow—as did Longtusk, who always bore more than his share.

After the successful drive, the Fireheads celebrated, and the mastodonts were allowed a few days to rest and recover.

But Longtusk noticed the Shaman, Smokehat, spending much time at the stockade, arguing with the keepers and jabbing his small fingers toward Longtusk.

Walks With Thunder came to him. Thunder walked stiffly now, for arthritis was plaguing his joints.

Longtusk said, "They seem to be planning another hunt."

"No, not a hunt."

"Then what?"

"Something simpler. More brutal . . . Something that will be difficult for you, Longtusk. The keepers are debating whether you should be allowed to lead this expedition. But the Shaman insists you go."

"You still read them well."

"Better than I like. Longtusk, this is it. The test. The trial the Shaman has been concocting for you for a long time—at least since that incident when you spared the life of the Dreamer."

"I do not care for the Shaman, and I do not fear him," said Longtusk coldly.

"Be careful, Longtusk," Thunder quoted the Cycle. *"The art of traveling is to pick the least dangerous path."*

Longtusk growled and turned away. "The Cycle has nothing to teach me. This is my place now. I am a creature of the Fireheads——nothing more. Isn't that what you always counseled me to become?"

Thunder was aghast. "Longtusk, you are part of the Cycle. We all are. Forty million years—"

But Longtusk, the perennial outsider, had spent the long winter since the death of Neck Like Spruce and her calf building his solitary strength. "Not me," he said. "Not any more."

Thunder sniffed the air sadly. "Oh, Longtusk, has your life been so hard that you care nothing for who you are?"

"Hard enough, old friend, that the Shaman with all his machinations can do nothing to hurt me. Not in my heart."

"I hope that's true," said Thunder. "For it is a great test that lies ahead of you, little grazer. A great test indeed . . ."

A few days later the keepers assembled the mastodonts for the expedition. Longtusk accepted pack gear on his back, and took his customary place at the head of the column of mastodonts.

The party left the settlement, heading north. Though Crocus still sometimes participated in the drives and other expeditions, this time she was absent, and the expedition was commanded by the Shaman.

Though they followed a well-marked trail that cut

across the steppe, showing this was a heavily traveled route, Longtusk had never come this way before. He did not yet know the destination or purpose of the expedition—but, he told himself, he did not need to know. His role was to work, not to understand.

The Dreamer Willow, enslaved by the Fireheads, was compelled to make the journey too. Willow's clothing was dirty and in sore need of repair, and his broad back was bent under an immense load of dried food and weapons for the hunters. The pace was easy, for the mastodonts could not sustain a high speed for long, but even so the Dreamer struggled. It was obvious his stocky frame was not designed for long journeys—unlike the taller, more supple Fireheads, whose whip-thin legs covered the steppe with grace and ease.

Over the year since his capture Willow had grown increasingly wretched. During the winter, the female Dreamer taken with him had died of an illness the Fireheads had been unable, or unwilling, to treat. Willow was not like the Fireheads. He had grown up in a society that had known no significant change for generations, a place where the most important things in all the world were the faces of his Family around him, where strangers and the unknown were mere blurs, at the edge of consciousness. Now, alone, he was immersed in strangeness, in constant change, and he seemed constantly on the edge of bewilderment and terror, utterly unable to comprehend the Firehead world around him.

It was said that no matter how far the Fireheads roamed they had not come across another of his kind. Longtusk supposed that just as the mammoths had been scattered and driven north by the Firehead expansion, so had the Dreamers; perhaps there were few of them left alive, anywhere in the world.

Longtusk could not release Willow from his mobile prison of toil and incomprehension. But he sensed that his own presence, a familiar, massive figure, offered Willow some comfort in his loneliness. And now, out of sight of the keepers, he let Willow rest his pack against his own broad flank and hang onto his belly hairs for support.

As the days wore away, and they drove steadily northward, the nature of the land began to change.

The air became chill, and the winds grew persistent and strong. Sometimes the wind flowed from west to east, and Walks With Thunder told Longtusk that such immense air currents could circle the planet, right around the fringe of the great northern icecaps.

And sometimes the wind came from the north, driving grit and ice into their faces, and that was the most difficult of all, for this was a katabatic wind: air that had lain over the ice, made cold and dry and heavy, so that it spilled like water off the ice and over the lower lands below.

They reached land recently exposed by the retreating ice. The ice had scoured away the softer soil down to bedrock, and it was a place of moraines of sand and gravel, rock smashed to fragments by the great weight of ice that had once lain here. There was little life—a few tussocks of grass, isolated trees, some lichen—struggling to survive in patches of soil, wind-blown from the warmer climes to the south.

The mastodonts became uneasy, for unlike the Fireheads they could hear the sounds of the icepack: the crack of new crevasses, the thin rattle of glacial run-off rivers and streams, the deep grind of the glaciers as they tore slowly through the rock. To the mastodonts, the icepack was an immense chill monster, half alive, spanning the world—and now very close.

Longtusk knew they could not stay long in this blighted land; whatever the Fireheads sought here must be a treasure indeed.

And it was as night began to fall on this wind-blasted, frozen desert that Longtusk came upon the corpse.

At first he could see only a hulked form, motionless, half covered by drifting dirt. Condors wheeled above, black stripes against the silvery twilight.

A hyena was working at the corpse's belly. It snarled at the mastodonts, but fled when a hunter hurled a boomerang.

Walks With Thunder was beside Longtusk. "Be strong, now . . ."

The mastodonts and hunters gathered around the huge, fallen form, awed by this immense slab of death.

It—she—was a female. She had slumped down on her belly, her legs splayed and her trunk curled on the ground before her. She was gaunt, her bones showing through her flesh at pelvis and shoulders, and her hair had come loose in great chunks, exposing dried, wrinkled skin beneath.

It was clear she was not long dead. She might have been sleeping.

But her eye sockets were bloody pits, pecked clean by the birds. Her small ears were mangled stumps. And Longtusk could see the marks of hyena teeth in the soft flesh of her trunk.

"She was pregnant," Walks With Thunder said softly. "See her swollen belly? The calf must have died within her. But she was starving, Longtusk. Her dugs are flaccid and thin. She would have had little milk to give her calf. In the end she simply ran out of strength. They say it is peaceful to go to the aurora that way . . ."

Longtusk stood stock still, stunned. He had seen no woolly mammoth since his separation from his Family—nothing but imperfect Firehead images of himself.

Nothing until *this*.

"We should Remember her," he said thickly.

Thunder rumbled harshly, "I thought you were the one who rejected the Cycle . . . Never mind. Did you know her?"

"She is old and dead. I can't recall, Thunder!"

The Fireheads were closing on the fallen mammoth with their stone axes and knives. Walks With Thunder wrapped his trunk around Longtusk's and pulled him backward.

The Shaman's hard eyes were fixed on Longtusk, calculating, as the Fireheads butchered the mammoth.

First they wrapped ropes around her legs. Then, chanting in unison and with the help of mastodont muscles, they pulled her on her back. Longtusk heard the crackle of breaking bones as her limp mass settled.

With brisk, efficient motions, a hunter slit open her belly, reached into the cavity and hauled out guts—long tangled coils, black and faintly steaming—and dumped them on the ground. There was a stink of blood and spoiled food and rot. But there were no flies, for few insects prospered in this cold desert.

Then the hunters pulled out a flaccid sac that bulged, heavy. It was the calf, Longtusk realized. Mercifully the hunters put that to one side.

The hunters cracked open her rib cage, climbed inside the body, and began to haul out more bloody organs, the heart and liver and kidneys, black lumps marbled with greasy fat.

Eviscerated, the Cow seemed to slump, hollowed.

When she was emptied, the butchers cut great slits in

the Cow's skin and began to drag it off her carcass. Where the tough hide failed to rip away easily, they used knives to cut through connective tissue to separate it from the pink flesh beneath. They chopped the separated skin into manageable slices and piled it roughly.

Then, with their axes, they began to cut away the meat from the mammoth's bones. They started with the hindquarters, making fast and powerful cuts above the knee and up the muscle masses. Then they dug bone hooks into the meat and hauled it away, exposing white, bloody bone. The bone attachments were cut through quickly, and the bones separated.

When one side of the Cow had been stripped, the ropes were attached again and the carcass turned over, to expose the other side.

The butchers were skilled and accurate, rarely cutting into the underlying bone, and the meat fell easily from the bones, leaving little behind. They assembled the meat into one immense pile, and extracted the huge bones for another heap.

When they were done the night was well advanced, and the Cow had been reduced to silhouetted piles of flesh and flensed bones, stinking of blood and decay.

The Fireheads built a fire and threw on some of the meat until the air was full of its stink. With every expression of relish they chewed slices of fat, bloody liver, heart and tongue. Even Willow, sitting alone at the fringe of the fire's circle of light, chewed noisily on the dark meat.

Then the hunters cracked open charred and heated bones and sucked hot, savory marrow from the latticework of hollow bone within.

And at last Longtusk understood.

"I have seen them devour the contents of such bones at the settlement."

"Yes," said Walks With Thunder. *"They were mammoth bones*, Longtusk. Fireheads rarely hunt mammoths. You are a big, dangerous beast, grazer, and the hunters' reward, if their lives are spared, is more meat than they can carry. That's why they prefer the smaller animals for food.

"But they need mammoths. For they need fat."

"The animals they hunt regularly, the deer and the horses, are lean, with blood-red meat. But *you*, little grazer, are replete with fat, which clings to your heart and organs and swims within your bones. The Fireheads must consume it, and they need it besides for their lamps and paints and salves, and—"

"All the years I watched them trek to the north, returning with their cargoes of great bones. All those years, and I never suspected they were mammoth . . . Thunder, *why didn't you tell me?"*

"It was thought best," said Walks With Thunder carefully, "that you should *not* know. I made the decision; blame me. What good would it have done you to have known? But now— "

"But now, the Shaman wants me to see this. He is forcing me to confront the truth."

"This is your test," said Walks With Thunder. "Will you fail, Longtusk?"

Longtusk turned away. "No Firehead will defeat me."

"I hope not," Thunder said softly.

But, as it turned out, the greatest test was yet to come.

The next day the hunters walked to and fro across the frozen desert, studying tracks and traces of dung. At last they seemed to come to a decision.

The Shaman pointed north. The mastodonts were loaded up once more.

"Why?" Longtusk rumbled. "They have their bones and their marrow. What else can they want?"

"*More*," called Thunder grimly. "Fireheads always want more. And they think they know where to find it."

It took another day's traveling.

The hunters grew increasingly excited, pointing out heaps of dry dung, trails that criss-crossed this dry land—and even, in one place, the skeleton of a mammoth, cleansed of its meat by the carrion eaters, its bones scattered over the dust.

. . . And Longtusk heard them, smelled their dung and thin urine, long before he saw them.

He rounded a low, ice-eroded hill. The land here was a muddy flat.

And around this mud seep stood mammoths.

With their high bulging heads, shoulder humps and thick straggling hair, the mammoths looked strange in Longtusk's eyes, accustomed after so long to the sight of short, squat mastodonts; suddenly he felt acutely conscious of his own sloping back and thick hair, his *difference*.

But these mammoths were bedraggled, clearly in distress.

The mammoths gathered closely around holes in the ground. They reached with their trunks deep into the holes and sucked up the muddy, brackish water that oozed there.

They were jostling for the seeping water. But there wasn't enough for everybody.

So the mammoths fought each other, wordlessly, dully, endlessly. The plain was filled with the crack of tusk on tusk, the slap of skull on flank. Calves, thin and bony, clustered around the legs of the adults, but they were pushed away harshly. The infants wailed in protest, too weak to fight for the water they needed.

Longtusk watched all this, trembling, scarcely daring to breathe. The familiarity of them—their hair, their curling tusks—was overwhelming. And yet, what was he? *He* was not some wretched creature grubbing in the dirt for a drop of water. But if not mammoth, what had he become? He felt himself dissolve, leaving only a blackness within.

There were perhaps forty individuals—but this was not a Family or a Clan, for there were Bulls here, closer to the Cows and calves than they would be in normal times. But these were clearly not normal times. One gaunt Cow walked across the muddy flat to a place away from the others. With nervous, hasty scrapes with her feet, she began to dig out a fresh hole. Just behind her, white flensed bones rose out from the muddy ground. She stepped carelessly on a protruding skull, cracking it.

Walks With Thunder grunted softly, "See the bones? Many have perished here already."

Longtusk quoted the Cycle: *"Where water vanishes, sanity soon follows."*

"Yes. But, beyond sanity, there is necessity. In times as harsh as this, mature Bulls survive, for they can travel far in search of water and food. The Cows are encumbered with their calves, perhaps unborn, and cannot flee. *But they are right to push away their calves*—so that those who do get water, those who survive, are those who can have more young in better times. And so the old and the young perish. Necessity . . . We did not come here by accident, Longtusk. The Fireheads knew they would find mammoths in this place of seeping water."

"But the mammoths would not be here in this cold desert," growled Longtusk, "if they had not been pushed so far north by the Fireheads."

Willow, the Dreamer, jumped into an abandoned hole.

He picked up a pawful of mud and began to suck at it, slobbering greedily, smearing his face with the sticky black stuff. Unlike the mastodonts, the wretched Dreamer had no keeper to care for him, and was probably in as bad a condition as these starving mammoths.

Now the wind shifted. As the mastodonts' scent reached him one of the Bull mammoths stirred, raising his muddy trunk to sniff the air. He turned, slowly, and spotted the Fireheads and their mastodonts. He rumbled a warning.

The Bulls scattered, lumbering, trumpeting their alarm. The Cows clustered, drawing their calves in close.

But the Fireheads did not approach or threaten the mammoths. They began to unload the mastodonts and to prepare a hearth.

Gradually, thirst began to overcome the mammoths' caution. The Cows turned their attention back to the seep holes, and quickly made use of the places vacated by the Bulls. After a time, some of the Bulls came back, raising their tusks and braying a thin defiance at the mastodonts.

Longtusk stepped to the edge of an abandoned hole. There was a little seeping water, so thick with clay it was black, but the hole was all but dry.

He was aware that a Bull mammoth was approaching him. He did not turn that way; he held himself still. But he could not ignore the great creature's stink, the weight of his footsteps, his massive, encroaching presence, the deep rumble that came to him through the ground.

". . . You smell of fat."

Longtusk turned.

He faced a Bull: taller, older than Longtusk, but gaunt, almost skeletal. His guard hair dangled, coarse and lifeless. One of his tusks had been broken, perhaps in a fight; it terminated in a crude, dripping stump. The Bull stood listlessly; white mucus dripped from his eyes. He must barely be able to see, Longtusk realized.

Longtusk's heart was suddenly hammering. Once the Bull's accent would have been familiar to him—*for it had been the language of Longtusk's Clan.* Was it possible . . . ?

"I am not fat," said Longtusk. "But you are starving."

The mammoth stepped back, growled and slapped his trunk on the ground. "You are fat and ugly and complacent, and you stink of fire, you and these squat hairless dwarfs. You have forgotten what you are. Haven't you— Longtusk?"

"*. . . Rockheart?*"

"I'm still twice the Bull you are." And Rockheart roared and lunged at Longtusk.

Longtusk ducked aside, and the Bull's tusks flashed uselessly through the air. Rockheart growled, stumbling, the momentum of his lunge catching him off balance. Almost effortlessly Longtusk slid his own tusks around the Bull's, and he twisted Rockheart's head. The huge Bull, roaring, slid sideways to the ground.

Longtusk placed his foot on Rockheart's temple.

He recalled how this Bull had once bested him, humiliating him in front of the bachelor herd. But Longtusk had been a mere calf then, and Rockheart a mature adult Bull. Now it was different: now it was Longtusk who was in his prime, Longtusk who had been trained to keep his courage and to fight—not just other Bulls in half-playful dominance contests, but animals as savage as charging rhinos, even hordes of scheming, clever Fireheads.

"I could crush your skull like a bird's egg," he said softly.

"Then do it," rumbled Rockheart. "Do it, you Firehead monster."

Firehead monster.

Is it true? Is that what I have become?

Longtusk lifted his foot and stepped back.

As Rockheart, gaunt and weak, scrambled to his feet and roared out his impotent rage, Longtusk walked away, saddened and horrified.

The Fireheads lingered close to the seep holes for a night and a day.

Longtusk found it increasingly difficult to bear the noise of this nightmarish place: the clash of tusks, the bleating of calves.

He said to Walks With Thunder, "Why do the Fireheads keep us here? What do they want?"

"You know what they want," Thunder said wearily. "They want hearts and kidneys and livers and bones, for fat to feed to their cubs. They prefer to take their meat fresh, from the newly dead. And here, in this desolate place, they need only wait."

"So we are waiting for a mammoth to die?"

"Why did you think, Longtusk?"

"These Fireheads believe themselves to be mighty hunters," Longtusk said bitterly. "But it isn't true. They are scavengers, like the hyenas, or the condors."

Thunder did not reply.

Somehow, in his heart, he had always imagined that his Family were still out there somewhere: just over the horizon, a little beyond the reach of a contact rumble, living on the steppe as they always had. But he had denied the changes in the land he had seen all around him, never thought through their impact on his Family. Now he faced the truth.

He recalled how so recently he had prided himself on his self-control, the fact that he was above mundane concerns, beyond pain and love and hope. He tried to cling to that control, to draw strength from it.

But the comfort was as dry and cold as the mammoths' seep holes. And he couldn't get out of his head the disgust and rage of Rockheart.

. . . The sun wheeled around the sky twice more before it happened.

There was a flurry of motion among the mammoths. The Fireheads, eating and dozing, stirred.

A mammoth Cow, barged away from a water hole, had fallen to her knees. Her breath gurgled in her chest. Other mammoths gathered around her briefly, touching her scalp and tongue with their trunks. But they were weak themselves, ground down by hunger and thirst, and had no help to offer her. Soon she was left alone, slumping deeper into the mud, as if melting.

"At last," rumbled Walks With Thunder brutally.

With fast, efficient cries, a party of Fireheads formed up, gathering their knives and axes and spears, and set off toward the Cow.

Drawn by a hideous curiosity, Longtusk followed.

The Fireheads reached the mammoth. They started to lay their ropes on the ground, ready to pull her onto her back for gutting.

The mammoth raised her head, feebly and slowly, and her eyes opened, gummy with the milky mucus.

The Fireheads stepped back, shouting their annoyance that she was not yet dead.

While the Fireheads argued, the Cow stared at Longtusk. She spoke in a subterranean rumble so soft he could barely hear it. "Don't you recognize me, Longtusk? Has it been so long?"

Memories swam toward him, long-buried: a calf, a ball of fluffy brown fur, not even her guard hairs grown, scampering, endlessly annoying . . .

A name.

"Splayfoot." Splayfoot, his sister.

"You're back in time to Remember me," she said. "You and your Firehead friends. You were going to be the greatest hero of all, Longtusk. Wasn't that your dream? But now I can smell the stink of fire and meat on you. *What happened to you?*"

One of the hunters—Bareface—stepped forward. He had a spear in his paw, tipped by shining quartz. He hefted it, preparing for a thrust into her mouth, a single stroke that would surely kill her. Evidently the Fireheads, impatient, had decided to finish her off so they could get on with mining her body for its fat and marrow.

But this was Longtusk's own sister. His sister!

Longtusk trumpeted his rage.

With a single tusk sweep he knocked Bareface off his feet. The Firehead fell, howling, clutching his leg; bone protruded white from a bloody wound. Longtusk grabbed the spear with his trunk and drove the quartz point deep into the mud.

He went to his sister and wrapped his trunk around hers. "Get up."

"I can't. I'm so tired . . ."

"No! Only death is the end of possibility. By Kilukpuk's dugs, *up* . . ." And he hauled her to her feet by main force. She scrabbled at the mud, seeking a footing. Her legs were trembling, the muscles so depleted they could barely support her weight.

But now another mammoth was here—Rockheart, almost as gaunt and weakened. Nevertheless he lumbered up to Splayfoot's other side, lending his support as Longtusk tried to steady her.

And, startlingly, here was Willow, the squat little Dreamer. He jammed his shoulder under Splayfoot's heavy rump and shoved as hard as he could. He seemed to be laughing as he, too, defied the Fireheads.

The Fireheads were recovering from their shock at Longtusk's attack on Bareface. They were reaching for weapons, more of the big spears and axes that could slice through a mammoth's hide.

But now Walks With Thunder charged at them, his gait stiff and arthritic. He trumpeted, waving his huge old tusks this way and that, scattering the Fireheads. "Go, little grazer!"

And as the water hole receded, and the motley party headed into an empty, unknown land, Longtusk could hear Thunder's call. "Go, go, *go!*"

Patriarch THREE

Longtusk and the Truth

There are many stories about Longtusk (said Silverhair).

There is a story that Longtusk flew over the ice, carrying his Clan to safety in a place called a nunatak.

There is a story that Longtusk dug his huge tusks into the ground, as we do when we search for water, only to find—not water—but warmth, coming out of bare rock, sufficient to drive back the ice and keep his Clan alive.

There is a story that he stamped his mighty feet and made his refuge of rock and heat fly off into the sky, carrying the mammoths with it, and the rock became the Sky Steppe, the last refuge of all. But Longtusk had to stay behind, here on Earth, to face his death . . .

Or perhaps Longtusk never died. Some say he returns, from out of the north, a hero come to save us when we face great danger. Perhaps it was he who brought our Family to the Island, before the sea rose and trapped us there. (But perhaps that was somebody else, another hero whose name we have lost, somebody inspired by Longtusk's legend . . .)

How can all the stories be true?

Can *any* of them be true?

Oh, Icebones, I understand. You want to know. And, more

than that, you *want* the stories to be true. I was just like you as a calf!

Longtusk is a wonderful hero. But we'll never know for sure. You understand that, don't you?

. . . What do I think?

Well, stories don't come out of thin air. Perhaps there's a grain of truth. Perhaps there really was a Longtusk, and something like the stories really did happen, long ago.

Perhaps. We'll never know.

If I could know one thing about Longtusk, though, it would be this.

How he died.

1

The Family

Under a gray sunless sky, without shadows, every direction looked the same. Even the land was contorted, confusing, the rock bare, littered here and there by gravel and loess, lifeless save for scattered tussocks of grass.

Longtusk, trunk raised, studied the vast, empty landscape around them. *There were no Fireheads*, he realized: no storage pits, no hearths, no huts, not even a mastodont, none of it in his vision for the first time for half his lifetime.

The Fireheads had filled and defined his world for so long. Their projects—predictable or baffling, rewarding or distressing—had provided a structure to every waking moment, even when he had defied them. Now the future seemed as blank and directionless as the land that stretched around him.

He felt disoriented, like a calf who had been spun around until he was dizzy.

"I don't think they are coming after us." He almost wished the Fireheads *would* follow him. At least that was a threat he could understand.

But it seemed he would not be given that much help.

207

And, for the first time since his capture as a calf, he had to learn to think for himself.

"Of course not," Rockheart was saying. "They have no need to—save revenge, perhaps. And those dwarfish pals of yours were making trouble."

"They aren't dwarfs," said Longtusk. "They are mastodonts."

"It doesn't matter," growled Rockheart. "You won't be seeing them again."

. . . Could that be true?

"You're the leader of this strange little herd of ours, Longtusk," Rockheart said sourly. "But I strongly suggest we head north and east."

"Why?"

"Because we might find something to eat and drink. Although we may have to fight for it." He eyed Longtusk. "You aren't in your Firehead camp now, being fed hay and water by your masters . . ."

Perhaps. But Longtusk didn't want to think about a future in which he became like the mammoths he had seen at the mud seep, fighting over dribbles of brackish mud, pushing away the weak and old and young.

"North and east," he said.

"North and east."

So they moved on.

After a time they found a place where grass grew a little more thickly. Longtusk pulled tufts of the coarse grass into his own mouth, and helped Splayfoot to feed. Her eyes half closed, Splayfoot ground up the grass with slow, feeble movements of her jaw, but he could see her tongue was spotted with black, and she was sucking at the grass as much as eating it.

He said, "She's very weak. She needs drink as much as food."

Rockheart growled, "There's no drink to be had here."

It struck Longtusk that Rockheart himself was barely in better condition than Splayfoot. But where Splayfoot was subsiding toward death, Rockheart was still functioning, working. At the mud seep he had even been prepared to challenge Longtusk—and now here he was playing his part in this unexpected journey, which looked as if it would prove long and difficult.

His respect grew for this indomitable, arrogant Bull.

Willow, too, was hungry and thirsty. There was no water here, and the little Dreamer couldn't eat grass, like the mammoths. He prowled around the area until he found a stunted dwarf willow, clinging to the ground. He prized up its twisted branches and studied them, eventually dropping them with scorn.

Rockheart said, "What's it doing?"

Longtusk replied, "It—*he*—is looking for long, straight bits of wood. I expect he wants to make a spear, maybe even a fire. He might catch a lemming or a vole."

Rockheart snorted in disgust, indifferent.

Rockheart and Splayfoot soon stopped eating, evidently having taken their fill.

Longtusk had barely scratched the surface of his hunger. He had been used to *much* more fodder than this at the Firehead settlement, and if he didn't take more he would soon be as scrawny and ragged as the others—and ill-prepared for the winter to come, when the mammoths would have to live off their stores of fat.

But to gorge himself was hardly a way to gain trust. So he took care to eat no more than Rockheart's shrunken stomach could manage.

Having fed as best they could, they moved on.

The sun was already sinking in the sky when they reached the trail.

It was just a strip of trampled land that cut across the gravel-littered rock barrens, passing roughly east to west. Longtusk, instincts dulled by captivity, might not have seen it at all. But Rockheart turned confidently onto the trail and began to head east.

Longtusk—supporting his sister, and occasionally allowing Willow to ride on his back—followed his lead.

They passed a stand of forest. The trees were firs, still young but already tall, growing fast and dense in a green swathe that stretched to the south. The forest had grown so thickly, in fact, that it had already overrun the old trail, and the mammoths had to divert north until the forest was behind them and they were cutting across open land once more.

Longtusk said, "It's a long time since I was here. But I don't recall the land being like this."

"Things have changed here, Longtusk—within the lifetime of calves a lot younger than you or me. I recall when this was all steppe, with grass, herbs, shrubs. *Now* look around: to the south you have the spreading forest, and to the north the bare rock. No place left for the steppe, eh?

"And even where there is steppe—though you might not think it—the climate is wetter than it used to be. There is more rain, more thick snow in the winter. Sometimes the land is waterlogged and boggy. In the summer nothing can grow but grass and lichens, and in the winter we struggle to keep out of snowdrifts so thick they cover our bellies. The land isn't right for us any more. Deer and moose can chew the trees, and reindeer and musk oxen browse on lichen and moss, dull cloddish brutes . . . but not *us*.

"But there are still a few places where the old steppe lingers, pockets of it here and there."

"And that's where you're taking us."

"That's where the mammoths live, yes—if we're lucky, friendly ones. That was the way we were heading, when we reached the mud seep. But we were weak, and . . .

"There are fewer of us now, and I suppose in the future there will be fewer still. But we persist. We have before."

"What do you mean?"

Rockheart eyed him. "You've been away too long. Have you forgotten so much of your Cycle?"

As winter followed summer, so the Earth had greater seasons, spanning the Great-Years. In the long winters the ice would spread, freezing the land and the air, and the mammoths could fill the expanding Steppe. Now it seemed the Earth's unwelcome spring was returning, and the steppe was overrun by forests and grass—and the mammoths had to retreat, waiting out the return of the cold, as they had many times before.

It was a time of hardship. But it would pass. That was the teaching of the Cycle. The ice had come and gone for more than two million years, and the mammoths had survived all the intervals of warmth in that immense stretch of time.

. . . But now Longtusk thought of the Fireheads: clustered around the mud seep, waiting for mammoths to die.

There were no Fireheads in the Cycle. There had been no Fireheads in the world when last the ice had retreated and advanced.

He had been away from his kind a long time, and he didn't presume to doubt Rockheart's ancient wisdom. But his experience, he was realizing slowly, was wider than the old tusker's. He had seen more of the world and its ways—and he had seen the Fireheads.

And *he* did not feel so confident that the future could be the same as the past.

He kept these thoughts to himself as they pushed on.

As night closed in the clouds thickened, and the wind from the icecap was harsh. Longtusk and Rockheart huddled close around Splayfoot, trying to shelter her and give her a little of their own sparse body heat; and Longtusk allowed the Dreamer to curl up under his belly fur.

Every so often Longtusk would rouse Splayfoot and force her to walk around. He knew that there was a core of heat inside the body of each mammoth, a flicker of life and mind that must be fed like the hearths of the Fireheads. If the cold penetrated too deep, if that flame of life was extinguished, it could never be ignited again.

Splayfoot responded passively, barely conscious.

In the morning they resumed their dogged walking, following Rockheart's trail.

But soon the light changed.

Longtusk raised his trunk, sniffing the air. He could smell moisture, rain or maybe snow, and the wind was veering, coming now strongly from the east. Looking that way he saw black clouds bubbling frothily.

There was a thin honking, a soft flap of wings far above him. Birds, he saw dimly, perhaps geese, fleeing from the east, away from the coming storm. He recalled what Walks With Thunder had told him of the eastern lands, where the icecap pushed far to the south. And he recalled Thunder's obscure, half-forgotten legends of a land embedded in the ice—a place that stayed warm enough to keep off the snow, even in the depths of winter. The nunatak.

He wondered how far those birds had flown—all the

way from the nunatak itself? But how could such a place exist?

The storm was rising, and he put the speculation from his mind. But he memorized the way those geese had flown, adding their track to the dynamic map of the landscape that he, like all mammoths, carried in his head.

By mid-morning the storm had hit.

The sky became a sheet of scudding gray-black clouds, utterly hiding the sun. The wind blew from the east with relentless ferocity, and carried before it a mix of snow, hail and rain, battering their flesh hard enough to sting. Soon they were all soaked through, bedraggled, weary, their fur plastered flat, lifting their feet from one deep muddy footprint into another.

Longtusk let Rockheart lead the way, and Willow followed Rockheart, clinging to his belly fur, his small round face hidden from the wind and rain. Longtusk plodded steadily after Rockheart, being careful never to let the big tusker out of his sight, even though it meant he walked so close he was treading in Rockheart's thin, foul-smelling dung. And behind Longtusk came Splayfoot, still weak, barely able to see, clinging onto Longtusk's tail with her trunk like a calf following its mother, as sheltered as he could manage.

But when the eye of the storm approached, the wind started to swirl around. Soon Longtusk, disoriented, couldn't tell east from west, north from south—and couldn't even see the trail. But Rockheart led them confidently, probing at the muddy ground with his trunk, seeking bits of old dung and the remnants of footprints, traces that marked the trail.

And it was while the storm was still raging that they came upon the mammoths.

*　　*　　*

They looked like a clump of boulders, round and solid, plastered with soaked hair. Longtusk saw those great heads rise, tusks dripping with water, and trunks lifted into the air, sniffing out the approach of these strangers. There were a few greeting rumbles for Rockheart and Splayfoot, nothing but suspicious glares for Longtusk.

There were perhaps fifteen of them—probably just a single Family, adult Cows and older calves. The Cows were clustered around a tall, gaunt old female, presumably the Matriarch, and the calves were sheltered under their belly hair and legs.

Longtusk could see no infants. Perhaps they were at the center of the group, out of his sight.

Rockheart lurched off the trail and led them toward the mammoths. Longtusk hadn't even been aware of the changes in the land around the trail. But now he saw grass, what looked like saxifrage, even a stand of dwarf willow clinging to the rock. It was an island of steppe in this cold desert of rock and glacial debris, just as Rockheart had described.

Willow found a shallow water hole, some distance from the mammoths, and went that way. Some of the mammoths watched him lethargically, too weak or weary to be concerned.

Rockheart and Splayfoot lumbered forward and were welcomed into the huddle with strokes of trunk and deeper, contented rumbles. Longtusk hesitated, left outside—outside, as he had been as a mammoth among mastodonts, as he had been as a mammoth at the cave of the Dreamers, and now outside even in this community of mammoths.

Longtusk dredged up memories of his life with his Family, before that terrible separation. He recalled how

214

the adults seemed so tall, their strength so huge, their command imposing, even their stink powerful. Now these wretched, bedraggled creatures seemed diminished; none of them, not even the old Matriarch at the center, was taller than he was.

Light flared, noise roared. There was a sudden blaze to Longtusk's right, and the mammoths, startled, trumpeted, clustered, tried to run.

It was lightning, he realized, a big blue bolt. It had struck out of the low clouds and set fire to an isolated spruce tree. The tree was burning, and the stink of smoke carried to his trunk—but there was no danger; already the fire was being doused by the continuing rain.

The other mammoths had raised their trunks suspiciously at Longtusk.

He hadn't reacted. It was only lightning, an isolated blaze; in his years with the Fireheads he'd learned that fire, if contained, was nothing to fear. But he realized now that the others—even the powerful Bull Rockheart—had shown their instinctive fear.

". . . He did not run from the fire. He didn't even flinch."

"Look how fat he is, how tall. None of us grows fat these days."

"See the burn on his flank. The shape of a Firehead paw . . ."

"He came with that little Dreamer."

"He stinks of fire. And of Fireheads. That is why he wasn't afraid."

"He isn't *natural* . . ."

But now the gaunt older Cow he had tagged as the Matriarch broke out of the group. Cautiously, ears spread and trunk raised, she approached him. Her hair was slicked down and blackened by the rain.

It had been so long, so very long. But still, there was something in the set of her head, her carriage—

Something that tugged at his heart.

Hesitantly, she reached out with her trunk and probed his face, eyes, mouth, and dug into his hair.

He knew that touch; the years fell away.

"I thought you were gone to the aurora," she said softly.

"Do I smell of fire?"

"Whatever has become of you, the rain has washed it away. All I can smell is you, Longtusk." She stepped forward and twined her trunk around his.

Through the rain, he could taste the sweet, milky scent of her breath.

"Come." Milkbreath pulled him back to the group, where the huddle was reforming. The other mammoths grumbled and snorted, but Milkbreath trumpeted her anger. "He is my son, and he is returned. Gather around him."

Slowly, they complied. And as the day descended into night and the storm continued to rage, slow, inquisitive trunks nuzzled at his mouth and face.

He felt a surge of warm exhilaration. After all his travels and troubles he was home, home again.

But, even in this moment of warmth, he noticed that there were no small calves at his feet, here at the center of the huddle—no infants at all, in fact.

Even as he greeted his mother, that stark fact dug deep into his mind, infecting it with worry.

2

The Decision

The storm blew itself out.

The next day was clear and cold, the sky blue and tall. The water that had poured so enthusiastically from the sky soaked into the ground, quickly, cruelly. But the grassy turf was still waterlogged, and drinking water was easy to find. The mammoths wandered apart, feeding and defecating, shaking the moisture out of their fur.

The spruce that had been struck by lightning was blackened and broken, its ruin still smoking.

Longtusk stayed close to his sister, and, with his mother's help, encouraged her to eat and drink. Slowly her eyes grew less cloudy.

His mother's attentiveness, as if he was still a calf, filled a need in him he hadn't recognized for a long time. He answered as fully as he could all the questions he was asked about his life since he had been split from the Family, and slowly the suspicion of the others wore away. And when he told of the loss of his calf and mate, the suspicion started to turn at last to sympathy.

But there were few here who knew him.

Skyhump, the Matriarch of the Family when he had been born, was long dead now—in fact there had been another Matriarch since, his mother's elder sister, killed by a fall into a kettle hole, and his mother had succeeded her.

And there was a whole new generation, born since he had left.

There was a Bull calf, for instance, called Threetusk—for the third, spindly ivory spiral that jutted out of his right tusk socket—who seemed fascinated by Longtusk. He would follow Longtusk around, asking him endless questions about the warrior mastodonts like Jaw Like Rock, and he would raise his tusks to Longtusk's in half-hearted challenge.

Longtusk realized that Threetusk was just how *he* had been at that age: restless, unhappy with the company of his mother and the other Cows of the Family—not yet ready to join a bachelor herd, but eager to try.

But things were different now. There was no sign of a bachelor herd anywhere nearby for Threetusk to join. Perhaps there was a herd somewhere in this huge land, in another island of nourishing steppe. But how was a juvenile like Threetusk, lacking knowledge of the land, to find his way there in one piece? And if he could *not* find a herd, what would become of him? . . .

The Family moved slowly over their patch of steppe, eating sparingly, drinking what they could find. After the first couple of days it was obvious their movements were restricted, and Longtusk took to wandering away from the rest, trying to understand the changed landscape.

He struck out south and east and west.

Each direction he traveled, the complex steppe vegetation soon dwindled out to be replaced by cold desert, or dense coniferous forests, or bland plains of grass. And to the north, of course, there was only the protesting shriek of the ice as it continued its millennial retreat.

And, hard as he listened, he heard no signs of other mammoths.

His Family was isolated in this island of steppe. Other mammoths, Families and bachelor herds, must also be restricted to steppe patches and water holes and other places where they could survive. And the nearest of those islands might be many days' walk from the others.

This isolation mattered. It made the mammoths fragile, exposed. An illness, a bad winter, even a single fall of heavy snow could take them all, with no place to run.

As they munched at their herbs and grass the others didn't seem aware of their isolation, the danger it posed for them.

And they didn't seem aware of the strangest thing of all: *there were no young calves here*—no squirming bundles of orange fur, wrestling each other or searching for their mothers' milk and tripping over their trunks.

Longtusk felt a profound sense of unease. And, when he spotted a new skein of geese flapping out of the east, it was an unease that coalesced into a new determination.

He plucked up the courage to speak to his mother.

"There was a Gathering," he said. "When I was a calf. Just before I got lost."

"Yes. The whole Clan was there."

"I saw Pinkface, the Matriarch of Matriarchs. Is she still alive?"

Milkbreath's trunk tugged at a resistant clump of grass. "There have been several Gatherings since you were lost."

Longtusk said slowly, "That isn't an answer."

Milkbreath turned to face him, and he was aware of a stiffening among the other Cows close by, his aunts and great-aunts.

He persisted. "When was the last Gathering?"

"Many years ago. It isn't so easy to travel any more, Longtusk. Especially for the calves and—"

"At the Gathering, the last one. Were there more mammoths—or less?"

Milkbreath snorted her disapproval. "You don't need to feed me my grass a blade at a time, Longtusk. I can see the drift of your questions."

Rockheart was at his side. "You shouldn't question the Matriarch. It isn't the way things are done. Not *here.*"

Milkbreath rumbled, "It's all right, Rockheart. His education was never finished. Times are hard, Longtusk. The Matriarch of Matriarchs gave us our instructions at the last Gathering. She could foresee the coming changes in the world, the worsening of the weather."

"The collapse of the steppe into these little islands?"

"Yes. Even that. She knew that Gatherings would be difficult or impossible for a long time. She knew there would be fewer of us next year, and fewer still the next after that. But we have endured such changes before, many times, as the ice has come and gone. And we have always survived. It will be hard, but our bodies know the way. That's the teaching of the Cycle."

"And what about the Fireheads? Did she speak of them?"

"Of course she spoke of the Fireheads, Longtusk. Fireheads come when we are weak and dying. They cut our corpses open for our bones and hearts . . ."

"But," he said, "there are no Fireheads in the Cycle. Maybe the Fireheads weren't here when the ice last retreated."

"What does it matter?"

"What I'm saying is that things are different now. The Fireheads are a new threat we haven't faced before . . ."

But the Matriarch continued to quote the Cycle. "When I die, I belong to the wolves—or the Fireheads. We must accept the Fireheads, as we accept the warming, and simply endure. In the future, all will be as it was, and there will be great Gatherings again."

Longtusk tried another approach. "When was the last time you heard from the Matriarch of Matriarchs?"

Rockheart growled, "Longtusk—"

"The last Gathering?"

". . . Yes."

"Then she is probably dead."

Some of the Cows rumbled and trumpeted in dismay.

"And she was wrong," said Longtusk grimly.

Rockheart tusked the ground, rumbling his challenge. "Do I have to fight you to shut you up?"

Longtusk ignored him. "I have seen the Fireheads. I have seen what they do. They wait for mammoths to die. If the mammoths take too long, they finish them off with their spears . . . The Matriarch of Matriarchs was right that the mammoths have endured warming before, and recovered. *But this is not the past.* The Fireheads make everything different—"

Rockheart's blow was a mere swipe at his tusks, a loud ivory clatter that echoed over the steppe. He said grimly, "You have forgotten your Cycle. *The Matriarch has given her orders, and we will follow.*"

Longtusk eyed Rockheart. He recalled how easily he had defeated this old tusker before—and yet here he was again, prepared to confront him, and Longtusk knew he could beat Rockheart down again, just as easily.

But that wasn't the way to succeed. Not today.

And he couldn't keep his peace, either, even though he longed to. He didn't want to be different! He only wanted to be one of the Family . . . All he had to do was stay silent.

But that wasn't the right path, either.

He summoned up the inner strength he had found during those long dark months in the Firehead camp, after the death of Neck Like Spruce and his calf.

He said, *"We cannot survive here, Matriarch.* This little patch of steppe is too small. Look around. You are thin, half-starved. A simple accident could kill us all—a flash flood, a lightning strike like the one which struck down that spruce.

"And some day the Fireheads will come here. They will—I know them! And—"

This time, Rockheart's blow was to his temple, and pain rang through his skull. He staggered sideways. He felt warm blood trickle down his flesh.

The Matriarch faced him, shifting from one foot to the other, distressed. "End this, Longtusk."

"Mother—Matriarch—*where are your calves?"*

Rockheart's tusks came crashing down on his. His ivory splintered, agonizingly, as if a tooth had broken, and the tip of his right tusk cracked off and fell to the ground.

"By Kilukpuk's black heart, fight," Rockheart rumbled.

"What makes you so wise?" Milkbreath said, upset, angry. "What makes you different? How do you see what others don't? How do *you* know what we must do?"

Longtusk, bleeding, aching, could see Rockheart prepare for another blow, but he knew he must not respond—not even brace himself.

". . . The calves are dead." It was Splayfoot, his sister.

Rockheart hesitated.

Gaunt, weakened, Splayfoot came limping toward

Longtusk. "The youngest died last winter, when there was no water to be had. That's your answer, Longtusk. He *is* different, Matriarch. He has seen things none of us can imagine. And we must listen. I would have died with the others at that drying mud seep—*as would you, Rockheart*—if not for Longtusk."

The Matriarch rumbled sadly, "Even when we have met Bulls, even when we have mated, our bodies have not borne calves. It is the wisdom of the body. If there is too little food and water the body knows that calves should not come."

"For how long?" Longtusk asked. "Look around you. How long before you *all* grow too old to conceive?" He glared at them wildly, and trumpeted his challenge. "Which of you will be the last to die here, alone?"

Rockheart, growling, prepared another lunge at Longtusk, but the Matriarch stopped him. Anguished, angry, she rumbled, "What would you have me do?"

Longtusk said, "There may be a way. A place to go. Beyond the reach of the ice—and even of the Fireheads." Shuddering, trying to ignore the pain of his temple and broken tusk, he looked to the east, thinking of the geese.

Rockheart roared his disgust. "And must we follow you, Firehead monster? Shall we call you Patriarch? There has never been such an animal. Not in all the long years of the Cycle—"

"He is right," Splayfoot insisted. "The spring blizzards kill our calves. The ice storms of the autumn kill those who are heavy with next year's calves. None of us can bear the heat of summer. And when the seeps and water holes ice over in the winter, too thickly for us to break through, we fight each other for the water, to the death . . . We can't stay here. *He is right.*"

Threetusk came pushing between them, his spindly

extra tusk coated with mud. He looked up at Longtusk with trunk raised. "Take me! Oh, take me!"

The arguments continued, for the rest of that day and into the night, and even beyond that.

The day was bright and clear and cold. The sun was surrounded by a great halo of light that arced above the horizon, bright yellow against a muddy purple sky. It was a sign of the icecap, Longtusk knew.

It was an invitation—and a challenge.

He drew a deep breath through his trunk, and the cleanness of the air filled him with exhilaration.

"It is time," he rumbled, loud enough for all to hear.

And the mammoths began to prepare for the separation.

The Family was to be split in two by Longtusk's project: calf separated from parent, sibling from sibling. And, though it was never stated, a deep truth was understood by all here—that the sundered Family would never be reunited, for those who walked with Longtusk into the cold mists of the east would never come back this way.

Willow pulled on all his clothing, stuffed his jacket and hat and boots with grass for insulation against the cold, and collected together his tools and strips of dried meat. Once he had understood that Longtusk was planning to move on, the Dreamer had been making his own preparations. He had made himself simple tools, spears and stone axes, and he disappeared for days at a time, returning with the fruits of his hunting: small mammals, rabbits and voles. He ate the flesh or dried it, stored the bones as raw material for tools, and used the skin, dried and scraped, to make himself new clothing.

Soon he had become as healthy and equipped as Longtusk could recall—much better than during his time as a creature of the Fireheads. It dismayed Longtusk to think that he, and the mastodonts, had received so much better treatment at the paws of the Fireheads than Willow, their close cousin.

He sought out his mother, the Matriarch.

She wrapped her trunk in his and reached out to ruffle the topknot of fur on his head, just as she had when he was a calf—even though he had grown so tall she now had to reach high up to do so. "Such a short time," she said. "I've only just found you, and now we are to be parted again. And this time—"

"I know."

"Maybe we'll both be right," she said. "Perhaps there really is a warm island of steppe floating in the icecap. And maybe the Fireheads and the weather will spare those who stay here, and we will flourish again. That way there will be plenty of mammoths in the future to argue about who was right and wrong. Won't it be wonderful?"

"Mother—"

She slipped her trunk into his mouth. "No more talking. Go."

Go, little grazer. Was he destined always to flee, to move on from those who cared for him?

This time, he promised himself grimly, this time is the last, whatever the outcome. Wherever I finish up will be my home—and my grave.

They gathered together: Longtusk, Rockheart, Splayfoot, the bold Bull calf Threetusk, and two young Cows. Just six of them, three Bulls and three Cows, to challenge the icecap—six mammoths, and Willow, the Dreamer.

As they stood in a dismal huddle at the fringe of the Family, the whole venture seemed impossible to Longtusk, absurd.

But here was Rockheart, the last to pledge his commitment to the trek: "You won't get through a day without me to show you the way, you overfed milk-tusk." Longtusk's spirit rose as he looked at the huge tusker—gaunt and bony, but a great slab of strength and determination and wisdom.

Now Rockheart raised his trunk. "You taste that?"

"Salt water. Blown from the sea . . ."

"Yes," said Rockheart. "But it comes from both north and south."

The mammoths would cross the land bridge between Asia and America much too close to its central line for Longtusk to be able to see the encroaching oceans to north and south. But sight is the least of a mammoth's senses, and, on this bright clear day, Longtusk could taste the traces of salt spray in the air, hear the rush of wind over the ocean, sense the crash of breakers on the twin shorelines.

The neck of land they had to cross seemed fragile to him, easily sundered, and he wondered again about the wisdom of what they were attempting.

But this was no time for doubt.

"From the old land to the new," he said boldly.

"From old to new," Rockheart rumbled.

Longtusk began to march to the east. He could feel the powerful footsteps of the others as they followed him.

It had begun.

3

The Trek

To show his own determination he chose to lead, that first day.

But at the start of the second day, without a word, he quietly deferred to Rockheart, letting the old tusker, with his superior instincts and understanding of the country, go first. That decision paid off many times—especially after the mammoth trails petered out, and the land became increasingly broken and unpredictable.

Willow preferred to walk during the day; it kept him strong and alert. But the mammoths, needing little sleep, would walk through much of the night, and then Willow would ride on Longtusk's back, muttering his strange dreams. The other mammoths watched in suspicious amazement, unable to understand how a mammoth could allow such a squat little creature onto his back.

There were animals here: musk oxen, horses, bison, even camels, passing in great herds on the horizon. They glimpsed some carnivores—wolves, lions, a saber-tooth cat that sent a shudder of recognition through Longtusk, and a short-faced bear, fat and ugly, which came lumbering from a limestone cave. The predators watched them pass, silently speculating after the manner of their kind, seeking weakness among potential prey.

They saw no other mammoths, no Fireheads, no Dreamers.

They paused to rest and feed in an isolated island of steppe vegetation: a mosaic of grass with flowering plants and herbs like marsh marigolds, harebells and golden saxifrage, and sparse trees like ground willow, few reaching higher than a mammoth's belly hair.

At Longtusk's feet, a small face peered out of a burrow. It was a collared lemming. The little rodent, seeing that the mammoths meant him no harm, crawled out of his burrow and began to nibble at the base of an Arctic lupine.

Longtusk realized sadly that, like the mammoths, the vanishing steppe was the lemmings' only true home. But the lemming's mind, though sharp, was too small for him to discuss the issue.

Mammoth and lemming briefly regarded each other. Then the lemming ducked beneath the ground once more.

A few more days' walking brought them to a more mountainous region. To the north there was the sharp tang of ice in the air, and when he looked that way Longtusk saw a small, isolated icecap, a gleaming dome that nestled among the mountains. It was shrinking as the world warmed; it might once have been part of a much more extensive formation.

Then they came to a place where the traveling became much more difficult. Longtusk, as the strongest, took the lead.

The land here was cut through by deep channels. These gouges ran from north to south, and so across their eastward path. Longtusk found himself having to climb down crumbling slopes into the beds of the channels, and then up ridges on the far side, over and over. The channels seemed to have been cut right down to the rock, and there was only thin soil and scanty vegetation, broken by dunes of coarse sand and ridges of gravel. There was little water to be had, for the soil was shallow. But there was thicker growth on the top of the ridges—some of which, surrounded by the deep valleys, had smooth outlines, like the bodies of fish.

Standing on top of such a ridge, cropping the sparse grass wearily, Longtusk looked about at the strange pattern of the land. It was like a dried-up river bed, he thought, a tracery of runnels and ridges in mud, cutting across each other so they were braided like hair, gouged out and worn smooth by running water.

But this was broader than any river valley he had ever seen. And most of the top soil and loose rock had been torn away, right down to the bedrock. If a river had ever run here it must have been wider and far more powerful than any he had encountered before.

To the north the bedrock rose, great shoulders of hard volcanic rock pushing up to either side of this channeled plain. He saw that the rocky shoulders came together in a narrow cleft. Ice gleamed white there, blocking the cleft. But it was from that cleft that these strange deep channels seemed to run.

When he raised his trunk that way he could smell water: fresh water, a vast body of it, beyond that cleft in the rock.

The mammoths discussed this briefly. The ice wedge was less than a day's walk away, and if there was water to be had the detour was surely worth the investment of their time. And besides, Longtusk admitted to himself, he was piqued by curiosity; he would like to know the story of this distorted, damaged land.

They followed one of the wider channels toward the ice plug, their muscles working steadily as the land rose.

At last Longtusk topped a ridge of rock, and he was able to look beyond the cleft and its plug of ice.

There was a lake here. It was broad and placid, and it lay in a natural hollow in the land. The water was fringed by rock and ice: the plug of ice that barred it from the damaged lands to the south, and by the shrinking icecap which lay at its northern end.

The mammoths walked cautiously down to the lake's gravel-strewn fringe. The water was ice cold, but they sucked it into their trunks gratefully. Threetusk and the young Cows splashed out into the water, playfully blowing trunkfuls of it over each other. After a time they loped clumsily out of the water, their breath steaming, their outer fur crackling with frost.

Willow, too, made the best of the water. He threw off his furs and scampered, squat and naked, into the lake. He cried out at the cold, but immersed himself and scrubbed at the thick hair on his belly and head with bits of soft stone, getting rid of the insects that liked to make their homes there.

There seemed to be little vegetation in this placid pool. But there were signs of life by the shore, holes dug by rabbits and voles and lemmings in the long grass that fringed the water's edge. And birds wheeled overhead, ducks and gulls.

". . . But there are no fish here," said Rockheart. "Strange."

"But no fish could reach this place," Longtusk said thoughtfully.

At the lake's northern shore, the ice gave directly onto

the lake, making a cliff that gleamed white. There was a constant scrape and groan from all across the ice cliff, and Longtusk could see icebergs, small islands of blue-white ice, drifting away from the cliff. The lake water looked black beside the blinding white of the ice.

It was obvious that the ice was flowing from its mountain fastness, with hideous slowness, down toward the lake. And where the ice met the water the icebergs were calving off, great fragments of the disintegrating ice sheet.

In fact, Longtusk saw, the lake had been created by the melting of the ice sheet as it crumbled into this hollow in the rock.

"This lake is just a huge meltwater pond," Longtusk said, realizing. "It is fed by melting ice. There are no fish here, because there is no way for a fish to get here. And the water is kept from draining away by *that*—" The plug of ice in the rocky cleft on the lake's southern side. "Fed by meltwater from the north, trapped by the ice plug to the south, this bowl in the land will gradually fill up—"

"Until," Rockheart growled, "that chunk of ice gives way."

"Yes. And then the lake will empty itself across the land, all at once—and wash away the soil and vegetation, scouring down to the bedrock."

Rockheart rumbled. "Like Kilukpuk's mighty tears."

"Yes. No wonder the land is so damaged. But then the ice plug forms again, and the lake begins to fill once more."

Rockheart grunted. "If that's true, we're lucky. We're in no danger here."

"What do you mean?"

"The water has some way to rise before it tops that ice dam."

"You're right. We'll be long gone by then." Good for Rockheart, Longtusk thought: practical as always, focusing on the most important issue—the mammoths' safety.

They left the lake, calling to the others.

A few more days and he could sense the broadening of the land to north and south, and he knew they had passed the narrowest point of this neck of Earth that stretched between the continents.

Thus, the mammoths walked from Asia to America.

Soon after that he could see the icecap.

It was a line of light, straight and pure white, all along the eastern horizon, as if etched there by the ingenious paw of a Firehead. He could hear the growl and scrape as the ice flowed over the rocky land, gouging and destroying, the mighty cracks as the ice itself split and crumbled, and the steady roar of the blunt katabatic winds which spilled from its chill domed heart.

It was a frozen sheet that covered half a continent, pushing far to the south, much farther south than in the land they had fled, on the far side of the land bridge. And it was this monster of ice that they must challenge before they reached safety.

He tried to maintain the pace and enthusiasm of his little group. But as they drew closer he could feel his own footsteps drag, as if the icecap itself was drawing out his strength, just as it sucked the moisture from the air.

They reached land that had clearly been uncovered only recently by the ice.

The rock was scoured clean, laced here and there with low dunes of glacial till and sand. Only lichen grew here: patches of yellow and green, bordered by black, slowly eroding the surfaces of the rock. The lichen might be extremely ancient; it took ten years for a new colony to become visible to the eye. He wondered what slow encrusting dreams these vegetable colonists shared, what slow cold memories of the surging ice they stored.

The land became steadily more treacherous. They worked their way past moraines, heaps of rubble left by the retreating ice. The rubble was of all sizes, from gritty sand to boulders larger than a mammoth. The moraines were cut through by meltwater rivers that varied unpredictably from trickles to mighty, surging flows, and the rubble heaps were unstable, liable to slump and collapse at any time.

As they pressed farther, a great wind rose, katabatic, pouring directly off the ice sheet and into their faces. It was a hard time. There was little to eat or drink and every step required a major effort, but they persisted. And Longtusk was careful to encourage his charges to gather as much strength as possible, for he knew that only harder days, if anything, lay ahead of them all.

At last they encountered the ice itself.

They reached the nose of a glacier. It was a wall of ice, cracked and dirty and forbidding. Blocks of broken ice, calved off the glacier like miniature icebergs, lay unmelting on rock that was rust-red, brown and black. Tornado-like columns of ice crystals spun across the barren rock in the wind, whipping up small lumps of sandstone that flew through the air, peppering the mammoths' hides.

This was the terminus of a huge river of ice that poured, invisibly slowly, from the vast cap that still lay to the east.

The mammoths paused to gather breath, hunted without success for food, and then began the ascent.

Longtusk picked his way onto the great ice river, stepping cautiously over a shattered, chaotic plain of deeply crevassed blue ice. The glacier was a river of raw white, its glare hurting his eyes, shining under the sky's clean blue. He could see the glacier's source, high above him, at the lip of the ice sheet itself. Where he could he chose paths free of crevasses and broken surfaces, but he could usually find easier ground near the glacier's edges, hugging the orange rock of the valley down which the glacier poured.

It was difficult going. Sometimes loose snow was whipped up by the wind and driven over the surface, obscuring everything around him up to shoulder height. But, above the snow, the sky was a deep blue.

At last the ice beneath his feet leveled out, and he realized he had reached a plateau.

It was the lip of the ice sheet.

He was standing on a sea of gleaming ice, which shone in every direction he looked, white, blue and green. The ice receded to infinity, flat white under blue sky—but perhaps his poor eyes could make out a shallow dome shape as the ice rose, sweeping away from him toward the east.

It was utterly silent and still, without life of any kind, the only sound the snort of his trunk, the only motion the fog of his breath.

He turned, ponderously, and looked back the way he had come.

This edge of the ice was marked by mountains, heavily eroded and all but buried, and he could see how the glacier spilled between the peaks toward the lower ground. Though locked into the slow passage of time, the glacier was very obviously a dynamic river of ice. Huge parallel bands flowed neatly down the valley's contours. The bands marked the merging of tributaries, smaller ice rivers that flowed into the main stream, each of them keeping their characteristic color given them by the rock particles they had ground up and carried. Where the glacier reached the lower land it spread out, cracking, making the jumbled surface of crevasses he had struggled to cross.

Everything flowed down from here, down to the west and the lower ground, as if he had climbed to the roof of the world. He was cold, exhausted, hungry, and thirsty; and he was still not confident of surviving this immense venture. But, standing here, looking down on the great frozen majesty of the icecap and its rivers, he felt exhilarated, privileged.

He turned to face the east, ready to go on.

He stepped forward experimentally. The ice was unforgivingly cold, seeming to suck his body heat out through the thick callused pads on his feet. It was harder than any rock he had encountered—but it was not smooth. It was choppy, rippled, like the surface of a lake under the wind. But the ripples were frozen in place, and the footing was, surprisingly, quite secure, thanks to those scalloped ripples.

There is nothing to eat here, he thought dryly. There is no shelter, and if I stay too long I will surely freeze to death. But at least I won't slip and fall.

He began to walk, and the others followed him. He could feel the ice's flow in his belly, a deep disturbing subsonic murmur as it poured with immense slowness toward the lip.

The cap was one of a string of great domes of ice that littered the northern hemisphere of the planet. As its center the icecap was kilometers thick, as humans would have measured it, and the bedrock beneath—ground free of life and locked in darkness—was crushed downward through many meters.

The dome was fed by fresh falls of snow on its upper surface. The new snow crushed the softer layers beneath, forcing out the air and turning them into hard blue ice. The collapsing center forced ice at the rim to flow down to lower altitudes, in the form of glaciers that gouged their way through river valleys and, where the ice met open water, they floated off to form immense shelves.

The ice was like a huge, subsiding mass of soft white dung, flattening and flowing, continually replenished from above.

The glaciers' flow was enormously slow—perhaps advancing by a mere mammoth footstep every year. But the icecap was nevertheless shrinking. Less snow was falling on the icecap than it was losing to its glaciers and ice shelves. The cap was inevitably disintegrating, though it would take an immense time to disappear.

At first, under blue skies, it was exhilarating to be here. But even from the start the icecap was not without its dangers.

Once, Longtusk walked over a place were the ice had frozen into a thin crust that seemed to lie on deeper snow. When he took a step the surface settled abruptly. He fell—not far, just enough to startle him. And then the crust around him continued to collapse, the cracks spreading for many paces as the surface settled. The crunching, crackling noise of the ice seemed to circle him. It was eerie, like the actions of a living thing in this place where nothing could live, and he was glad to pass onto firmer ice.

. . . Even the light was strange.

Sometimes, when the sun was low in the sky, there were rings and arcs surrounding it, glimmering in the sky, and even false images of the sun to either side of it, or nestling on the horizon. It was like the blurred multiple images Longtusk would sometimes see when his eyes were wind-battered and filled with tears, so that he had to peer at the world through a lens of water.

When the nights were clear they were blue, as the moonlight was reflected from the ice. Even when there was no Moon, and only stars shone, the nights would still be bright and blue, so powerfully did the ice capture and reflect even the stars' trickle of light.

On the third day the sky clouded over, and a white mist descended.

The light grew bright but soft, the details of the sky and even the ice under his feet hazing. Soon the horizon was invisible and the sky was joined seamlessly to the ground, as if he was walking inside some huge hollowed-out gull's egg. The light was very bright, enough to hurt his eyes, and gray-white floaters drifted like birds across his vision. There was no shadow, no relief, no texture. He could make out the line of mammoths behind him, robust stocky forms laboring across the ice, their heads wreathed in steam. They were the only objects he could see in the whole world, as if they were all floating in clouds, disengaged from the Earth.

But the mist thickened further still. In this sourceless, shadowless light, even footprints were nothing but thin tracings of blue-white against the greater white of the washed-out world, all but impossible to see with his sore and watering eyes.

They endured a day and a night in the mist: a night they spent in utter darkness, huddled together against the wind, trying to ignore their own mounting hunger and thirst and the cold of the huge thickness of ice beneath their feet, which threatened to suck every scrap of warmth from their bodies.

Doubts assailed Longtusk, suspended here in this

harsh fog of ice crystals and mist. How could he have imagined that he could lead a party on such an impossible undertaking? He had only a fragment of legend to inspire him—only his memory of the flight of the birds to guide him. And in this white-out fog, even his acute mammoth senses were baffled by the clamor of wind and the creak of ice under his feet.

They were all in distress, Longtusk realized, for mammoths were not built to endure such long treks over such inhospitable terrain without food and water. It was obvious that the journey was taking a heavy toll on poor Splayfoot; she was sinking once more into that ominous half-consciousness from which he feared, one day, she might not have the strength to climb out.

And Rockheart too was suffering. He was more gaunt and bony than ever, his eyes milky and sore, his tusks protruding from the planes of his face like icicles. He had never looked older. But he wasn't feeble yet, as he proved as he propelled Splayfoot forward with a mighty shove of his forehead at her rump.

They continued. They had, after all, no choice.

At last, after another half day, the mist cleared as suddenly as it had descended. The world emerged again, reduced to elementals: a flat white surface under a blue dome, nothing but white and blue and flatness, an empty, stripped-bare land across which the mammoths toiled.

. . . But the landscape was not quite empty.

The Dreamer Willow walked a little way away from the mammoths, blinking in the sudden glare. He peered into the east, and he pulled a strip of rabbit skin around his eyes to protect them from the sun's glare.

Then he came running to Longtusk, jabbering in his guttural, incomprehensible language, and pointed to the eastern horizon.

Longtusk squinted that way. He could see nothing but a blur where the ice merged with the sky. But that meant little; Willow's eyes, like a Firehead's, were those of a predator, much sharper than any mammoth's.

Nevertheless he felt encouraged, and they pulled forward with increased enthusiasm.

They smelled it before they saw it.

". . . Water," said Splayfoot, wondering. "It smells almost warm."

Rockheart, wheezing, walking stiffly, had raised his great scarred trunk. "Growing things. And something else, something sour. Sulfur, perhaps."

Willow was growing increasingly agitated. His bow legs working, he ran ahead of the mammoths and then back, urging them forward.

And then Longtusk saw it.

The mountains, protruding from the ice, seemed to float between blue sky and white ice. Gray-black scree, shattered by frost, tumbled over pure white glaciers—and, etched sharply against the black mountains, he saw pale green stripes that could only be vegetation.

It was the nunatak.

Heartened, trumpeting with excitement, he hurried forward.

Under his feet, rock began to push out of the ice and its thin covering of snow. The exposed rock was rust brown, the color of a calf's hair. It was littered with loose snow, which was blown by the prevailing wind into white streaks.

For a time walking became a little easier. But the long, steady climb up the shallow rise added to their efforts, and soon they were all breathing hard, the young Cows trumpeting their dismay.

After a time the land began to descend once more. Longtusk found himself walking down a broad, widening valley that curved between rounded, icebound hills. The smooth curving profiles of the hills were barely visible, the blue-white of the ice against the duller white of the sky. But here and there the land was sprinkled with fragments of black rock. The rock made it easier to see the shape of the land around him: the sweep of the valley floor, the tight rounded profiles of the hills.

He came to a piece of the black rock, lying in his path. He nudged it cautiously with his foot. It was frothy, jet black, and sharp-edged—surely sharp enough to cut through the skin of an incautious mammoth's foot or trunk. He trumpeted a warning.

Now they left the hills behind and the valley flattened out into a wide plain. There was more rock here, he saw: dark fragments scattered across the plain, half buried by the ice. Here and there the fragments were piled up in low unstable heaps. It was as if some giant creature had burst from the land itself, scattering these lumps of rock far and wide.

Now the plain of broken rocks gave way to a broader area, smooth flat ice largely free of the rock lumps. Longtusk guessed they were approaching a frozen lake; rock lumps that fell here must have sunk to the bottom of the water and were now hidden beneath the ice layers.

Cautiously they skirted the lake, sticking to the shore.

But the land here was no longer flat. It was broken by vast bowls, like immense footprints—not of ice, Longtusk realized, but carved out of the rock itself, and coated by thin layers of ice and snow. The mammoths were forced to wend their way carefully between these craters, calling to each other when they were out of sight of one another.

Longtusk wondered what savage force had managed to punch these great wounds in the ground. This was, he thought, a strange place indeed, shaped by forces he couldn't even guess at.

At last he came to a place where the ground was bare of snow and ice. He walked forward warily.

The ground was *warm.*

He walked over a gummy brown-gray mud that clung to his footpads; here and there it was streaked orange, yellow, black. The mud was littered with shallow pools of water and rivulets which ran over sticky layers of gray scum. Where snow lay on the ground, he could see how it was melting into the hot pools and streams, folding over in huge complex swathes.

In places the water was so hot it actually boiled, the steam stained a muddy gray by particles of dirt, and there was a sour, claustrophobic stink of sulfur. The steam, curling into the air, formed towers of billows and swirls, pointlessly beautiful. In fact it rose so high it blocked out the sun, like a cloud that reached from the ground to the air, and Longtusk shivered in the cold, reduced light.

He found a place some way from the steaming, active areas. He tasted the water. It was hot—not unpleasantly so—and it tasted sour, acidic. He spat it out.

Nearby was a place where it wasn't water that boiled but mud, gray-brown and thick. The mud had built itself a chimney, thick-walled, that rose halfway to his belly like some monstrous trunk. The steam here was laced with dark gray dust that plastered itself over the walls of the fumarole. The water had bubbled with a high rushing noise, but the slurping mud made a deeper growling sound, like the agitated rumbling of old Bull mammoths arguing over some obscure point of pride.

. . . And there was life here.

Lichen and moss clung to the bare rock, and grass, brown and flattened, struggled to survive in swathes over ground streaked yellow by sulfur. The plants were coated with layers of ice—frosted out of the steaming, moisture-laden air—as if the plants themselves were made of ice crystals.

Curiously he reached down and plucked some of the frozen scrub. The ice crumbled away, revealing thin, brittle plant material within; he crushed it with his trunk until it was soft enough to cram into his mouth. It was thin on his tongue, but nourishing.

His heart pulsed with hope and vindication. It was a harsh, unnatural place, he thought, a place of steamy claustrophobic heat and rushing noise in the middle of the stillness of this perpetual winter—*but this was the nunatak,* just as Thunder's legend had promised. He trumpeted in triumph—

But somebody was calling.

Rockheart had fallen. The Cows had clustered around him, while Threetusk and Willow stood to one side, awkward, distressed.

Longtusk hurried down the slope.

Rockheart had slumped to his knees, and his trunk drooped on the muddy ground. His breath was a rattle.

"Rockheart! What happened? Why did you fall?"

His rumbled reply was as soft as a calf's mewling. "We made it, milk-tusk, didn't we? By Kilukpuk's dugs, you were right . . ."

And Longtusk saw it. Rockheart—understanding that Longtusk would need his experience, knowing he was too weak for the trip—had come anyway, burning up the last of his energy. He had driven the others on until they had reached this island of rocky safety.

And now he could rest at last.

Convulsed by guilt, Longtusk picked up Rockheart's trunk. "Rockheart! You mustn't—not *now*—"

But it was too late. Rockheart's last breath bubbled out of his lungs, and he slumped to the warm rock, lifeless.

Longtusk trumpeted his grief, and his voice echoed from the rocky walls of the nunatak.

4

The Nunatak

It was a fine bright spring morning, one of the first after the long winter. The nunatak was a bowl of black rock and green life under a blue-white sky.

Everywhere mammoths grazed.

Longtusk was working on his favorite patch of willow, which grew in the lee of a pile of sharp-edged volcanic boulders. The adults knew he favored this spot, and left the miniature forest for him.

But the calves were another matter.

The calf called Saxifrage was playing with her mother, Horsetail, Longtusk's niece. Horsetail lay on her side, her trunk flopping, while Saxifrage tried to clamber onto her flank, pulling herself up by grasping the long furs of her mother's belly.

When she spotted Longtusk, Saxifrage gave up her game, jumped off and approached the old tusker.

But her attention was distracted by a length of broken tusk, snapped off by some young male in an over-vigorous fight. Perhaps she had never come across such a thing before. She picked it up and began to inspect it. She grabbed it with her trunk, turned it over, and rubbed it against the underside of her trunk, making a rasping sound against the rough skin there. She put it in her mouth, chewed it carefully, and turned it over with her tongue. Then she threw it in the air and let it fall to the ground several times, listening intently to the way it rattled on the ground. At last she walked over it and touched it delicately with the tender soles of her hind feet.

Longtusk was entranced.

He couldn't help contrast the calf's deep physical exploration of the unfamiliar object with the way a Firehead cub would study something new—just *looking* at it. For a mammoth calf, the look of something was only the most superficial aspect of it: the beginning of getting to know the object, not the end.

Longtusk rumbled softly. Even after so long in the nunatak, such behaviors still charmed and fascinated him. He'd spent too much of his life away from his own kind, he thought sadly, and that had left scars on his soul that would never, surely, be healed. He wondered if there was anything more important in the world than to watch a new-born calf with her mother, lapping at a stream with her tongue, too young even to know how to use her trunk to suck up water . . .

Now Saxifrage recalled he was there. She abandoned the tusk fragment and ran to him, dashing under his belly.

He tried to turn, but his legs were stiff as tree-trunks nowadays, his great tusks so heavy they made his head droop if he wasn't careful; and in his rheumy vision the calf was just a blur of orange-brown fur, running around his feet and under his grizzled belly hair.

As the calf made another pass he looped down his trunk, grabbed her around the waist and lifted her high in the air, ignoring the protests from his neck muscles.

She trumpeted her delight, a thin noise just at the edge of his hearing.

He set her down before him once more, and she stepped through the forest of his curling tusks. Her calf fur was orange, bright against his own guard hairs, blackened and gray with age.

She said, "Longtusk, I'm going to be your mate."

He snorted. "I'd be impressed if I hadn't heard you say the same thing to that old buffer Threetusk yesterday."

"I didn't! Anyway I didn't mean it. Why do they call him Threetusk? He only has two tusks, a big one and that spindly little one."

"Well, that's a long story," said Longtusk. "You see, long ago—long before you were born, even before Three-tusk became the leader of the bachelor herd, in fact—he got in an argument with one of his sons, called Bark-trunk—"

"Why was he called that?"

"It doesn't matter."

"Where is Barktrunk? I never met him."

"Well, he died. That was before you were born too. But *that's* another story. You see, the first time Barktrunk came into musth—"

"What does musth mean?"

Longtusk growled. "Ask your mother. Now, where was I? Barktrunk. Now Barktrunk did some digging—just over there, where those rocks are piled up—and he found a new spring of water, and he said we should all drink it at once. He wanted to show us how important and clever he was, you see. Especially the Cows."

"Why the Cows?"

"Ask your mother! Anyway—what was I saying?—yes, the water. But Threetusk, his father, came over and tasted a little of the water, just on the tip of his trunk, and he said no, this water has too much sulfur. He said so to everybody, right in front of Barktrunk."

"I bet Barktrunk didn't like *that*."

"He didn't. And they got into a fight. Now in those days Threetusk was big and strong, not the broken-down grass-sucking old wreck he is *now*, and you can tell him I said so. It should have been easy for Threetusk to win. But there was an accident. Barktrunk came at him like this"—he feinted stiffly—"but Threetusk dodged, and knocked his head like *this*"—a deft sideways swipe, but slower than a glacier, he thought sourly—"and that was when it happened. Threetusk got one of his tusks stuck in a cleft in the rock. Just over there. When he was trying to get free the tusk broke off. Maybe that was one of the bits of it you were playing with just now. And then—"

But Saxifrage was running around in circles, trying to catch her own tail. Longtusk rumbled softly; he had lost his audience again.

"You listen to Longtusk," said Horsetail, Saxifrage's mother, who had come lumbering up. Named for the long graceful hairs that streamed across her rump, this daughter of Splayfoot was the Matriarch now—she had been since Splayfoot's death, some years ago, when his sister's proud heart, strained by her dismal experiences, had at last failed her. Horsetail pulled her calf under her belly fur, where Saxifrage began to hunt for a nipple. "I'm sorry, Patriarch," she said respectfully. "Everybody knows you need time to work on those willow leaves these days."

"Not that much time," he growled. "And I do wish—"

"Try not to bite, Saxifrage!"

I do wish *you'd* listen to me, he thought.

But, thinking back, he was sure *he* had ignored almost

all of what everybody had had to say to him, back when he was a calf—even Walks With Thunder, probably.

Remarkable to think that the last time he saw him, Thunder had actually been younger than Longtusk was now. How on Earth had he got so old? Where had the years gone? And . . .

And he was maundering again, and now the calf was nipping at his toes.

Saxifrage said, "Longtusk is going to mate with me when I'm old enough."

Horsetail rumbled her embarrassment, flapping her small ears.

Longtusk said, "I'm flattered, Saxifrage. But you'll have to find someone closer to your own age, that's all."

"Why? Mother says you're a great hero and will go on forever, like the rocks of the nunatak."

Again Horsetail harrumphed her embarrassment.

"Your mother's right about most of that," said Longtusk wryly. "But—not forever. Look." He kneeled down before the calf, ignoring warning stabs of pain from his knees, and opened his mouth. "What's in here?"

Saxifrage probed with her trunk at his teeth and huge black tongue. "Grass. A bit of old twig stick under your tongue—"

"My teeth, calf," he growled. "Feel my teeth."

She reached in, and he felt the soft tip of her trunk run over the upper surfaces of his long lower teeth.

He said, "Can you feel how worn they are? That's because of all the grass and herbs and twigs I've eaten."

"Everybody's teeth get worn down," said Saxifrage, wrinkling her trunk. "You just grow more. My mother says—"

"But," said Longtusk heavily, "I've gotten so old I

don't have more teeth to grow. This is my last set. Soon they will be too worn to eat with. And then . . ."

The calf looked confused and distressed. He reached out and stroked the topknot of her scalp with his trunk.

She said, "Will you at least *try* to keep from dying until I'm big enough? I wouldn't have thought *that* was too much to ask."

Longtusk eyed Horsetail; that was one of her favorite admonitions, he knew. "All right," he said. "I'll try. Just for you."

"Now come on," said Horsetail, tugging at her calf's trunk. "Time for a drink. And you really mustn't bother the Patriarch so much."

"I told you," he said. "She wasn't bothering me. And don't call me Patriarch. I'm just an old fool of a Bull. That Patriarch business was long ago . . ."

But Horsetail was leading her calf to a stream which bubbled from the rocks; a group of mammoths was already clustered there, their loosening winter coats rising in a cloud around them. "Whatever you say, Patriarch."

Longtusk growled.

Now there was a tug at his belly furs. He turned, wondering which calf was troubling his repose now.

It was the old Dreamer, Willow. Standing there in his much-patched skins, with grass crudely stuffed into his coat and hat, Willow was aged, bent almost double, his small face a mass of wrinkles. But, with a gnarled paw, he still stroked Longtusk's trunk, just as he had when they'd first met as calf and cub.

And Longtusk knew what he wanted.

Longtusk turned slowly, sniffing the air. After all these years he had learned to disregard the pervading stink of sulfur which polluted the air around this nunatak. There was little wind, and though there was a frosty sharpness to the air, there was no sign that the weather was set to change.

All in all, it was a fine day for their annual trek.

Rumbling softly, with Willow limping at his side, Longtusk set off.

Longtusk climbed a shallow rise, away from the glen where the mammoths fed. At first he walked on soil or rock, but soon his feet were pressing down on ice and loose snow.

The going got harder, the slope steepening.

At first Willow was able to keep up, limping alongside the mammoth with one paw wrapped in Longtusk's belly hair. But soon his wheezing exhaustion was obvious.

They paused for breath. Longtusk turned, looking back over the nunatak and the life sheltered there.

From afar, the mammoths were a slow drift of dark points over a field of tan grasses. Occasionally the long guard hairs of a mature Bull would catch the light, glimmering brightly. Their movements were slow, calm, dense, their attitudes full of attention. They were massive, contemplative, wise: beautiful, he thought, wonderful beautiful animals.

The nunatak was everything he could have hoped for, that fateful day when he took his leave of his own Family. But still—

But still, how brief life had been. Like a dream, or the blossoming of a spring flower on the steppe—a splash of color, a burst of hope, and then . . .

Willow stroked his trunk absently, bringing him back.

He'd been maundering again. Morbid old fool.

With considerable effort on both their parts, Willow managed to clamber onto his back. Longtusk couldn't help but recall the liquid grace with which Crocus, the Firehead cub, had once flowed onto his back, how they had run and pranced together.

With a deep rumble he turned away and headed up the cold, forbidding slope. His breath steamed, and his aging limbs tired quickly.

The old Dreamer was already snoring gently.

Soon Longtusk neared the crest of a ridge. The snow thinned out, and he found himself walking on rock that was bare or covered only by a scattering of snow. The land flattened out, and he stood atop the ridge, breathing hard.

He was standing on the rim of a crater.

He stepped forward cautiously. It was a great bowl, cut into the Earth, like the imprint of an immense foot. The rim curved around the huge dip in the land to close on itself, a neat circle.

The crater wall, coated with snow and ice, was sculpted to smoothness by the wind, like the sweep of a giant sand dune. The shadows were subtle and soft, white shading to blue-gray—save at the rim itself, where a layer of bare brown rock was exposed. The winds off the ice sheet kept this curving ridge swept clear of new snow falls, so that ice could not form. He let his eye be drawn to the crater's far side, where there had been an avalanche, and the smooth snow surface was marked by great ripples descending toward the crater's base.

The floor of the crater was surprisingly flat. He knew there was a lake down there. In the brief summer it would melt, turning into a placid pond of blue-gray water, cupped by the crater, visited by birds—in fact, the geese who had guided him here to the nunatak. If a mammoth were down there now, walking across that frozen surface, she would look no larger than a grain of sand, dwarfed by this immense structure of rock and ice.

Longtusk raised his trunk and trumpeted, high and thin. His voice echoed from the iced-over walls of the crater, and pealed out over the frozen lands around the nunatak.

Willow stirred on his back, grumbling, and subsided back to sleep, clinging to Longtusk's fur instinctively.

Longtusk walked a little farther around the crater's rim. He came to a broad ridge in the icebound land, leading away from the crater. He walked this way now, feeling for the firm places in the piled-up snow.

Soon he saw what he was looking for. It was a splash of coal-black darkness, vivid against the snow that surrounded it. This was another crater, but little more than ten or fifteen paces wide. And further craters lay beyond, dark splashes on the snow, as if some wounded, rocky giant had limped this way.

He let himself slide over crunching rubble into the small crater. The rock was warm under his thick footpads. Where snow fell from his coat it melted quickly, and steam wisped up around him. The rock here was fragmented, crumbled. It was jet black, sharp-edged, and the fragments he picked up had tiny bubbles blown into them, like the bones of a mammoth's skull.

This crater did not have a neat rounded form, no cupped lake in its base. The walls here were just crude piles of frothy black rock. In places he could see flat plates of rock which lay over drained hollows, like the remnants of broken eggs. Everything was sharp-edged, new. This small crater was obviously much younger than its giant cousin nearby. Perhaps these small frothy rocks, frozen fragments of the Earth's chthonic blood, were the youngest rocks in the world.

And yet even in this new raw place, there was life.

He picked up a loose rock. He tasted moss and green lichen, struggling to inhabit this unpromising lump: sparse, nothing but dark green flecks that clung to the porous stuff—but it was here. And these first colonists would break up the hard cooling rock, making a sand in which plants could grow. Perhaps one day this would be a bowl of greenery within which mammoths and other animals could survive.

He came up here once a year—but always with Willow as his sole companion. Mammoths are creatures of the plains, and the members of his little Clan were suspicious of this place of hills and ice. And there wasn't a great deal to eat up here. But Longtusk embraced the stark, silent beauty of this place.

For he knew that these craters were a sign of Earth's bounty—the gift that had created this island of life and safety, here at the heart of the forbidding icecap.

One night—many years ago—the mammoths had seen, on the fringe of their nunatak, a great gush of smoke and fire which had towered up to the clouds. The mammoths had been terrified— all but Longtusk, who had been fascinated. For at last he understood.

Over most of the world, the heat which drove life came from the sun. But here, far to the planet's north, that heat was insufficient. Even water froze here, making the icecaps that stifled the land.

Instead, here in the nunatak, the heat came from the Earth itself.

In some places it dribbled slowly from the ground, in boiling springs and mud pools. And in some places the heat gathered until it burst through the Earth's skin like a gorged parasite.

That was the meaning of the great eruption of fire and smoke they had seen. That was why the land was littered by enormous blocks of black rock, hurled there by explosions.

And the craters—even the biggest of them—were surely the wounds left in the Earth by those giant explosions, like scars left by burst blisters. In this small crater he could actually see where smaller bubbles had formed and partially collapsed, leaving a hard skin over voids drained of rock that had been so hot it had flowed like water.

It was the Earth's heat which had shaped this strange landscape, and it was the Earth's heat which cradled and sustained the nunatak.

He left the small craters behind and began a short climb to another summit.

Soon he was breathing hard. But he'd been climbing up here every spring since they'd first arrived, and he was determined that *this* would not be the year he was finally defeated.

He reached the summit. This rocky height, windswept bare of ice like the crater rim, was one of the highest points in the nunatak, so high it seemed he could see the curve of the Earth itself.

All around the nunatak was ice.

The icecap was a broad, vast dome of blue-white, blanketing the land. The ice was smooth and empty, as if inviting a footstep. Nothing moved there, no animals or plants lived, and he was suspended in utter silence, broken not even by the cry of a bird.

Mountains protruded from the ice sheet like buried creatures straining to emerge, their profiles softened by the overlying snow. The mountains—a chain of which this nunatak was a member—were brown and black, startling and stark against the white of the ice. Their shadows, pooled at their bases, glowed blue-white.

Over the years Longtusk had come to know the ice and its changing moods. He had learned that it was not without texture; it was rich with a chill, minimal beauty. There were low dunes and ridges, carved criss-cross by the wind, so that the ice was a complex carpet of blue-white traceries, full of irrelevant beauty. In places it had slumped into dips in the crushed land beneath, and there were ridges, long and straight, that caught the low light so that they shone a bright yellow, vivid against ice. Here and there he could see spindrift, clouds of ice crystals whipped up by the wind and hovering above the ground, enchantingly beautiful.

The ice was a calm flat sea of light, white and blue and yellow, that led his gaze to the horizon. The ice had a beauty and softness that belied its lethal nature, he knew; for nothing lived there, nothing outside the favored nunatak.

But much had changed in the years—by Kilukpuk's dugs, it had been forty years or more—that he had been climbing this peak.

To the west he looked back the way they had come on their epic trek, so long ago: back across the fragile neck of land that connected the two landmasses. On the land bridge's northern side there was a vast, glimmering expanse of water, dark against the ice. It was where he recalled the ice-dammed lake had been.

But that lake had grown immeasurably—it was so large now it must have become an inlet of the great northern ocean itself.

Ice was melting into the oceans and the sea level was rising, as if the whole ocean were no more than a steppe pond, brimming with spring water. And the ocean was, little by little, flooding the land.

Meanwhile, on the southern horizon, there was brown and green against the ice white: a tide of warmth and life that had approached relentlessly, year by year. The exposed land formed a broad dark corridor that led off to the south—and into the new land, the huge, unknown continent that lay there—a passageway between two giant, shrinking ice sheets.

The world was remaking itself—the land reborn from the ice, the sea covering the land—all in his lifetime. It was a huge, remarkable process, stunning in scale.

And he knew that the changes he saw around him would one day have great significance for his little Clan.

He had long stepped back from his role as Patriarch. There had never before been a Patriarch in all the Cycle's long history, and he had never believed there should be one for longer than strictly necessary.

So he was no longer a leader of the Clan. Still, he had traveled farther and seen more than any of the mammoths here on the nunatak.

And he knew that this nunatak would not always remain a refuge.

Sometimes he wished he had someone to discuss all this with. Somebody like Rockheart, or Walks With Thunder—even Jaw Like Rock.

But they were all gone, long gone. And Longtusk, always the outsider, now isolated by age, was forced to rely on nothing but his own experience and wisdom.

. . . Willow, on his back, was growing agitated. He was muttering something in his incomprehensible, guttural tongue. He leaned forward, over Longtusk's scalp, and pointed far to the west.

Longtusk raised his trunk, but could smell nothing on

the dry air but the cold prickle of ice. He squinted, feeling the wrinkles gather around his eye sockets.

On the far horizon, he saw something new.

It was a line scratched across the ice. It ended in a complex knot, dark and massive yet dwarfed by the icecap. And a thin thread rose up from that knot of activity, straight and true.

It was too far away to smell. But it was unmistakable. *It was smoke:* smoke from a fire. And the line that cut across the ice was a trail, arrowing directly toward the nunatak.

On his back, Willow was whimpering his alarm—as well he might, Longtusk thought.

For the signs were unmistakable. After all these years, the Fireheads were coming.

As the sun sank deeper in the sky, the light on the ice grew softer, low and diffuse. Blue-gray shadows pooled in hollows, like a liquid gathering. It was stunning, beautiful. But Longtusk knew that this year he could not stay to see the sunset.

The nunatak's long dream of peace was, so quickly, coming to an end.

He turned and, with elaborate care, began his descent from the summit.

"We have no choice but to abandon the nunatak." He looked down at the Family—the fat, complacent Cows, their playful calves, all gazing up at him, trunks raised to sniff his mood. "We have been safe here. The nunatak has served us well. But now it is a refuge no more. And we must go."

"You're being ridiculous," Horsetail said severely. "You're frightening the calves."

"They should be frightened," he said. "They are in

danger. Mortal danger. The Fireheads are on the western horizon. I could see their trail, and their fire. They will overrun this place, enslave you, ultimately kill you. And your calves." He eyed them. "Do you understand? Do you understand any of this?"

The Cows rumbled questions. "Where should we go?" "There is nowhere else!" "Who is *he* to say what Cows should do? He is a Bull. And he's *old*. Why, if I—"

He had expected arguments, and he got them. It was just as it had been when he had argued with Milkbreath, his own mother, trying to convince her that the flight in search of the nunatak was necessary.

He was too old for this.

One more effort, Longtusk. Then you can rest. Think of Rockheart. *He* had kept going, despite the failure of his huge body. He pulled his shoulders square and lifted his tusks, still large and sweeping, so heavy they made his neck muscles pull.

Horsetail, the Matriarch, said sadly, "I'm trying to understand, Longtusk. I truly am. But you must help me. *How* can they come here? We are protected by the ice."

"But the ice is receding."

"Where would we flee?"

"You must go south and east. At first you will cross the ice"—a rumbling of fear and discontent—"just as your grandmothers did. Just as *I* did. But then you will reach a corridor. A passage through the ice sheets, to the warmer lands beyond, that has opened up in the years we have lived here. It won't be easy—"

"But Longtusk, *why*? Why would the Fireheads come here? On this rock, we are few. Even if these Fireheads are the savage predators you describe, why would they go to such efforts, risk their own lives, just to reach *us*?"

Now Threetusk, dominant Bull of the bachelor herd, loped toward Longtusk. He said grimly, "Perhaps the Fireheads come because there is no room for them in the old lands. Perhaps they are seeking mammoths here because there are none left where they come from."

There was a general bray of horror.

"Or perhaps," Longtusk said sadly, *"it is me."*

Horsetail rumbled, "What do you mean?"

"I defied her," he said, unwelcome old memories swimming to the surface of his mind.

"Who?"

"The most powerful Firehead of them all. She thought I was hers, you see. And yet I defied her . . ."

He knew it was hard for them to understand. All this was ancient history to the other mammoths, an exotic legend of times and places and creatures they had never known—maybe just another of Longtusk's tall stories, like his tales of she-cats and rhinos and Fireheads with caps of mammoth-ivory beads . . .

It was not their fault. He had wanted to bring his Clan to a safe place, and these generations of fat, complacent mammoths were what he had dreamed of seeing. It wasn't *their* fault that he had succeeded too well—that their lives of comfort and security had prepared them so badly for the ordeal ahead.

But he recalled Crocus.

He recalled how she had hunted down the Firehead who had killed her father. He knew she would not have forgotten, or forgiven.

As long as he was alive, nobody was safe here.

Horsetail and Threetusk approached him and spoke quietly so the others couldn't hear.

Horsetail said, "You aren't the only one who has seen the corridor to the south. But it is harsh, and we don't know how long it is, or what lies at its end. Perhaps it is cold and barren all the way to the South Pole."

"When we set off for the nunatak," he said evenly, "we didn't know how far that was either. We went anyway. *You* know, Threetusk—you're the only one left who does. You will have to show them how to survive."

Horsetail said severely, "We have old, and sickly, and calves. Many of us will not survive such a trek."

"Nevertheless it must be made."

"And you?" asked the Matriarch. "Do you believe *you* could walk through the corridor?"

"Of course not." He brayed his amusement. "I probably wouldn't last a day. But I'm not going."

Threetusk said, "What?"

Briefly, briskly, he stroked their trunks. "I know the Fireheads. You don't. And I have thought deeply on their nature. And this is what I have concluded. Listen closely, now . . ."

Saxifrage watched this, fascinated, the rumbling phrases washing over her.

Later, boldly, she stepped forward from under her mother's belly and tugged her trunk. "What did he say? What did he say?"

But Horsetail, grave and silent, would not reply.

They filed past him, down the sloping rock face and onto the ice, bundles of confusion, fear and resentment— much of it directed at *him*, for even though the smoke columns from the Fireheads' hearths were now visible for all to see, they still found it impossible to believe they represented the danger he insisted.

Nonetheless, they were his Clan. He wanted to grab them all, taste each one with his trunk. For he knew he would not see them again, not a single one of them.

But he held himself back. It was best they did not think of him, for the ice and the dismal corridor to the south would give them more than enough to occupy their minds.

And besides, he still had company: the little Dreamer, Willow. He had tried to push the Dreamer, gently, off the rock and after the column of mammoths. But Willow had slapped his trunk and dug his old, bent fingers in Longtusk's fur, his intentions clear.

Company, then. And a job to complete.

Longtusk waited until the long column of mammoths had shrunk to a fine scratch against the huge white expanse of the ice.

And then he turned away: toward the west, and the Fireheads.

5

The Corridor

It was, Threetusk decided later, an epic to match any in the long history of the mammoths.

But it was a story he could never bear to tell: a story of suffering and loss and endless endurance, a blurred time he recalled only with pain.

It was difficult even from the beginning. Away from the warmth of the nunatak, the hard, ridged ice was cold and unyielding under their feet—crueler even than he recalled from the original trek so long ago. Where snow drifted the going was even harder.

The land itself was unsettling. The mammoths could hear the deep groaning of the ice as it flowed down from its highest points to the low land and the sea. A human would have heard only the occasional crack and grind, perhaps felt a deep shudder. To the mammoths, the agonized roar of the ice was loud and continuous, a constant reminder that this was an unstable land, a place of change and danger.

And—of course—there was nothing to eat or drink, here on the ice. They had barely traveled half a day before they had used up the reserves of water they carried in their throats, and the calves were crying for the warm rocks they had left behind.

But they kept on.

After a day and a night, they came to a high point, and they were able to see the way south.

To the left the ice was a shallow dome, its surface bright and seductively smooth. To the right, the ice lay thick over a mountain range. Black jagged peaks thrust out of the white, defiant, and glaciers striped with dirt reached down to the ice sheet like the trunks of immense embedded animals.

And the two great ice sheets were separated by a narrow band of land—colorless, barren, a stripe of lifeless gray cutting through blue-white.

It was the corridor.

They found a glacier, a tongue of ice that led them down from the icecap to the barren strip of land. The climb down the glacier was more difficult than Threetusk had imagined—especially when they got to the lower slopes, and the glacier, spilling onto the rock, spread out and cracked, forming immense crevasses that blocked their path.

Nevertheless they persisted, until they reached the land itself.

Horsetail stood by Threetusk, frost on her face, her breath billowing in a cloud around her. They gazed south at the corridor that faced them.

They stood on bare rock, sprinkled with a little loose stone, gravel and rock. There were deep furrows gouged into the land, as if by huge claws. Here and there, against the ice cliffs that bounded the corridor, there were pools of trapped meltwater, glimmering. Little grew here: only scattered clumps of yellow grass, a single low willow, clutching the ground.

A wind blew in their faces, raising dust devils that whirled and spat hard gray sand into their eyes. Saxifrage, the calf, plucked at a spindly grass blade without enthusiasm, bleating her discomfort.

Threetusk said, "It's as if the land has been scraped bare of everything—even the soil—down to the bedrock. There may be water, but little to eat."

"The calves are probably too fat, as Longtusk always says," Horsetail said briskly. "We'll let them rest a night. There is some shelter, here in the lee of the glacier. Then, in the morning—"

"We go on."

"Yes."

Longtusk had a single intention: not to allow the Fireheads to complete their journey, in pursuit of his mammoths, across the land bridge. And he believed he knew how to do it, where he must go to achieve it.

With Willow on his back snoring softly, Longtusk, with stiff arthritic limbs, picked his cautious way down off the nunatak rocks. He took a final, regretful step off the warmth of the black rock, and let his footpads settle on hard ice.

It would begin as a retracing of the great trek which had brought him here.

. . . But everything was different now.

The ice was, in places, slick with a thin layer of liquid water, making it slippery and treacherous, so that he had to choose his steps with care. And there seemed to have been a fresh frost overnight; ice crystals sparkled like tiny eyes on the blue surface of the hard older ice.

The nunatak receded behind him, becoming a hard black cone of rock, diminishing. It was as if he was leaving behind his life: his ambiguous position in the small society of the Clan, his prickly relationships with Threetusk, Horsetail and the others, the endless complexity of love and birth and death. Not for much longer would he have to carry around his heavy load of pain and loss and memory.

His life had reduced, at last, to its essence.

Soon—much sooner than he had expected—he found himself clambering down a snub of ice and onto bare rock.

He walked cautiously over rock that had been chiseled and scoured by the retreating ice. Beyond the edge of the cap itself the ice still clung in patches. But it was obvious that the ice's shrinking had proceeded apace.

He found a run-off stream. It bubbled over shallow mud, cloudy with rock flour. He walked into the brook. It barely lapped over his toes. He drank trunkfuls of the chill, sterile meltwater; it filled his belly and throat.

The water had cut miniature valleys in the flat surface of the mud. The gouges cut across each other, their muddy walls eroded away, so that the incised mud was braided with shallow clefts. Here and there a patch of ground stuck out of the stream, perhaps sheltered by a lump of rock. These tiny islands were shaped like teardrops, their walls eroded by the continuing flow, and grasses, thin and yellow, clung to their surfaces. Longtusk found himself intrigued by the unexpected complexity of this scrap of landscape. Like so much of the world, it was intricate, beautiful—but meaningless, for there were no eyes but his to see it.

He moved on. His feet left shallow craters in the mud; downstream of where he had stood the water, bubbling, began to carve a new pattern of channels.

Soon he reached a new kind of landscape. It was an open forest, with evergreen trees growing in isolated clumps, and swathes of grass in between.

He let down Willow. With brisk efficiency, the Dreamer built and set simple traps of sharpened sticks and sinew.

One of the traps quickly yielded a small rabbit. The Dreamer skinned it, cooked it over a small fire, ate it with every expression of enjoyment—and then, in the warmth of the afternoon, he lay down and began to snore loudly.

Longtusk explored.

The trees were spruce, fir and pines, growing healthy, straight and tall. Farther to the south he saw hardwoods, oak and elm and ash. There was sagebrush abundant in the grassy patches between the trees. The air was too warm for Longtusk and he sought out snow and loose ice to chew and swallow and rub into his fur; the melting snow in his belly cooled him, and bits of ice trapped in his fur evaporated slowly, acting like sweat.

It was not long before he detected the thin scent of water: a great body of it, not much farther to the west. Birds wheeled overhead, some of them gulls. And that water smell was tinged with the sharpness of salt.

It was the meltwater lake he had seen from the nunatak's summit: still dammed by its plug of ice, now joined to the ocean, grown immeasurably since he had passed by on his original trek to the nunatak. And it was his destination.

He walked back into the forest, through the shade of the young, proud trees. He saw spoor, of horses and bison and other animals. Perhaps the warmth, and the abundance of life here, had something to do with the nearness of that body of water.

But it was no place for mammoths, and the other creatures of the steppe. He felt a huge sadness, for a world was evaporating.

After a night's rest, they moved on.

The Clan walked between divergent walls of ice.

The twin icecaps were lines of white on the horizon.

Sometimes they were too far away to see—but they could always be heard, groaning as if in pain at their endless collapse and crumbling.

The wind gathered strength, always coming from the south, howling in their faces, as if daring them to progress. Even if it was the ice that had made this place barren, it was the wind that kept it so; any soil which formed was whipped away in a cloud of dust, and only the hardiest plants could find root and cling to the rock.

The ground changed constantly. Where soil and dirt collected in hollows, protected from the wind, the surface was boggy and clinging. At times they had to cross islands of ice, left behind by the retreating icecaps and yet to melt. Worse, there were stretches of stagnant ice covered over by a thin crust of detritus, a crust which could conceal pits and crevasses where the underlying ice had melted and drained away.

The going became harder still.

Now they seemed to be descending a shallow slope, as if the whole land inclined to the south. The rock was cut through by valleys—some no more than narrow gullies, and some respectably large channels. Sometimes there were torrents of water, gushing down one valley or another, often carving a new course altogether. Threetusk didn't understand where these sudden floods came from; perhaps some dam of ice had burst, or a river valley's wall had been breached.

Where they could, the mammoths followed the broader valleys. But more often than not the valleys cut across their path, and they were forced to spend energy climbing over sharp-crested ridges.

Soon all the mammoths were exhausted, and several were weakening. They had plenty to drink now, but never enough to eat. Still the wind blew, harsh and fierce.

And then the first calf died.

He was a Bull, small and playful, younger than Saxifrage. He simply fell one day, his papery flesh showing the bones beneath, his eyes round and terrified.

"I have no milk!" his mother wailed. "It's my fault. I have no milk to give him . . ."

"We have to leave him," Threetusk said grimly to the Matriarch.

"I know," said Horsetail. "But after this it will be harder to keep them together. Already the Cows with small calves want to strike out alone, to find pasture they don't need to share with the others."

"That's natural. It's what mothers do."

"We must wait until the calf dies," she said. "His mother needs to Remember him. And then we go on."

"Yes."

After that, more deaths followed: calves, the old, and one mature Bull whose leg was crushed in a fall.

Each day the sun climbed lower in the sky. Threetusk knew the summer was ending, and if they couldn't feed and water in preparation for the cold to come, winter would kill them all as surely as any Firehead would.

And still the mammoths walked on into the teeth of the unrelenting wind, leaving a trail of their dead on the unmarked land.

The land began to rise—gently at first, then more steeply. The grass-covered soil grew thin, until at last a shoulder of rock protruded, bare and forbidding. Still Longtusk climbed, the air growing colder. He stepped with caution up the steepening slopes, avoiding heaps of sharp, frost-shattered scree.

He recalled this place from the trek. He had reached the range of low, glacier-eroded hills which marked the southern border of the ice-melt lake. And as he climbed, the land opened up around him, and he saw the great ice dam before him, lodged in its cleft in the hillside—still containing its mass of meltwater, after all these years.

To his right, to the north, he saw the lake itself—much bigger than he recalled, a shining sheet of gray-blue water stretching to a perfectly sharp horizon. There was ice scattered on it, floes and slushy melt and even a few eroded-smooth icebergs. But the icecap which had first created this lake was much receded now.

The water lapped at a shallow shore of gravel and bare rock, and he saw birds, coons and ducks, swimming among reeds. There were gulls nesting in the steeper cliffs below him. And he could smell the tang of salt, much more strongly now. The northern ocean, which ran all the way to the pole itself, must have broken in on this lake, turning it into an immense pool of brine, an inlet of the ocean itself.

To his left—to the south of the hills—the land swept away. It was a rough plain, marked here and there by the sky-blue glimmer of pools and the glaring bone-white of old ice. Far away he could see a flowing dark patch, clouded by dust, that might be horses or bison. If he listened closely he could hear the thunder of hooves, feel the heavy stamp of that moving ocean of meat.

But this blanket of life—grown much thicker since the last time he passed here—did not conceal the deeper rocky truth of this landscape. He could see how the land was folded, wrinkled, cut deeply by channels and gorges. Most of these channels were dry, though thin ribbons of water gleamed in some of them. They flowed south, away from the lake-ocean behind him, and in places they cut across each other, braided like tangled hair.

It was a land shaped by running water—just like the muddy rivulet where he had drunk. But no rivulet had made this land, not even a great river; only the mightiest of floods could have shaped this immense panorama.

He turned back and forth, trunk raised, sniffing the air, understanding the land.

He knew what he must do here. And he knew, at last, how he would die.

He set off for the ice dam itself.

". . . Threetusk."

He paused, lifting bleary, wind-scarred eyes. The wind had eased, for the first time in—how long?

He raised his trunk and looked back at the column of mammoths, wearily trudging in his footsteps. They had been walking over a rocky plateau that had been even more barren and unforgiving than the rest of the corridor. Had they lost anyone else since he last counted? But he couldn't even recall the names of those who had fallen . . .

Horsetail was pulling at his trunk. He saw how thin she had become, the bones of her skull pushing through tangled fur.

But she was saying, "Threetusk—*smell.*"

Wearily he raised his trunk and sniffed the air.

There was water, and grass, and the dung of many animals.

They blundered forward.

They came to a ridge. He stepped forward cautiously.

The land fell away before him, a steep wall of tumbled rocks. To his left, a waterfall thundered. It was glacier melt: the ghost of snows that might have fallen a Great-Year ago, now surging into the land below.

And that land, he saw, was green.

Pools glimmered in the light of the low sun. He saw clouds of birds over some of the pools, so far away they might have been insects. The land around the pools, laced by gleaming streams, was steppe: coarse grass, herbs, lichen, moss, stunted trees.

And there were animals here, he saw dimly: horses, what looked like camels—and, stalking a stray camel, a pack of what appeared to be giant wolves.

"We made it," he said, wondering. "The end of the corridor. We had to battle through the breath of Kilukpuk herself. But we made it. We have to tell Longtusk—tell him he was right."

Horsetail looked at him sadly. "Where Longtusk has gone, I don't think even a contact rumble would reach him." She sniffed at the ground, probing with her trunk. "We need to find a way down from here . . ."

Threetusk looked back, troubled. The journey had been so hard that it had been some time since he had thought of the defiant old tusker they had left behind.

What *had* become of Longtusk?

6

The Tears of Kilukpuk

Cautiously, Longtusk walked forward onto the ice dam. In places the ice, melting, had formed shallow pools; some of these were crusted over, and more than once a careless step plunged his foot into cold, gritty water.

He reached the center of this wall of ice, where it was thinnest—and weakest.

The ice dam was old.

On its dry southern side its upper surface was gritty and dirty, in places worn to a grayish sheen by years of rain. Its northern side had been hollowed out by lapping water, so that a great lip of ice hung over a long, concave wall. The ice under the lip gleamed white and blue, and more ice, half-melted and refrozen, gushed over the lip to dangle in the air, caught in mid-flow, elaborate icicles glistening.

He could feel the groan of this thinning dam under the weight of the water—a weight that must be rising, inexorably, as the sea level rose, spilling into the lake. The ice dam settled, seeking comfort, like a working mastodont laboring under some bone-cracking load. But there was little comfort to be had.

Instability—yes, he thought; that was the key.

A memory drifted into his mind: how Jaw Like Rock had taken that foolish keeper—what was his name? Spindle?—riding on his back standing up. Jaw had stopped dead, and stood square on the broken ground. Spindle had tried to keep his balance, but without Jaw's assistance he was helpless, and he had fallen.

It had been funny, comical, cruel—and relevant. For the water of the lake was poised high above the lower land, contained only by this fragile dam, just as the keeper's weight had been suspended over Jaw.

Strange, he hadn't thought of old Jaw for years . . .

"*. . . Baitho! Baitho!*"

Fireheads were approaching Longtusk, stepping onto the narrow rim of this worn ice dam. And one was calling to him in a thin, high voice.

On his back Willow hissed, full of hatred and fear.

Longtusk could see them now. There was a knot of Firehead hunters with their thick, well-worked clothing thrown open, exposing naked skin to the warmth of the air. Most of them had held back on the rocky ridge. But two Fireheads were coming forward to meet him, treading carefully over the ice dam, holding each others' paws.

And beyond the Fireheads, snaking back to the west, there was a column of mastodonts. Longtusk could hear the low rumbles of their squat, boulder-like bodies, feel the soft pound of their big broad feet on bare rock.

Ignoring the Fireheads, he sent out a deep contact rumble. "Mastodonts. I am Longtusk."

Replies came as slow pulses of deep sound, washing through the air.

"Longtusk. None here knows you."

"That is true. We are young and strong, and you must be old and weak."

"But we know of you."

The voices were colored by the rich, peculiar accent of the mastodonts, brought with them all the way from the thick forests of their own deep past.

"Walks With Thunder," Longtusk called. "Is he with you?"

"Walks With Thunder has gone to the aurora."

"It was a magnificent Remembering."

"He died well . . ."

He growled, and a little more sadness crowded into his weary heart. But perhaps that was all he could have hoped for, after so long.

"Longtusk. There are legends of your courage and strength, of your mighty tusks. My name is Shoulder Of Bedrock. Perhaps you have heard of my prowess as a warrior. I would welcome sharpening my tusks on yours . . ."

He rumbled, "I regret I have not heard of you, Shoulder of Bedrock, though I have no doubt your fame has spread far. I would welcome a contest with you. But I fear it must wait until we meet in the aurora."

The mastodonts rumbled their disappointment.

"Until the aurora," they called.

"Until the aurora . . ."

The two Fireheads approached him. One wore a coat of thick mammoth hide, to which much black-brown fur still clung, and it—no, he—wore a hat of bone from which smoke curled into the air. And the other, smaller, slighter, wore a coat that gleamed with the blue-white of mammoth ivory.

The male was Smokehat, of course. The Shaman's face was a weather-beaten, wizened mask, etched deep by resentment and hatred. The Shaman's tunic was made of an oddly shaped, almost hairless piece of hide. It had two broad holes, a flap of skin sewn over what looked like the root of a trunk, and its hair had been burned away in patches, exposing skin that was pink and scarred . . .

It was a face, Longtusk realized—the face of a mammoth, pulled off the skull, the trunk cut away and stretched out so that empty eye holes gaped. And not just any face: that swathe of purple-pink hairless scarring was unmistakable. This was a remnant of Pinkface, the Matriarch of Matriarchs.

This one brutal trophy, brandished by Smokehat, told him all he needed to know about the fate of the mammoths in the old land to the west.

And with the Shaman was Crocus, Matriarch of the Fireheads, the only Firehead in all history to ride a woolly mammoth. Her hair blew free in the slight wind—once fiery yellow, now a mass of stringy gray, dry and broken. Longtusk felt a touch of sadness.

There was a sharp pain at his cheek, a gush of warm blood. He looked down in disbelief.

Smokehat's goad, long and bone-tipped, was splashed with Longtusk's blood. The Shaman had slapped him as if he were an unruly calf.

"Baitho!" On your knees . . .

Longtusk reached down with his trunk, plucked the goad from the Shaman's paw, and hurled it far into the dammed lake.

The Shaman was furious. He waved a bony fist in Longtusk's face with impotent anger.

But now a stream of golden fluid arced from over Longtusk's head and neatly landed on the Shaman's bone hat. Smokehat, startled, stood stock still. The burning embers in his hat started to hiss, and thick yellow fluid trickled down his face.

There was a bellow of guttural triumph from Longtusk's back. It was Willow, of course. With surprising skill, he was urinating into the Shaman's hat.

The Shaman, howling with rage, dragged the hat from his head and threw it to the ground. He jumped up and down on it, smashing the bones and scattering the embers. But then he yelped in pain—perhaps he had trodden on a burning coal or a shard of bone—and he fled, limping and yelling, acrid urine trickling over his bare scalp.

Crocus covered her face with her paws, her shoulders shaking. Longtusk recalled this strange behavior. She was laughing.

Now she looked up at him, blue eyes made only a little rheumy by age, startlingly familiar. She reached out and buried her fingers in the long fur dangling from his trunk. She made cooing noises, like a mother bird, and he rumbled his contentment. The years evaporated, and he was a growing calf, she a cub freezing to death in the snow, a vibrant young female riding his back with unprecedented skill.

But her face was a mask of wrinkles, and he saw bitterness etched there: bitterness and disappointment and anger. Her life—the demands of leadership, the hard choices she had had to make—all of it had soured her.

And her coat was grotesque.

He recalled the simple tooth necklace she had worn when he first found her. But now, as if it had grown out of that necklace like some monstrous fungus, her coat, draped down to the ground, was sewn with many thousands of beads. There were strings of them across her forehead and in a great sheet that followed her hair down her back; there were rows and whorls sewn into the panels at front and back; there were more strings that dangled from her forelegs and belly to the ground, like the long hairs of a mammoth.

And every one of the beads was of mammoth ivory.

Within her suit she shone, blue-white like the ice. But Longtusk felt sure that not all the mammoths who had sacrificed their tusks for this monstrosity had gone to the aurora Great-Years before, abandoning their bones to the silt of a river bank. If the Fireheads had ever respected the mammoths, it was long ago. This coat was a thing of excess, not beauty: a symbol of power, not respect.

The Crocus he had known would never have worn such a monstrosity. Perhaps the girl he had known had died at the moment her father fell to the Whiteskins' arrow, all those years ago. Perhaps what had lived on was another creature: the body alive, the spirit flown to the aurora.

Now she dug beneath her coat and pulled out a double loop of thick plaited rope. She held it toward him, cooing.

It was a hobble.

It was a hated thing, a symbol of his long submission, and he realized he had been right: she had pursued the mammoths over such immense distances so that she could regain her dominance over him.

He lifted his tusks and roared, and his voice echoed from the curving dam of ice.

Crocus looked up at him, her eyes hardening. Perhaps she intended to call her hunters to put him down, to end once and for all the life of this unruly mammoth.

But it didn't matter. For she didn't know, couldn't know, that his life was already over.

He stamped his foot. The ice cracked.

The surface of the ice immediately crumbled, cracking in great sheets around them. He felt himself fall, his legs sinking into deeper loose material beneath.

Willow tumbled off his back and landed in the soft ice.

Crocus fell to her knees, her heavy bead suit weighing her down, old and bewildered.

Longtusk shook himself free of the loose ice and continued to stamp, here at the dam's narrowest and weakest point.

Compared to the forces here—the weight of water, the power of this huge ice dam—even the strength of a powerful Bull mammoth was as nothing, of course. But what was important was how he applied that strength—for, like Spindle riding the back of Jaw Like Rock, the ice dam was unstable, overloaded by the brimming lake.

And he heard the dam groan.

Worn thin by years of erosion, already under immense pressure from the weight of the water it contained, stress cracks began to spread through its weakening structure, and Longtusk, in the deep senses of his bones, felt the rhythm of those cracks, and changed his stamping to speed their propagation.

There were ripples on the lake. Birds were taking to the air, alarmed.

And on the other side, water began to gush out of the dam's dirty, eroded face—just a fine spray at first, noisy rather than voluminous; but soon the cracks from which it emerged were widening, the water flow increasing.

Willow got to his feet, and he reached out with a hairy paw to help Crocus. Crocus hesitated, then took it in her own paw. Then the two of them grabbed onto Longtusk's belly fur.

And so the three of them were locked together, Longtusk realized—Longtusk, Willow and Crocus; mammoth, Dreamer and Firehead—locked together at the end of their lives, just as had once been foreseen by a Dreamer female, long, long ago.

He wondered if they understood what he had done.

The center of the dam collapsed.

Huge slabs and boulders of ice arced into the air, followed by a powerful torrent of water. Suddenly the air was filled with noise: the roar of the water, the shriek of tortured ice. The dam was high, and the first blocks took a long time to fall to the green land below, fanning out amid a spray of rumbling, frothing, gray-blue water. Longtusk thought he saw a deer there, immense antlers protruding proudly from his head, looking up in utter bewilderment at the strange rain descending on him.

The first ice blocks hit the ground, exploding into fragments and gouging out deep earth-brown craters. But the craters lasted only a heartbeat, for when the waters splashed over the earth the land turned to shapeless mud and washed away.

The deer had vanished. He had been the first to die today. He would not be the last, Longtusk knew.

The dam, once broken, was crumbling quickly. Gray-brown water cut down through the unresisting ice like a stone knife slicing through the flesh of a mammoth. And as the breach widened, so the gush of water extended, deepening and broadening. But its violence did not diminish, for the great mass of water pressed against the dam with an eagerness born of centuries of containment. It shot through the breach horizontally, darkening the land before falling in a shattering rain.

Willow was tugging at Longtusk's fur and pointing back the way they had come, toward the rocky hillside.

The Dreamer was right. It would be safer if they returned there, away from the collapsing ice dam itself.

Longtusk turned and began to make his cautious way back along the shuddering dam. The whole ice surface was cracking and unstable now. Crocus was whimpering with fear, and the Dreamer put his strong arm around her, in this last extreme helping this distant cousin to safety. Low and squat, Willow seemed to find it easier to stand on the dam's shaking surface than the taller, more elegant Firehead.

Above the rush of water, the scream of the cracking ice, Longtusk heard a remote, thin trumpet. It was a mastodont. He looked back, and saw that the mastodonts and their Firehead keepers had fled to the safety of the land, and were fanning out over the hillside there. He couldn't see if the Shaman was among them. He didn't suppose it mattered; with Crocus gone, so was his grisly power.

He hoped the mastodonts would survive, and find freedom.

At last the three of them scrambled onto the rocky hillside. It felt scarcely less unsteady than the ice, so powerfully did the gushing water shake it.

He looked over the flooding land to the south. New rivers surged along the dry old valleys, like blood surging through a mammoth's veins. Already the ridges of soil and gravel, slowly and painfully colonized by the plants, were being overwhelmed and swept away.

But now the ice dam collapsed further. Immense blocks, blocks the size of icebergs, calved off the eroded walls and fell grandly to the battered land—and the flooding reached a new intensity.

A wall of gray water surged from the huge breach, a river trying to empty a sea. This new mighty flow simply overwhelmed the puny canyons and valleys hit by the first flooding, drowning them as if they had never been. A great bank of mist and fog rolled outward from the breached dam, looming up to the sky as swirling clouds.

Beyond the advancing wave front, bizarrely, the sun still shone, and the land was a placid blanket of folded earth peppered with trees. Longtusk saw a herd of bison, a black lake of muscle and fur. They looked up from their feeding at the wall of water that advanced on them, towering higher than the tallest trees.

The herd was gone in an instant, thousands of lives snuffed out as their world turned from placid green to crushing black.

And still the water came, that front of gray advancing without pity over the green, spreading out over the land in a great fan from the breached dam, as if trying to emulate the sea from which it had emerged.

. . . Now, though, the flow began to diminish, and the water surging over the land began to drain away. Longtusk saw that the breached dam had, if briefly, reformed; slabs of ice and boulders, presumably torn from the basin of the trapped lake, had jammed themselves into the breach, stemming the flow, which bubbled and roared its frustration at this blockage.

As the flood waters subsided, draining into shallow pools and river valleys, the drowned land emerged, glistening.

It was unrecognizable.

Where before there had been green, now there was only the red-brown and black of the bedrock. Under the dam, where the water had fallen to the ground, a great pit had been dug out, gouged as if by some immense mammoth tusk, already flooded with water and littered with ice blocks. It was not that the surface of the land had been washed away, a few trees uprooted—*all* of it, all the animals and trees and grass and the soil that had sustained them had been scoured clean off, down to the bony bedrock, and then the bedrock itself broken and blasted away. Even the hills had been reshaped, he saw, their flanks eroded and cut away. It was as if a face had been flensed, scraped clean of hair and skin and flesh down to the skull.

Mighty rivers flowed through the new channels, and in folds of the land lakes glimmered—huge expanses, lakes that would have taken days to walk around. It was a new landscape, a new world that hadn't existed heartbeats before. But he knew there was no life in those rivers and lakes, no plants or fish, not even insects hovering over their surfaces. This was a world of water and rock.

And now there was a new explosion of shattered rock and crushed ice. The temporary dam had failed. The water leaped through and engulfed the land anew, immediately overcoming the lakes and rivers that had formed and gleamed so briefly, a world made and unmade as he watched.

Surely this mighty flood would not rest until it had gouged its way across this narrow neck of land to reach the brother ocean to the south, sundering the continents, cutting off the new lands from the old.

And with the Fireheads trapped in the old world, the mammoths would be safe in the new.

But such small calculations scarcely seemed important. Longtusk felt the shuddering of the planet in his bones, a deep, wild disturbance. The Earth was reshaping itself around him, the sea asserting its mighty fluid dominance over the land. Before such mighty forces his life was a flicker, no more significant than droplet of spume thrown up as the water surged through the broken dam.

. . . And yet he lived, he realized, wondering. They still stood here—the three of them, Willow, Crocus and himself, the Firehead and the Dreamer still clutching his soaked fur.

For a heartbeat he wondered if they might, after all, live through this.

But now Crocus cried out, pointing.

The hillside they stood on was crumbling. Its surface was cracking, falling away into the gray-brown torrent that gushed below. And the exposed gray-black rock was crumbling too, exploding outward, great shards of it being hurled horizontally by the power of the water. Its lower slopes must have been undercut by the flood.

The land itself was disappearing out from under him, faster than any of them could run.

So it is time, he thought.

Willow plucked at his ears. He bent his head, and the Dreamer slid proudly onto his back. Another story was ending here, thought Longtusk: this squat, aged Dreamer was probably the last of his kind, the last in all the world, and with his death his ancestors' long, patient Dreams would end forever.

Crocus was weeping. She was frightened, like the cub he had once found in the snow, lost and freezing and bewildered. She looked up at Longtusk, seeking comfort.

He wrapped his trunk around her. She curled up in the shelter of his powerful muscles, pulling his long thick fur around her. She closed her eyes, as if sleeping.

. . . The land disappeared with a soft implosion, startlingly quickly, and there was nothing under his feet.

He was falling, the Dreamer's legs locked around his neck, Crocus cradled in his trunk. The air gushed around him, laden with noise and moisture.

He could hear the rush of water beneath him, smell its triumphant brine stink as the sea burst across this narrow neck of land, sundering continent from continent.

Is this how it feels to die? Is this how it feels to be born? Defiantly he lifted his mighty tusks. *Milkbreath! Thunder! Spruce!*

And then—

7

The Cousins

It was later—much later—before Threetusk truly understood what had happened. And, as he grew older yet, the
strange events of those days plagued his mind more and
more.

He found her cropping grass with the painful, slow
care of the old.

"You look terrible," said Saxifrage, as she always did.

"And, Matriarch or not, you're just as uppity as when
you were a calf and I could lift you in the air with my
trunk."

She snorted with contempt. "Like to see you try it
now." But she reached up and nuzzled her trunk tip into
his mouth.

Her flavor was thin, stale, old—yet deliciously familiar
to Threetusk. They had sired four calves together. Threetusk had known other mates, of course—and so, he
knew, had Saxifrage—but none of his couplings had
given him such warm joy as those with her. And (he
knew, though she would never say so) she felt the same
way about him.

But Saxifrage was a Matriarch now, and her Family
stood close by her: daughters and granddaughters and

285

nieces, calves playing at the feet of their mothers, happy, well-fed and innocent.

Even in this huge and empty new land, birth and life and death had followed their usual round for the mammoths, and Threetusk found the world increasingly crowded by unfamiliar faces. Sometimes he was startled to discover just how old he was: when he tried to kneel in the water of a spring, for instance, and his knees lanced with arthritic pain; or when he grumbled about the smoothness of his teeth—and then recalled they were the last he would ever grow.

He settled in beside her, and pulled at the grass. "I've been thinking," he said. "We're the only ones who recall it all. The crossing. The only ones who were *there*. To these youngsters, all of it—Longtusk, the refuge, the corridor—is as remote as a story in the Cycle."

"It already *is* in the Cycle."

"Yes," he said. "And if I knew Longtusk he'd bury his head in a mud seep rather than hear some of the legends that are growing up around him."

"But he *was* a hero . . . You know, you never told me the last thing Longtusk said to you. That day when he announced we had to leave the nunatak, and he took aside you and my mother, Horsetail."

"I've been thinking," he said again.

She rumbled, irritated at his evasion. "Bad habit for your age."

"About ice and land bridges and corridors . . . You see, it isn't so easy to reach this new land of ours. First you have to cross the land bridge, *and* you have to get through the ice corridor. You have to time it just right; most of the time one or other of them will be closed, by sea or ice—"

"So what?"

"So it's difficult, but not impossible, for others to make the crossing. Although for now we're protected by the ocean, there might come a time in the future when the land bridge opens again, and *they* come pouring across . . ."

Saxifrage shivered, evidently as disturbed as he was by the notion that the Fireheads might come scouring down this innocent country, burning and hunting and building and *changing*.

"It won't happen in our time," Saxifrage said. "And—"

But they were interrupted by a thin trumpeting on the fringe of the gathering. It sounded like a calf—a badly frightened calf.

"Circle!"

Saxifrage's Family immediately formed a defensive ring around their Matriarch.

Impatiently Saxifrage pushed her way out of the ring, determined to see what was going on. Threetusk followed in her wake.

A calf stood in the protection of her mother's legs, agitated, still squealing with fright. It was immediately obvious why she was distressed.

The Family was standing at the edge of an open, grassy flood plain. A forest bounded the southern side of the plain. And something had emerged from the fringe of trees on the far side of the clearing.

It might have been a mammoth—it was about the size of a healthy adult Bull, Threetusk supposed—but it was almost hairless. Its skin was dark brown and heavily wrinkled, and it sprouted patches of wiry black hair. Its head was strangely small, and its trunk was short and inflexible.

And it had four short, straight tusks, one pair in the upper jaw, one in the lower.

It was staring at the herd of mammoths, clearly as surprised and alarmed as they were.

"It's a calf of Probos," said Saxifrage, wondering. "A cousin of the mammoths—like Longtusk's mastodonts. There have been rumors of creatures like us here: distant sightings, contact rumbles dimly heard. But . . ."

A young Bull mammoth had gone to challenge the strange animal.

Threetusk struggled to hear their encounter. "His language is strange. I can barely understand him. *Gomphothere.* His kind are called gomphotheres. We are cousins. But we have been apart a long, long time—"

Saxifrage grabbed his trunk. "Threetusk, don't you see? *This is proof.* Your ideas about the bridge and the corridor opening and closing *must be right.* The way must have opened in the past and let through that gomphothere thing—or his ancestors anyhow. And if the way opened in the past, it will surely open again in the future. Oh, Threetusk, you were right. It won't happen in our lifetimes. But the Fireheads are coming." She shuddered. "And then what will become of us?"

". . . We shouldn't call them Fireheads," he said slowly.

"What?"

"That's what Longtusk said to Horsetail and me. On that last day." He closed his eyes and thought of Longtusk. It was as if the years peeled away like winter fur.

We know their true name. They are already in the Cycle. Driven by emptiness inside, they will never stop until they have covered the Earth, and no animal is left alive but them— heap upon heap of them, with their painted faces and their tools and their weapons. They are the demons we use to scare our calves; they are the nemesis of the mammoths. They are the Lost . . .

Saxifrage said, "Some day in the future the ice will return, and the steppe will spread across the planet once more. It will be a world made for mammoths. But will there be any mammoths left alive to see it?"

The young mammoth's tusks clashed with the gomphothere's, a sharp, precise ivory sound. The gomphothere trumpeted and disappeared into the forest.

Epilogue

On this world, a single large ocean spans much of the northern hemisphere. There are many smaller lakes and seas confined within circular craters, connected by rivers and canals. Much of the land is covered by dark green forest and by broad, sweeping grasslands and steppe.

But ice is gathering at the poles. The oceans and lakes are crawling back into great underground aquifers. Soon the air will start to snow out.

The grip of the ice persisted for billions of years before being loosened, it seemed forever. And yet it comes again.

This is the Sky Steppe.

This is Mars.

The time is three thousand years after the birth of Christ. And in all this world there is no human to hear the calls of the mammoths.

Afterword

The picture drawn here of the processes which led to the extinction of the mammoths and other Ice Age fauna is largely based on the careful studies of Gary Haynes and others; see Haynes' *Mammoths, Mastodons and Elephants* (Cambridge University Press, 1991) and Peter Ward's *The Call of Distant Mammoths* (Copernicus, 1997). Details of human cultural involvement with mammoths may be found in *Mammoths* by Adrian Lister and Paul Bahn (Macmillan, 1994). A fine reference on human Ice Age culture is Bahn's *Journey Through the Ice Age* (Weidenfeld & Nicolson, 1994). A good reference on the strange world of the Ice Age, with its land bridges and ice corridors, is *After The Ice Age* by E.C. Pielou (University of Chicago Press, 1991).

The idea of humans taming mammoths or mastodonts in such ancient times is speculative but not impossible. We have records that elephants have been tamed since 2000 B.C. in the Indus Valley and China, and used in war since 1100 B.C.

A valuable source on Neanderthals and their culture is James Shreeve's *The Neanderthal Enigma* (Penguin, 1995). It's sadly unlikely that any Neanderthals survived as late as the period in which this book is set. But hominid fossils are hard to find, and much of Beringia is now submerged by the ocean . . .

Any errors, omissions or misinterpretations are of course my responsibility.

Stephen Baxter
Great Missenden
May 1999

AUG   6 2001